WELCOME TO THE FAREWELL PARTY . . .

Hi! We hate to mention this, but in about three months, the earth is going to pass into a cone of absolutely undiluted heat and light from the sun. We're doing what we can, of course, but that doesn't amount to much.

Oh, sure, you can have a car and food and clothes and we'll even supply everyone with several thousands of dollars to make certain that you can afford these luxuries.

What? You're still afraid? Well, we're developing this pill, it's quick, painless . . . Yes, yes, we will be saving the great works of Man, a rocket is being loaded . . .

Apocalypse? A Messiah? Well, maybe . . .

THE

FAREWELL PARTY

FRANKLIN BANDY

CHARTER
NEW YORK

A DIVISION OF CHARTER COMMUNICATIONS INC.
A GROSSET & DUNLAP COMPANY

To Brian Garfield,
who has a great sense of humor,
for his helpful suggestions.

Prologue

President Sonnabend Fargo was a deeply religious man. He folded his trembling hands on the polished mahogany conference table and lowered his head for a moment of silent prayer.

Finally he raised his head. "I'm sorry gentlemen. The people will have to be told the truth."

Willoughby Stern, Secretary of State, coughed softly. "Mr. President, may I suggest that this information be withheld until say, a week or so before the, ah, happening?"

Fargo shook his head.

"Mr. President, we'll have three months of absolute chaos. No one will work. Nothing will function. Food will run out, garbage will cover the streets." Stern clutched his stomach. He had a pain there ever since he had learned the news. "Typhoid and other diseases will sweep the country. Crime will run rampant."

Fargo nodded. "Nevertheless, they must be told. And immediately. Three months is little enough time for a man to make his peace with God."

Calder Wilson, Secretary of Defense, scratched his chin nervously. "Mr. President, I agree with the Secretary of State. Why, we might even be attacked by Russian missiles."

"To what purpose?"

"Well—"

"Gentlemen," said Fargo, "we have no *right* to withhold this information. Furthermore, it is naive to even suppose that we could do so. We have no

1

monopoly on the astronomical sciences. Within days, perhaps even hours, other men in other nations will arrive at the same conclusion. Isn't this correct, Doctor Friedenbaden?''

Freidenbaden ducked his head. "Quite true, Mr. President.''

"The people must be told the exact truth. Otherwise, rumors will spread. Half-truths will create even more chaos. We've had enough of that. I will not go down in history as a president who dealt in deceit.''

Stern chuckled, still clutching his stomach. "History, Mr. President?''

Fargo smiled. "That's right, Willy. There won't be any, will there?''

Hiram Gillies, the president's chief aide, said, "At least, Mr. President, give us twenty-four hours to work up a plan. We've got to sell the people on accepting this information in the right way. In a non-violent way. We've got to convince them to continue in essential jobs, at least on a limited schedule. We've got to—''

Fargo held up his hand. "Of course. We must set up a committee. Religious leaders, business, media and civic leaders—and our governors, of course. A master plan must be developed. It will take more than twenty-four hours. I'll give it a week. No more. That's the deadline, gentlemen.'' He stood up.

His cabinet members pushed back their comfortable, upholstered chairs and got slowly to their feet.

"Thank you, gentlemen,'' said Fargo, and left the room.

It was hard to accept, but the world was coming to an end. The world was a terminal case, with about three months to live. The scientific details were complex. Explained in terms that the general public could understand, however, they were simple enough.

While the sun is known as a dwarf star, it is enormous in mass compared to the earth. Its circumference is nearly three million miles. Earth's is a tiny twenty-five thousand plus. The sun's surface temperature is 6,000 degrees Centigrade, adequate for the earth's comfort. Its interior temperature, however, is estimated to be 26,000,000 degrees. Astrophysicists have long known that if the sun's surface coat ever peeled away, every planet in the solar system would shortly be a cloud of burning gases.

For some reason inexplicable to scientists, an elliptical strip about forty thousand miles at its widest and approximately one hundred thousand miles in length, had either been peeled or burned away by the interior heat. The effect of this was to create a gigantic searchlight hole beaming 26,000,000 fiery degrees on luckless planets orbiting past.

One by one, every planet in the solar system was destined to sail into quick oblivion. The earth, in its annual orbit, would pass into this cone of inconceivable heat on September 28th.

The earth would become a molten glob, then a cloud of hot gases. Nothing could survive. Nothing would be left. Not even the pillars of Stonehenge or the faces carved on Mount Rushmore. The Pyramids would become runny wax turning to obnoxious gases. The Pan Am building would settle into the earth like Jell-O under a desert sun.

The human cycle was finished.

I

Archibald John Tate II stood in the shower washing his long golden hair with special herbal essence shampoo. Whistling softly, he rubbed some of the foam into his beard and moustache, thoughtfully combing out a few slivers of aluminum with his fingers. Putting up aluminum siding was dirty work, but not as dirty as roofing. Roofing was not only filthy, it was tough. When a man carried eighty-pound bundles of shingles up a ladder all day it produced a certain apathy in the evenings. Aluminum siding was tolerable.

Chris had announced that today was to be another *first day of the rest of their lives*. She was pregnant. Fine. But it created one hell of a problem with his guitar lessons. They couldn't go on living with his parents. A baby was, like, too much. Or so his parents said.

The hundred and fifty a week he was earning was okay as long as they did not have to pay for room and board. It wouldn't go far in a separate establishment. If they had to move out, the guitar lessons were finished. They were expensive. Harold Harold, his teacher, was a musician of considerable fame in the Rock World.

It was like giving up. He'd be cutting aluminum siding the rest of his life.

Chris banged on the door. "Jack, will you hurry up."

"Yeah. Okay." It was four A.M. If they didn't get to Burden's Gap before seven, the line would be so long they wouldn't make it up to the *Well of Resplendent Aurae* that day.

He shut off the shower and dried himself, depressed, but glad to be free of aluminum siding for the day.

Chris asked, "Would you like some toast and coffee?"

He shook his head. "No, I'd better not." He had taken a Man's Laxative before going to sleep, and you could never tell what might happen. "Let's go."

He watched her while she tucked a thermos into a plastic picnic hamper and fussed with it, checking the contents. She was a slender girl with waist-length straight black hair, green eyes and a dimpled smile. It was the old, old trap. Sex and the hungry man. And now a bambino fucking up his guitar lessons. But she refused to have an abortion, and that was that. So much for the "pill." Maybe they could sue the pharmaceutical company. Maybe his father would reconsider.

Stumbling in the pre-dawn summer night, he carried the hamper out to his rusty old van and shoved it onto the floor in the back. Closing the door as quietly as he could, he went to the driver's side and climbed in.

"I love to see the dawn come up," said Chris.

He lit a Marlboro, hoping it wouldn't stir up the Man's Laxative, and rattled the starter.

"Well, we're off to another *first day*," he said.

Chris reached over and hugged him. "Flying into the dawn."

The ancient Ford van rumbled and groaned along, a prehistoric earthbound bird with arthritis. They labored east into the sunrise.

"I wonder how many *first days* of the rest of our lives we've had?" he asked.

"I know."

"How?"

"They're in my diary. Forty-three."

He crushed the Marlboro out, burning his finger.

"Maybe we're going to be running out of *first days*."

Chris turned to him. "Today is going to be the real thing. I have a feeling about it."

They spotted a hitchhiker with long hair and a guitar case. The van wheeled partly onto the road's shoulder and stopped. They waited while he opened one of the side doors and climbed into the back, flopping onto the mattress which rested on a raised platform.

"Thanks, man. Where you headed?"

"Burden's Gap."

"Is that any where near Albany?"

"No, but it's on the way."

"Far out."

The hitchhiker stretched out on the mattress. "Man, am I tired. Hitched all the way from Albuquerque."

"Is Albany your home?" Chris asked.

"Yeah." He raised himself on one elbow. "Broke. Got to go home to Mom and Pop, head bowed in contrition."

"Tough," said Jack.

"What's Burden's Gap? How far is it from Albany?"

"Maybe seventy miles. I'm not sure," said Jack.

"Our church has a shrine there," said Chris.

"Yeah? What church is that?"

"It's the Church of Empirical Mysticism."

The hitchhiker thought about it for a minute. "Mellow!" He sank back on the mattress and spoke to the ceiling. "What's the shrine for?"

"Luck," said Chris. "Ask and ye shall occasionally receive."

"Cosmic." He went to sleep, breathing in a mild, bubbly snore.

They rode along in silence for a while, the thick green of the turnpike trees reeling past with unchanging monotony. Jack encouraged the silence, because he was still feeling wounded, with small jabs of anger pricking the wound, and he didn't want to say anything hurtful to Chris and spoil the day. She was leaning against his shoulder dozing, and there was no need for conversation anyway.

He lit another cigarette as they approached the turn-off for Burden's Gap, then slowed the van, pulling onto the grass verge.

"Hey, this is as close as we go to Albany."

The hitchhiker woke up. "Okay." he struggled to a sitting position and groped for his backpack and guitar. He climbed out. "Thanks. Sorry I'm so broke and can't contribute a little bread for gas."

"That's okay," said Jack, smiling.

"Good luck in Albany," said Chris.

The *Well of Resplendent Aurae* was located at the top of a small stone mountain, a granite outcropping approximately a hundred feet high. Wide steps carved out of the rock traversed the face of the hill. The steps led to the top in a slope so gradual that even the few middle-aged members found it no strain on wind or limbs.

It was six forty-five when they pulled into the almost-empty parking lot, delighted to see that there were only five supplicants ahead of Jack. He yanked the handbrake, jumped out and hurried away to the small registration house to stake his claim for position number six.

Chris lit a cigarette and waited.

In five minutes he was back, a clean, white toga draped over his arm. "Number six."

Chris smiled. "That's good. We won't have to wait so long."

"Number six is lucky. It's always been lucky for me." He climbed into the back of the van and stripped off his jeans, shirt and underwear. Naked, he pulled the toga over his head. It was a knee-length garment, trimmed with red embroidery at the neck and bottom hem. Designs from tarot cards were printed down the front.

He jumped down, the loose garment billowing slightly, and walked around to the front seat to sit with Chris.

The attendants on duty at the well started work at seven o'clock. Allowing fifteen or twenty minutes per supplicant, Jack would complete his mission before nine. If everything went smoothly at the well. On occasion a supplicant fell in. When this happened, it was considered a bad luck day, and operations were shut down.

"I hope nobody falls in," said Jack. "I think I'll have a cup of coffee."

"Nobody will fall in. Hadn't you better wait?"

"No. I think I can handle it. I feel I'm in complete control."

Chris shrugged. "I'd wait."

They went to the back of the van, found the thermos and filled two cups. Lighting a Marlboro, he sipped. "Man, this is great."

Chris shook her head doubtfully. She sipped her own coffee. They strolled over to join the group at the bottom of the steps. Locating a spot close enough to maintain his presence in line, but apart enough for privacy, they sat down on the grass. He arranged his toga self-consciously.

"You're bugged about the baby," said Chris, putting her cup on the ground.

He shrugged. "It's a little early to be starting a family all right."

"You'll see. It'll all work out."

He clenched his teeth for a moment. "It'll work out

with me cutting aluminum the rest of my life."

She reddened. "I'm *not* having an abortion. No baby of *mine* is going to be flushed down the toilet."

He was suddenly ashamed of himself. An abortion might be a bad-luck thing anyway. What was it Grandpop had said? When a union is blessed with children . . .

"Your parents won't throw us out," said Chris.

"They won't?"

"No, they won't."

They sat for a while avoiding each other's eyes. Then he put his arm around her shoulders. "Don't worry. We'll make out."

She smiled, tucking her head closer.

They sat watching the supplicants trudge up the side of the gigantic rock. The four hundred steps, each only three inches high, had to be negotiated at a dignified pace. This morning's crop were all young, so the ascent took only about six minutes.

Number three came down looking grim, his long hair tangled by the early morning wind. Passing them he paused and nodded glumly. "A bad scene, man. I didn't make it."

Jack shook his head. "Tough."

"There's always tomorrow," said Chris.

"Yeah." He walked on, saying over his shoulder, "Only tomorrow I'm back in the same old cheese factory."

Jack said, "I have a stomachache."

"I know," said Chris.

"You don't like to say, 'I told you so.' "

"I never say I told you so."

Jack groaned, holding his stomach.

"Practice visceral learning. Tell your intestines to be quiet."

"*You* be quiet," he moaned softly.

"Hang on. Only one more to go."

Number five finally came down, taking his time, a smug smile on his fat face.

Jack got carefully to his feet and started up, taking each step with delicate caution. He was afraid even to wave to Chris. There was nitroglycerine rolling around inside.

At the top the two attendants greeted him, smiling, as he tipped them the customary five dollars each.

The *Well of Resplendent Aurae* was actually a ten-foot-wide crack in the top of the rock. Inside the crack was a sheer drop of one hundred feet to the well, a large black, circular hole with a stone border. A wooden platform, roofed with red shingles, bordered the chasm, extending a couple of feet over the edge. Aside from a simple bench for the attendants, who were dressed in plain white togas, and a small table, the platform was bare.

"Are you ready to make your plea?" asked one of the attendants.

"I am," said Jack, hardly daring to talk. He walked to the edge, stared down into the dizzy abyss, then bowed from the waist. Straightening up, he said, "Oh *Well of Resplendent Aurae,* hear this plea. Exert thy powerful influence to help me get a job paying at least two hundred and fifty dollars a week so that I may continue my guitar lessons under the master, Harold Harold, leader of the *Hesitant Dead.* I'm assured that my talent is superior, and that with adequate professional training I shall be able to make a great contribution to society by bringing happiness to millions. Many thanks, oh *Well of Resplendent Aurae,* for listening to this humble request."

He took a deep breath, visceral control still a painful effort, then turned to face the attendants. Lifting his toga in the rear, he pulled the cloth around and fastened it in front with a safety pin. He held out his arms to the attendants. Each buckled a leather strap to one wrist, and held the other end in a tight loop. Jack backed slowly to the edge of the platform. then lowered himself, his rubber-soled shoes braced against the edge, until his rear was positioned directly over the well. He swayed there for a moment, supported only by the leather straps, his bowels frozen by the uncomfortable strain.

"Relax," said one of the attendants.

He relaxed. Suddenly it came. He defecated with a mighty roar. Rolls of thunder bounced around the chasm walls in resounding echoes. It seemed to go on and on, while the attendants grinning with amazement leaned back straining at the straps. Finally the cacaphony subsided, dying on a few weak sputters.

He was empty, and free as a bird. He could fly right out of the chasm. The attendants pulled him back to the platform.

"Man, you really had it in you," said one.

Jack smiled. "The Man's Laxative separates the men from the boys. That's what they say on television." He sighed. "A boy it would have killed."

The other attendant handed him a box of Kleenex. "You were right on target, as neat a plea as I've ever seen. May the *Well* grant your wish."

Jack thanked him and trotted happily down the four hundred steps.

II

At six A.M. the alarm began its unremitting buzz. John Tate fumbled for the cut-off knob, then levered himself out of bed and into his robe. He staggered down the hall to the bathroom, still half-blind with sleep.

The tub-shower had five inches of water remaining from Jack's four A.M. bath. Stopped up again. Muttering, he struggled to uncap a plastic bottle of Liquid Blast, the child-proof cap making it even safer from half-asleep adults. He finally succeeded in opening it, and poured it slowly into the water above the drain opening, careful not to splash any of what might be pure sulphuric acid on his hands.

The number of longhairs in this house who shampooed daily was unbelievable. No wonder the drains were always stopped up. He lit a Vantage, only 10 milligrams of 'tar,' and waited for the acid to eat through the hair. It usually did.

So he was going to be a grandfather. Wasn't forty-five a bit young to be a grandfather? They had told Jack he would have to move, and establish his own home, if he was going to start a family. But if it really meant giving up the guitar lessons, he supposed they would have to relent. Achievement was important to the male Tates. They tended to live in hope for tomorrow instead of joy for today. Had Jack been studying with Heifetz, they would have made any sacrifice to keep him going. While they couldn't take Harold Harold very seriously, many millions did. What the hell. *Autres temps, autres moeurs*! The lessons would continue. Even if it meant a new Tate squalling in the semi-ruin of their falling-down house.

The water gurgled slowly out and he was able to take his shower.

"Why are you going to the office on Saturday?" his wife Virginia asked.

"Because it's there."

"Very not-funny."

He sipped his coffee. "I feel nervous here. I sit at my typewriter and all I can think about is the termites eating the floor right out from under us."

Ginny poured herself another cup. "I don't know about termites, but there's a mouse in the walls. He's eating his way into your closet."

John lowered the *Times*. "How do you know this?"

"Look in the back of your closet. He's gnawing his way through the plaster. Where the hot water pipe goes through the wall. Everyday there's more plaster powder on the floor. The hole gets a little bigger everytime I look."

He returned to the *Times*. "Rats have to gnaw. Their upper teeth grow right through their jaws if they don't. They have to keep them ground down by gnawing."

"I would prefer he didn't gnaw his way into my bedroom."

He lowered the paper again. "Ask Billy to set a rat trap."

"There's been one there for a week."

"I see."

He stood on the station platform thinking what a fraud he was. Dressed in a spanking clean blue and white striped suit, blue shirt and red and black patterned tie, his light brown hair styled modishly long, his face tanned, not from golf, tennis or the beach, but from hours of running the power mower over their hopelessly large lawn, he looked like a successful man in complete command.

Actually he was a panic-stricken semi-failure who hovered constantly on the brink of financial disaster. Or so he saw himself. Others saw him as a moderately successful advertising copy writer who had also managed to publish four novels. None had caused any stampedes to the book stores, or occasioned golden offers from Hollywood or television.

He stood with his back to the tracks, idly watching new arrivals wheel into the parking lot. A Mercedes pulled up to the platform. Wife driving husband to station. He sat on the passenger side cuddling a Yorkshire terrier. Nuzzle, more nuzzling, lips moving in baby-talk. With the rumble of an approaching train, the man flung open the door of the car, kissed the terrier on the mouth, nodded to his wife, and hurried up the steps to the platform.

John Tate shrugged. Moving along the platform as the train slowed to a halt, he tried to position himself near a door. Being Saturday it would be a local, and crowded. Among the first to push his way onto the train, he saw that there were nothing but detestable center seats available.

He took one anyway, and it was the usual tight squeeze. The seats might accommodate three twelve-year-old girls comfortably, but not three broad-shouldered men. John was six-foot-two and solidly built, with only an ounce or two of fat here and there. The man on the aisle, he noticed, had only one arm, the empty sleeve on John's side, making things less crowded. How about that, Conrail? You can't win them all in the discomfort battle, can you?

The one-armed man's stub was poking him insistently, like somebody else's hard-on. Since John was completely heterosexual, the feeling was vaguely uncomfortable. Why would his stub be aroused? Maybe it was just that stubs did that, without the weight of an arm to hold them down? Embarrassed, the one-armed man tugged at his empty sleeve, attempting to control his aroused stub, to hold it down. It wouldn't be controlled, and continued to probe the muscles of John's arm. The one-armed man gave up and went to sleep, leaving only his stub awake and active. John closed his eyes and tried to nap, but the stub kept pressing harder and harder into his arm. It burned. It had zeroed in on a nerve, a forbidden spot on the acupuncturist's chart, a deadly zone. If it penetrated, he would die.

He shifted his position, but the stub followed eagerly, probing a new muscle. "I will count ten," John said to himself, "and when I reach ten I will go to sleep. I will dream of a beautiful young girl, naked, with long black hair, who is poking my arm with her finger, urging me to love her." He savored the mental image of "one," printed in big lower-case letters, then "two," and slowly on up to "ten." When "ten" came slowly on the screen of his mind he found himself slipping into the deep pit of relaxation and shallow breathing that precedes sleep. But sleep never came, really. A psychiatrist had told him to conquer his insomnia this way. It never worked. It just *almost* worked. That was the story of his life. It *almost* worked. The dark haired girl was touching his arm shyly. He bent over to kiss her stomach, but she faded away as the train roared into the tunnel under Park Avenue.

He stuck a Vantage in his mouth, dislodging the stub as he twisted to get his hand in his pocket.

"You can't smoke in here," said a woman behind him, "this is a no-smoking car."

"I am not smoking, Madam."

"As long as you know."

"I know. I promise not to light it."

He pulled himself to his feet, nipped his case from the rack, climbed over the sleeping one-armed man and made his way to the platform where he could light his cigarette.

He hadn't expected to find anyone in the office on a Saturday morning. Certainly not on a fine summer day. But the place had one other occupant. He could hear the muted thunk of the IBM composer.

He tossed his case onto a chair in his own office and went to investigate.

Biting her lower lip, Marilyn Henley sat hunched over the machine, her long, straight black hair closing in enough to almost blot out her vision.

"What are you doing in here on a Saturday?" he asked.

She looked up, brushing her hair back. "Typing my boyfriend's resume. He got fired again."

"Oh."

"Mr. Harlowe said it would be all right to do it on the composer. The copies will be sharper."

He lit another Vantage. "Sure, why not."

"What are you doing here?"

He shrugged. "Oh, I don't know. I just felt like coming in—"

She went back to her typing. "I made a pot of coffee."

"Good," he said, and went to get himself a cup. He carried it to his office and sat down, feeling vaguely uneasy. He had expected the place to be empty and quiet. It was quiet, but it was a long way from being empty. Marilyn alone was more disturbing than having the entire staff there.

Marilyn was slender, with small breasts, and a face that, while not beautiful, was attractive and vital.

Friendly, with a quick smile. She was a strange girl. Evenings and weekends she worked in an elegant massage parlor. She was twenty-two. Only three years older than his own daughter, Marcia Louise.

Wanting to help, John had tried some well-meaning, avuncular advice on her, but had quickly abandoned it in the face of her amused reaction. Taking the opposite tack he had asked, "Why work thirty-five hours a week at Wendell Harlow Associates to take home a hundred and ninety dollars when you're earning a tax free five hundred in the massage parlor?"

She had thought about it. "I don't know. I guess I need to keep a respectable job. Maybe I'm not cut out to be a full-time whore."

"You're not a whore."

She had smiled. "No? Try waving a hundred dollar bill under my nose."

"I thought—"

"That we only gave hand jobs?"

"Well—"

Later she had slipped into his office, and beginning to speak awkwardly, had asked him not to tell anyone. Mr. Harlowe would probably fire her.

"Of course not. I won't say anything," he had promised.

He suspected that Wendell Harlow already knew. His own source had been Jim Ferguson, a big-mouthed space rep who had inadvertently patronized the parlor. Ferguson had probably told Harlow even before telling John. Besides, Wendell was not a narrow-minded man. Especially when it came to money. It was not easy to find a highly intelligent girl for two hundred and forty a week who could manage fast and faultless typing on the composer, act as secretary, file clerk and receptionist, and had graduated cum laude from a good university. And if she got arrested in a raid, so what? The papers wouldn't mention the company name. They never did. Wendell had probably weighed the pros and cons and decided that the pros had it.

"If he finds out, or has found out, I assure you it won't be me who gives you away."

"You mean Jim Ferguson?"

John nodded.

Marilyn just shrugged.

He zipped open his leather case, removed his notes, and rolled some paper into his IBM Selectric. It was about six hundred dollars better than the manual typewriter he had in his study. But electrified or manual, typing was still a chore. He envied writers who could lie on a sofa and dictate into a microphone. He had to see what he wrote in cold type before it made any sense to him.

He sat listening to the damned Selectric hum. Some days it hummed nicely, and on others it rasped unpleasantly. Today it was rasping. The hell with it, he figured, and flipped the off switch.

The problem was, if he had a hundred dollars, would he? He simply couldn't afford it. There were too many Tates to feed and educate. The question was academic. He never had a hundred dollars in cash. And if he took that much out of their joint checking account he would have to invent some stupid excuse and the whole thing would be more trouble than it was worth. On the other hand, if he found a hundred dollar bill on the sidewalk, would he?

Marilyn came into his office waving the two-page resume. "All done. I'm going."

He nodded, smiling. "Lock the door on your way out, okay?"

She perched on the edge of his desk. "Maybe you'd like a quickie hand job for twenty?"

They had kidded this way before. "Nope. Only the real thing, and for free."

"How about a succulent blow job for thirty-five?"

"How about my eating you, and you pay *me* thirty-five?" he asked.

She stared at him, unsmiling. "I don't have to pay for *that*."

He lit a cigarette. "I would imagine not."

"I'll make you a special rate. A real fuck for fifty." She was serious. He wondered at the girl's insistence.

"Honestly, Marilyn, I wish I could. I was just thinking before you came in that I wished I could afford your rates. But things are very tight. And now Chris is going to have a baby. Another mouth to feed."

"Chris?"

"My son Jack's wife."

She closed the office door, then unzipped her skirt, stepping out of it. She went back to her perch on the edge of the desk, now only wearing flowered bikini shorts and a lightweight turtleneck sweater.

"On credit then. Ten dollars down and ten a week."

"No."

She pulled off the bikini shorts, then struggled to get the sweater over her head. Completely naked, she stalked around the desk and began to search his pockets, her long black hair falling in his face.

"Come on you cheapskate, I know you've got ten dollars." She found his wallet in his hip pocket and extracted a ten dollar bill. She took it to her purse, which she had dropped on a chair with the resume, and tucked it in.

"That's about my speed. Ten dollars for entertainment," he said, replacing his wallet.

"Ten dollars a week for four more weeks." She strolled over and shoved her small breasts into his face.

"I'm already paying off loans to Bowery, Chase

Manhattan, Citibank, Marine Midland, Master Charge and Visa.''

"Tough." She pushed the swivel chair back and sat on his lap. "I'm giving you half off, today only.'' It was the kind of ad they wrote at Wendell Harlowe Associates. "You expect me to sell at a loss? You think we buy cunt by the mile and can sell for much less, maybe?'' She framed his face with her hands, kissing him roughly, digging her tongue between his lips. The chair strained back and almost toppled. They slipped off to the floor. He was being raped, he decided, and might as well enjoy it. Besides, he rationalized, rejection would be too impossibly humiliating for her at this stage.

The romp had to pause for an awkward interruption while he undressed. Tie, shirt, undershirt, shoes, pants, shorts. It was only a matter of a minute or two, but it seemed unendurably long. She remained sprawled on the soft gray carpet, propped on one elbow, watching him with professional disinterest. Out of the corner of his eye he saw and resented. For a moment he had somehow felt that all the talk of money had been a joke, even the ten dollars, and that she had for some peculiar reason been in the mood, had wanted him, or something.

He lowered himself to the floor and stretched out beside her, fondling her, kissing her small breasts. She bore it with unconcealed impatience. He moved downward, thrusting his face between her legs.

She tried to push him away. Grasping her tanned legs tightly, he held on.

She struggled, dislodging him. "No!"

He forced his way back, gripping her legs and shifting the weight of his chest to her twisting stomach. Gradually she stopped pushing and began to respond in spite of herself, holding his head tightly against her. He could hear her breathing quicken, and feel her stomach trembling. When she tightened her legs in approaching climax, he jerked his head away and mounted.

When it was over she pushed at him roughly. "You *shit*."

He rolled to one side and raised himself on one elbow to look at her.

She scrambled to her feet, her face mottled and angry. While he lay there smirking, she stepped forward and stomped hard on his stomach with her bare heel.

"Ooouf! What the hell—" He pulled himself groggily to his knees.

Hopping away, she grabbed a heavy volume from his desk and heaved it at him. It struck a glancing blow on the back of his head, more jolting than painful. He got quickly to his feet.

Backing up, she grabbed the wooden "IN" box from his desk. Holding it up with both hands, she advanced. He quickly shielded his face with his arm. The box crashed, sending shock waves of pain.

Enraged, he ripped the box out of her hands and threw it on the floor, then slapped her face hard with his open palm. She tried to hit him with her fist, but he caught her wrist and deflected it. He closed in, grabbing her right arm and twisting it behind her back, raising it upward until she screamed. Her throat was caught in the crook of his left arm. She tucked her head to one side and bit hard.

"Stop it or I'll break your goddamned arm," he said, pushing her arm upward again.

She screamed and stopped biting.

He jerked her around and gave her a resounding slap on the rear. She tripped and fell to the floor, catching herself on her hands. He dived, flattening her to the carpet face down. Striding her back, and sitting on her, he began to slap her buttocks, raising his arm high and bringing it down with hard, whip-like whacks again and again until his arm was tired and he was panting, breathless and dizzy. Only then did he realize that she was screaming, and that her buttocks were dark cherry red.

He stopped and got slowly to his feet. "What were you trying to do, kill me?" He was still panting heavily.

She continued to lie there. "You raped me," she said, turning her head away.

He found his shorts and pulled them on. Rape? Because he wouldn't settle for one of her quick tricks, mechanical and unfelt? He put on his undershirt, feeling his injured forearm. He studied the bite marks on his other arm. The skin was broken, though not deeply.

"I hope you had your rabies shots this year," he said, putting on his shirt.

"Oh, shut up. I could *kill* you."

"Why?"

"Oh, go to hell."

He put on his trousers, socks and shoes. As he tightened his belt, he felt his stomach twinge from where she had stepped on him. Incredible. If she had had a knife, she probably would have stabbed him. Why?

She got to her feet silently, found her bikini shorts and pulled them on, her red buttocks quivering like gelatine. He watched cautiously as her skirt and sweater followed.

Was she one of those women who got her kicks from being beaten up, or beating up? No. It was sheer, monumental anger.

She stepped into her sandals, picked up her purse and her boyfriend's resume, snatched open the office door and left.

He went to the men's room and rinsed his mouth. His feelings were a mixed turmoil of guilt, triumph, self-loathing, satisfaction and amazement. Underneath was a soft fog of depression. The incident had literally left a bad taste.

III

At seven A.M., Archibald J. Tate the elder pulled himself creakily out of bed. In recent years he hadn't needed an alarm clock. His kidneys took care of that.

He walked the few feet to his private bathroom, his joints scraping small flashes of pain like screams from an unoiled machine. They always did the first thing in the morning. He stood for a while waiting for the old drainpipe to function. It came through, eventually. For seventy-five, he wasn't in bad shape, he told himself.

He took a hot shower, shaved, trimmed his distinguished looking white moustache, and then brushed his silver hair until it was positioned exactly right.

Walking down the steps, he found his bones in better shape. They generally were after a hot shower. Actually they had been pretty good recently, probably because last winter had been so summery. Something to do with sunspots.

"Good morning, Papa," said Ginny as he entered the large, old-fashioned kitchen. "How about a soft-boiled egg and toast?" Some mornings he took only toast, and that disturbed her.

"That sounds fine, dear," Her solicitude always reassured him, made him feel wanted. In addition to being damned attractive, she had a wide streak of good humored kindness and generosity. John had been a lucky boy. Boy? God, he was middle-aged. In fact, he was about to become a grandfather. That made Archibald a great-grandfather? Unbelievable.

It was Ginny who had been most vocal in insisting

that he live with them after Eleanor had died. He'd have been miserable, he admitted, living alone or in some damned senior citizen's colony. He still went to his law office in New York every weekday, even though there weren't many cases anymore. Practically all of his clients were dead. It was embarrassing that John wouldn't let him pay board. He could afford it.

He picked up his personal copy of the *Times,* idly watching Ginny instead of reading it. She was wearing a lightweight flowered house coat. The thin fabric clung to her body, emphasizing a certain thickness about the middle. Her hair, fashionably long and naturally blonde, had recently been dyed a lighter shade of gold, and made her look somewhat younger. He approved.

"Well, Papa, what's new and disastrous today?" she asked, dropping two slices of bread into the toaster.

He glanced at the headlines. "The same old stuff I'm afraid." He chuckled. "Some idiot wants to impeach Fargo because he spoke to a lobbyist on the gold course." Ever since the scandals of the early seventies the press followed a president's every move with the suspicious scrutiny of a man watching his television set being repaired.

Ginny lifted the soft-boiled egg from the water. "Well, he damned well shouldn't be talking to lobbyists."

"Except consumer advocates."

"That's different."

In the early eighties the people's lobby idea had finally caught on. Common Cause now had ten million members paying fifteen dollars a year. Ralph Nader's organization had almost as many. Three hundred million dollars carried a lot of clout. It was hard to make any real money in politics anymore. You couldn't turn a dishonest penny without having eight different groups investigating you, or filing a class action suit against you.

It amused old Archibald. A card-carrying Humanist, he had spent his life fighting for liberal causes. Now that things were really getting interesting, he was no longer useful. He simply didn't have the energy. A nice easy legal aid case was about his speed, bargaining for a plea for some poor clod who had been caught red-handed. He wished he was twenty-five years younger.

He finished his toast and egg, and drank his cup of weak tea. Then he lit a Carlton, five milligrams of 'tar,' and attacked the *Times*.

Billy came pounding down the steps. A platoon of Russian infantry would have been quieter. Archibald got up and slipped quickly away to John's study at the rear of the house. Billy was a little too much the first thing in the morning.

"Hey, Mom, where did you hide my clean jeans?" he yelled. "I don't want any damned eggs. You got any English muffins? I mean the *regular* ones, not those crappy ones you buy? If you don't have that, I'll have French toast, and don't fry it so damned brown. Is the bacon any good, or is it that greasy stuff that's all fat?"

Muttering under her breath, Ginny cracked some eggs and began to make French toast. "Did you take a bath last night?"

"No, I didn't take a bath last night, and if you don't quit bugging me I won't take one tonight."

He was seventeen. She had to keep reminding herself that they were all impossible at that age. He had his brother's shoulder length hair, but brown instead of golden. Like all the Tates, he was tall, over six feet, and so rib-protruding thin that Ginny seethed in continuing frustration over his eating habits.

Then there was the drug thing. She wondered

whether he was on something that made him so uncivilized. Or was it just being seventeen? Jack had been
a problem at that age too. In some ways worse. With-
drawn, moody, hysterical when crossed.

"I have a pain right here in my right leg," said Billy,
pointing to his calf.

"Probably a sore muscle," said Ginny.

"It's very bad."

"Take some aspirin."

"I don't like aspirin."

Ginny banged the frying pan down on the stove.
"Well then suffer, damnit."

"I want to see Dr. Howard."

"Well *see* Dr. Howard."

"Call him."

"Call him yourself."

Between his visits to Dr. Howard everytime he had
so much as a cut finger, and his visits to Dr. Grossman
for acne treatments, the doctor bills added up.

She slapped down his plate of French toast and
bacon, poured him a cup of coffee and left the room to
avoid further abrasion.

He wolfed down his food, mouth only inches away
from the plate, drank half of his coffee, then lit a
Marlboro and inhaled deeply. He scraped back his chair
with maximum noise, got up, and walking with a limp,
headed for his father's study. He had seen the old man
sneaking away.

"Grandpop."

"Yes?" Archibald peered cautiously over his
Times.

"I have this friend and, well, last night he got
busted. I was wondering—"

"What for?"

"Well he was selling pot. But he was only doing it as
a favor—"

Archibald rattled his paper, irritated. "You know how I feel about selling. If it was just possession, I'd take it on—"

Billy puffed hard on his Marlboro. "You don't understand. He only buys it to do his close friends a favor. Guys like me. He doesn't *make* anything selling it. He just gets it for his friends."

Archibald had heard that story before. And sometimes, of course, it was true. "If he only sells to his close friends, how is it he sold some to a narc?"

"He thought he was a friend."

"A close friend?"

"Well—"

Archibald lit another Carlton. "Tell him to call the Legal Aid Society. If they want to assign me to it, I'll take it. Otherwise, to hell with it."

Billy went away muttering.

When it came to pot, the distinction he made between selling and possession was probably silly, Archibald decided, but the attitude had hardened along with his arteries, and he couldn't shake it. The main reason for his distaste was that most pushers moved hard drugs as well as pot, and the old man believed that selling drugs was slow murder.

He could hear Billy telephoning. "This is Bill Tate. I want to make an appointment with Dr. Howard. I have this pain in my right leg and—"

IV

Marcia Louise Tate rapped softly on the front door of the old brick house. After waiting a moment or two she pressed the button and listened to the chimes echoing loudly.

Jeff's father answered the door. He was wearing a striped shirt and puffing on a curved stem pipe. The humidity caused the door to stick, and he had some difficulty pulling it open.

"Good evening. It's, uh, Marcia, isn't it?"

"Hi. Is Jeff home? I know it's late, but—"

He glanced at his wrist watch. "Eleven. That's not so late. Come in."

She came into the hall quickly, her eyes on the steps leading to the second floor. "Is Jeff here? If he isn't—"

"He's here, but sit down a minute, I'd like to talk to you."

"If he's here, I'll just run up—"

"Sit down. He's sound asleep with all the lights on and the radio turned up as loud as he can get it." The bass beat of a rock piece was throbbing through the ceiling. "He won't miss you for a couple of minutes." He motioned towards a sofa. "Sit."

She sat down on the edge of the sofa, pushing her long blonde hair away from her eyes nervously.

He sat down opposite her, fingering his pipe thoughtfully. He was a fat-faced man in his forties.

"You're the girl who had the dog raising an uproar when you were sneaking out of here the other morning about six." He smiled. "She's a very brave watch dog.

29

When she thinks there's a stranger around she crawls under my bed and barks her head off. It's disconcerting.''

He took a pipe knife from his pocket and fiddled with the bowl, tamping down the tobacco. ''The point I want to make is that you don't have to sneak around here. Neither Ellie nor I is going to bite you. While we feel that this sort of casual intimacy is sort of hard on little girls, we'd rather have you here than turning-on in some crummy motel.''

She put her hands on her knees, which were pressed tightly together. ''Why do you think it's hard on girls?''

He relit his pipe. ''Well, we happen to believe that women have a very strong nesting instinct. That underneath everything they want security very powerfully, a comfortable, safe place for their children, a father for them that they can depend on.'' He puffed, staring at her through the smoke.

''What's all that got to do with fucking?''

He winced. ''Fucking, as you so bluntly put it, is tied in very strongly with conceiving and bearing children. In fact, as far as nature is concerned, that is its primary purpose. The pleasure involved is purely incidental.''

She relaxed a little. ''If I ever decide to have children, I'll look for that safe nest you're talking about. It's a decision women have more power over now.''

He pointed his pipe stem at her. ''I think you're missing the point. Men have a very strong sex drive, but their nesting instincts are practically zilch. You girls make it too easy for them to avoid that responsibility.''

''You think a man has to be trapped into providing a secure nest?''

''Well—''

"If you ask me, that's a hell of a way to establish a relationship."

He smiled. There was no way to get through to them other than with cynicism, and then they had you with their damned idealistic honesty. "Do me a favor, will you?"

"What?"

"Get friendly with our dog. Her name is Priscilla. She's a very affectionate little mutt." He stood up and whistled softly. "Priss, come here."

The little brindle beagle came trotting into the living room, tail wagging. She went over to inspect Marcia. Marcia petted her, smiling, then bent to scratch her neck and stomach.

She stood up. "May I go upstairs now?"

"Sure. Lecture's over."

"I'll try not to wake you."

"Thanks."

He watched her running up the steps, her round little buttocks bouncing, and envied his son.

Jeff's room was a shambles. The window fan was roaring at full speed, but could not compete with stereophonic rock blasting from the two big speakers. He was sprawled on his bed, alseep face down, wearing jeans and a faded T-shirt. A bright overhead light and two high-wattage lamps had the small room brighter than a photographer's set.

She slapped him smartly on the rear.

He woke up and turned over, yawning.

"Your father's a nice old fart. He wants you to marry me and give me a *nest*."

Grinning, he pulled her down on top of him.

V

For three days, the news media had been releasing a barrage of announcements. These stated that at nine o'clock on Sunday evening President Fargo would make a speech of great importance to all America. Full-page ads appeared in all newspapers. All radio and television stations carried the announcement every two hours. Theaters published notices that programs would be interrupted for the speech. Baseball games and other athletic events would pause for President Fargo. Every restaurant and other place of public gathering would be required to carry it. The tone of these announcements was so serious, so ominous, that wild rumors were sweeping the country. The press and public officials confirmed these rumors to many by denying them vehemently.

The Chinese had perfected a death ray and were demanding the unconditional surrender of the whole world.

President Fargo had cancer.

The mercury content in foods had risen to the point where no one could eat anything but soybeans, and even they were suspect.

All the gold in Fort Knox had been stolen.

Fargo had been caught financing a gigantic heroin smuggling ring and was going to resign.

Lesbianism was going to be declared a capital crime with mandatory life imprisonment.

With the exception of Billy, the Tate family gathered in front of the television set with considerable apprehension. Billy was upstairs playing records.

"Shut that damned thing off and get down here!" John yelled up the steps.

The music stopped and Billy came downstairs sulkily.

"And now," said the announcer, "we bring you the President of the United States."

The camera shifted to Fargo sitting at his desk in the Oval Office. He grasped his hands tightly to keep them from trembling. The camera moved to a close-up of his face.

"My fellow Americans. Tonight I must bring to you news so incredibly shocking that you will find it difficult to believe. Unfortunately, it is true. It has been checked and double-checked and triple-checked by leading scientists both here and abroad. We have confirmation from Russia, England, France and Germany. And, oh yes, China.

"I bring you news of a disaster of unparalleled magnitude. I implore you to remain calm and listen to the plan we have prepared for mitigating this disaster. As Americans we have always been noted for our ability to take swift, well-planned action in emergencies."

He told them about the sun.

The Tates listened and watched in stunned silence.

His voice beginning to crack, Fargo told them about the plan.

So that the American people could live out their something less than three months in dignity and comfort, essential services had to be maintained. Fire, police, the armed forces, doctors, hospitals, undertakers, sanitation workers, cemetery employees, water supply personnel and those providing other vital services would have to carry on. An adequate three month food supply had to be assured. Entertainment would be expanded and free. Citizens were urged to spend as much time as possible praying in the church or synagogue of their choice. People with nonessential jobs would have to give them up. Everyone would pitch in to provide vital services.

Lists of essential occupations would be posted in every Post Office by eight A.M. tomorrow, and of course, newspapers and other media would also carry this information. Those in now useless occupations would be required to report to their local state employment offices for reassignment.

The announcement ended with the playing of "America the Beautiful" and a final close-up of President Fargo trying desperately to smile.

The camera switched back to the announcer. "And now we'll have a brief message from Mr. Hiram Gillies, President Fargo's press relations aide." The camera moved to Gillies, who was smiling. "Now for the *good* news." He chuckled, "You didn't think there could be any, did you? You're probably sitting there before your television set stunned, gloomy, and maybe you're thinking about what a horrible end we have in store. Being burned to death isn't much to look forward to, is it? Well, President Fargo isn't going to let that happen to you. Our pharmaceutical companies have developed a little capsule for you, and within a month we'll have enough to distribute one to every American. When you take it you'll go to sleep painlessly in less than fifteen seconds, and within five minutes—well, need I say more? Believe me folks, we won't feel a thing.

"And here's some more good news. Almost everything you require for your comfort and happiness will be free. With only three months to go, we have more than enough of everything for everybody. Within reason, of course. We can't pass out Rolls-Royces, of course. But there'll be lots of goodies, folks and all *free*.

"So take heart. Let's all go out with dignity and courage."

The announcer said, "We'll now return to the studio where our analysis panel will give you their impressions of President Fargo's message. Here's Frank Rowell. You all know Frank. And Sally Metz of *Afternoon,* and Arbus Foley, our intrepid Washington correspondent."

The camera zeroed in on the panel, providing close-ups as the names were mentioned. Having received a pre-broadcast release of the President's message, the panel had had plenty of time to digest its import. After digesting it, which took a relatively short time, they sent out for a couple of bottles.

"Well, Arbus, you know the president better than any of us. Let's have your impressions of this momentous message."

Arbus Foley rolled his big, glassy eyes upward. "I shought, well, it sheemed to me that the president looked a little peaked. I shink he's been worrying a lot."

"Yes. Well, Sally?"

Sally Metz's tongue came lazily out as she licked her lips thoughtfully. "Well, now, I think Arbus's thought, that is, well, it has a lot of merit. President Fargo was definitely, and I can emphasize this without fear of being in error, he was definitely peaked."

"Frank?"

Rowell's mouth was hanging open. He snapped it shut and glared at the camera. "President Pargo was not peaked. He was tried. I mean tired."

John Tate stood up. "Those monkeys are stoned to the eyeballs. And It's not a bad idea."

He went to the closet in his study and brought out a
fresh bottle of Scotch. Bringing it to the small bar
cabinet in the living room, he found a glass and poured
a stiff drink. He walked over and handed it to Ginny,
who was sitting frozen, her shoulders hunched, her
eyes glazed.

He put his arm around her shoulders. "Here Honey,
drink this. It's not—" He was about to say, 'it's not the
end of the world.'

She accepted the drink numbly, then sipped it with
wide-eyed curiosity, as though she had never tasted
Scotch before.

John went back to the bar. "Dad?" he asked, motioning with a glass in old Archibald's direction.

Archibald came to attention. "Pour one for youself,
John. I'll—I'll get myself one in a minute."

John poured several ounces into an old-fashioned
glass and turned to face his family. "Everybody help
themselves." He lifted the glass and downed a long
swallow, which traveled warm and aromatic down his
gullet to this stomach.

He walked over to Jack, holding his glass tightly.
"Son, give me one of those damned Marlboros."

Still slightly fogged, Jack reached into his pocket
and found the cigarette pack. He handed it to John, then
settled back with a deep sigh. "There sure as hell won't
be anymore fucking aluminum siding to put up, that's
one thing."

"Let me have one of those too, John, as long as
you're up," said Archibald. He coughed, as though
anticipating the first drag. "I had sort of hoped to live
another ten years. My father, uh, my father lived to be
eighty-seven."

Billy laughed shrilly. "I had sort of hoped to live
another sixty years," he said, imitating his grandfather's voice sarcastically. "Oh *shit*!"

The old man looked hurt. "Of course. I know it's much harder on you youngsters. I've lived most of my life. But strangely enough, I'd like to keep on living, too."

"Of course you would, Grandpapa," said Marcia. "Don't pay any attention to Billy. He's a pig."

Billy said, "I'm getting screwed worse than anybody here. I'm only *seventeen.*"

Ginny burst into tears, spilling her drink onto the floor. "My *babies,* she sobbed.

John went over to comfort her. He took her glass and refilled it.

"Think of it in terms of, well, we'll all be leaving at the same time." He stuttered slightly. "W-w-we'll all be together." Tears were misting his eyes. He turned his back on them and took another long swallow, then lit the Marlboro. He remembered that Archibald had asked for one and took the packet to him.

"In thinking about death, I've always gotten some comfort from Lucretius," said John. "Most people somehow feel that when they die they'll still be hovering around somewhere regretting the years they were cheated of, watching those still alive having the good times they'll never have again." He paused to take another drink. "This, of course, is natural but ridiculous. Death is complete oblivion. There can't be any regrets, any envy. You're *not around* to look back and regret the years you were not able to live. While you're here, you're here. I'm okay, you're okay. When you're gone, you simply do not exist."

Chris toppled forward onto the floor in a faint.

They scrambled around reviving her with washcloths soaked in cold water.

She sat up. "I think I must have been holding my breath or something." She looked up at Jack, who was hugging her tucked against his chest. "I'd like to have that abortion, Jack. If you can find a doctor who'll bother.''

Jack burst into tears.

Marcia said, "I like that about our all leaving together.'' Her mouth twisted. "I—I want Jeff to leave with us,'' she sobbed.

VI

The *Times* carried a banner headline in Monday morning's first edition, "WORLD TO END IN SEPTEMBER." Pages of Space Agency photos and scientific explanations followed. For once the strictly foreign news was pushed out of the first few pages, though there was an interview with the Pope on page one.

He had met with the College of Cardinals to discuss an encyclical letter which would define the church's position. The Pope was seeking divine guidance. Either God was punishing the world for the rampancy of sin and disrespect, or the impending holocaust was due to a temporary ascendancy of the forces of evil. The Pope admitted that either or both might be the cause. Perhaps it was the beginning of Armageddon, he said, with the whole great universe to become locked in mortal struggle. He prayed that God would provide an answer.

Then there was the question of the capsule the American pharmaceutical companies were producing, which they had tentatively labeled *Oblivion 123*. One of the tenets of the Catholic faith was that self-destruction was a mortal sin. In light of these special circumstances, this tenet would be reexamined. Particularly since cremation was also proscribed.

The *News* was direct, with three-inch letters proclaiming "WORLD TO BURN!" The *Village Voice* put out a special extra, and its banner headline asked "WORLD TO END?" Prominently featured was an interview with a black militant leader who claimed it was all a white plot to promote black genocide. "After all us blacks take our pills, there'll be a big fire all right. In those crematoriums they're throwing up in Jersey.''

It was true that the Government had started construction of a twenty-acre crematorium in Jersey, but it was purely a health measure. Thousands would probably become despondent and jump the gun by a month or so. Then, you never could tell how well the undertakers and cemeteries would be functioning in handling the regular flow. The crematorium was a crash project, with high priority.

John Tate, Archibald and Jack drove down to the Village State Employment Office. They hadn't been able to get near the Post Office to read the lists of essential occupations. However, John was certain that copywriter wouldn't be one of them, and Jack couldn't see that anyone would want aluminum siding. Archibald went along out of curiosity. Lawyers could never be unessential, he maintained. Anyway, as a senior citizen he probably wouldn't be required to do much of anything.

The station parking lot was half-empty, and since John had a commuter parking permit for his rusty old Corvair, they decided to leave the car there and walk the five blocks to the Employment Office.

Main Street, where the office was located, was packed from curb to curb with people, making auto traffic out of the question. They stood on the fringe of the crowd wondering whether to stay or go.

A man came out of the Employment Office with a bull horn. ''Everybody go home,'' he yelled. ''Listen to the radio for other arrangements. This is impossible.''

Apparently most of the population was unessential.

''Hell, I'm going down to New York,'' said John. ''No point in moping around out here.''

Archibald nodded. ''I'll join you.''

Jack decided he'd go out to the job. Unessential or not, he suspected that the guy whose house they were working on would like to have it finished. It would look pretty peculiar if they left it half covered with siding and half covered with beaten-up old shingles.

"Don't you think we ought to finish the guy's house, Dad?" he asked.

John reached for the Corvair keys. "I certainly do. I wouldn't want to spend my last three months in a house only half-covered with aluminum siding."

Jack took the keys. "It's not only that, he's probably been looking forward for weeks to seeing his house look new and beautiful. This is simulated redwood grain, and it really is terrific."

John smiled. "*You'd* like to see it finished too, right?"

"Well, sure."

They waved to Jack as he hurred off, then strolled into the station. A small group of commuters stood around, looking uncertainly at the closed ticket window and chatting nervously. John approached a neighbor, Willard Cohn.

"Hi, Will. Any trains running?"

Cohn shrugged. "Who knows? Rumor has it that one went through about an hour ago."

"Hmmmm."

"I've about decided to give it up and drive in. Want to take a chance with me? The roads may be bumper-to-bumper."

John said, "Might as well. You know my father, don't you?"

"Sure. How are you, Mr. Tate?"

"About the same as everyone else, I guess. Confused. How are you?"

"Depressed."

They laughed.

As they walked to Cohn's big Lincoln Continental John asked, "How's Celia taking it?"

He busied himself unlocking the doors. "Surprisingly well. I think the women have more guts than we have."

John offered the front seat to his father, who declined. "Yeah. Ginny and the girls have gone to investigate the supermarket situation. With this 'everything free' bit, they figure the hoarders will clean them out in minutes."

They climbed in. "Say, I didn't think of that. I'd better call Celia when I get to New York." He stepped on the starter. "Also the liquor store."

"I'm in pretty good shape there," said John. He had been in London in April, and before leaving had ordered three cases of Glenlivet shipped home. Even with duty it was considerably cheaper than at his liquor store. Two and a half cases were still left in the basement. Thirty quarts of golden, soul-satisfying pure malt Scotch. It was a comforting thought. He expected to be semi-stoned reasonably often during the next three months.

Cohn wheeled the big comfortable car out of the parking lot and headed for the Thruway. "I don't know why I'm going in. My business is about as unessential as you can get." He manufactured perfumes.

"Me either," said John. "It's something to do. No point in finishing the novel I'm working on."

"Ha." It wasn't a laugh, just a comment. "You can't even finish it for posterity. That's a damned shame," said Cohn. "I suppose it'll sink in eventually, but I just can't seem to grasp it. That there'll be absolutely nothing left."

John said, "It's completely mind-boggling all right. The biggest mind-boggle of all time."

Old Archibald leaned forward. "Do you think there

could be any possibility of error?"

John turned his head. "I wish I could believe that."

Cohn said, "I'm afraid the science boys know what they're talking about. After all, if they can put ship after ship on the moon—"

John lit a cigarette. He had swiped a pack of Marlboros from the carton in Jack's room. "Maybe we should refuse to accept it anyway. Maybe Bishop Berkeley was right. Maybe we're here only because we think we're here. Maybe the earth's going to burn up only because we *think* it's going to burn up."

Cohn stepped on the gas, shifting into the faster left lane. "It was pretty damned warm all last winter. I didn't wear my overcoat once, but I *thought* about wearing it a lot. In late January, for instance, when it was eighty-five degrees."

John laughed, without much mirth. "Don't underestimate the power of the mind."

"Don't you have a radio in this gilded palace?" Archibald asked Cohn.

"Oh, sure. Why didn't I think of it?" He touched a button on the instrument panel.

The announcer's voice leapt at them. "Let me repeat. *Do not* go to your local State Employment Office. Go to your regular job or stay home. The authorities are not yet equipped to handle the placement of nonessential workers. For one thing, they have been unable to ascertain how many are required. As of the moment, it seems that more than two-thirds of the essential workers are staying on the job. We'll have more information on this for you later. In the meantime, *do not* go to your State Employment office.

"This morning President Fargo replied to the charges brought by black leader Harrison Ricketts that the world's end announcement was a plot to promote black genocide. Here's President Fargo."

The president's taped voice came booming from the speaker. "This is the most ridiculous nonsense I have ever heard. Can Mr. Ricketts seriously believe that the governments of *six* of the earth's major powers would cooperate in such an insane scheme? Let me point out that no one, I repeat, *no one* will be forced to take *Oblivion 123*. If Mr. Ricketts actually believes this nonsense, I suggest that he advise all blacks to refrain from taking the capsule. After they see a few million whites pass away in quiet, painless dignity, I presume that this and the increasing heat may change their minds. Personally I don't think Mr. Ricketts really believes this absurd charge. I think he just wants to stir up trouble. And given our situation, it is absolutely incomprehensible to me that anyone would wish to give us any more trouble than we already have. And one final word, Mr. Ricketts. We are all facing death. This childish accusation is an insult to every American. Go soak your head in cold water and grow up, will you?''

The announcer chuckled. "President Fargo is not his usual suave self this morning. Obviously the president has a lot on his mind, and none of it can be very pleasant.''

A rock number was announced, and Cohn switched off the radio.

Traffic was curiously light. Perhaps many were staying home to comfort their families, John thought, with some feeling of guilt. On the other hand, the idea of really being able to comfort anyone in a situation so irrevocable was somewhat naive. *Oblivion 123* or not, each person would die very much alone.

Cohn dropped them near Grand Central. Archibald's office was on Madison Avenue, and John's on Third Avenue. They parted, agreeing to meet at five for the trip back.

Manhattan seemed as crowded as ever. But the usual

bustle was missing. People were not hurrying along, eyes straight ahead. They walked slowly, staring at each other curiously and sneaking glances at the sky and skyscrapers above like tourists fresh from Three Gullies, Idaho.

Marilyn Henley was wearing a flowing, ankle-length gown of monk's cloth. Her only adornment was a thick gold cross suspended on a bulky chain.

John looked her up and down, trying to find some trace of Saturday's wild sexuality. "What have we here, a priestess?"

"I'm going to join Jesus," she said.

"Oh."

"You owe me nothing, sinner," she said.

"What? Oh, thanks." It was mildly comforting to be reminded that Chase Manhattan, Citibank, Marine Midland, Bowery, Visa, and Master Charge wouldn't be collecting much either.

"So you're going straight, eh?"

"What else?"

He lit a Marlboro. "I've been considering the possibility of going ape. Plunging into the kind of wild orgies I've read about but never dared."

She shook her head. "Don't damn your immortal soul more than it's already damned. Jesus is giving us one last chance."

"Chance for what?"

"Chance to repent."

He'd spent a lifetime repenting, John thought, in the form of worrying about whether he was doing the right thing. He'd lived every day for tomorrow, or next year, and now he couldn't quite figure out how to live for today.

The corridor door popped open and Wendell Harlowe came rushing in. He was a tall man with stylish gray hair, and a resonant actor's voice. "John! I'm glad you made it in.'' He leaned against the wall, looking dazed. "We've just been handed the biggest campaign the company's ever had. A *five* goddamned million dollar budget!'' He grinned wildly. "Five million dollars to be spent in *two months*. That's an annual budget of thirty million. This puts us right in there with the biggest kids on the block.''

John stared at him, momentarily speechless. "I thought we were strictly unessential.''

Harlowe kicked one of the reception room chairs around and sprawled in it. "Haven't you heard the latest? It's business as usual.''

John sat down. "What about this everything-free thing? Who needs to advertise something they're going to give away?''

"Oh that. I talked to Washington early this morning. They're going to give out scrip. If you're poor, and don't already have a television set, or a car, for instance, you get one. If you're earning less than ten thousand, you get a ton of food scrip. Buy all the steaks you want. The rest of us still pay cash.''

"Oh.'' No free goodies. Diddled again by the dirty digit of fortune.

"Do you realize the agency will gross $750,000 on this account alone?''

"What are you going to do with it?''

Harlowe shook his head, his face sober. "Oh hell, it's something to do, isn't it? I never had a five-million dollar budget. And on one lousy little product.'' He smiled. "Anyway, the whole megillah may be a mistake.''

"What's the product?''

Harlowe fished out a package of cigarettes. John noticed that he had switched to Winstons. "You know Mort Lochman? Lochman Novelty and Die Stamping Corporation?''

"Sure."

"He had a real whang-bang of an idea. During the Vietnam thing they subcontracted some bullets for the army. Just the casings. Now he's got about a million of these damned things lying around. He's got the dies. He can make fifty million of them." He paused to light his cigarette, savoring the stronger smoke. "Now here's the gimmick. He gold-plates these bullets, attaches a gold-plated chain, and zingo, you've got a prestigious container for your *Oblivion 123* capsule. We figure at least twenty million people will buy them at $7.99. Cost of manufacture, $1.13."

John nodded. "I see it all. When it comes time to bite the bullet, BITE GOLD!"

"Right! Now you're swinging, man."

John said, "I'm not sure I want to bother with it." He had close to fifteen thousand in a savings account, and he couldn't visualize their needing more than five thousand a month. Prices certainly wouldn't climb, what with giving all that stuff to the poor. Also, if he was unemployed, they could qualify for the free goodies.

Harlowe stood up. "John, I'm depending on you to handle the copy. Hell, you've already come up with a ball-buster of a headline. Bite the bullet, bite gold. I love it."

John lit one of his Marlboros. He sat smoking and shaking his head sadly.

"Look at it this way, John. What the hell are you going to do with your time anyway? Write another novel for that great big incinerator in the sky?"

"No. Certainly not that."

"Travel? You've been all over the world. And conditions today. *I* wouldn't want to try Europe or the Orient."

John leaned back, studying the ceiling. "No, I plan

to stay and die right in dear old Green Valley.''

"So what are you going to do? Sit around and go quietly crazy?''

"I might get to know my family better.''

Harlowe strolled over and stood looking down at him. "Do you *really* believe that?''

No, he didn't believe it. He'd never know them any better than he knew them right now.

Well, what the hell. Writing the kind of horseshit this product needed would be no problem. A week at the most. And, as Wendell said, it would be something to do.

He had a sudden inspiration. "There are a lot of good books I've always wanted to read but never got around to. Like Spengler's *Decline of the West.*''

Harlowe turned and went back to his chair. "Spengler. For Christ's sake. Better you should reread *Valley of the Dolls.*

He was probably right. Read for entertainment, not enlightenment. Enlightenment wasn't worth much now, was it?

"Write the copy. There'll be a fat bonus in it for you.''

"In advance?''

Harlowe cocked an eyebrow. "Don't you trust me?''

"Sure. But it's the time element. An extra ten thousand, say, to blow over the next three months, provides a little incentive. Ten thousand two months from now? Who needs it? I have an idea the weather is going to be a bit tropical.''

"Ten thousand!''

"Wendell, there'll be a hell of a lot of writing. TV spots, radio, newspaper ads, and maybe even some for the weekly magazines. No time for the monthlies, of course.''

"Hmmm.''

"Hell, your commissions the *first week* will be about $90,000."

Harlowe's eyebrows twitched as he did some fast figuring. Finally he said, "Yeah. Okay, it's a deal. But it's got to be fast. I want to start taping some spots tomorrow, or the next day at the latest."

John went into his office and shucked his jacket. Thrusting some paper into the Selectric, he began work on the gold bullet television commercials. It was a simple enough proposition. Vanity and safety. The *Oblivion 123* safety blanket. You'd want to keep your precious pill safe and with you at all times. Your painless passage to eternity. The alternative was too ugly to even contemplate. Wear your gold bullet proudly, go out with dignity when the time came.

No time for elaborate production. A straight taped pitch from a well-known actor or actress, product demonstration, and hurry to your nearest stores before they're all sold out, because under the unusual conditions prevailing we cannot guarantee an uninterrupted supply.

In an hour he had finished five 30-second spots, all with 8-second take-outs for station-break announcements. He tucked them away in his file cabinet. No need for Wendell to see how easy it was. He could have them later in the afternoon.

Sharon McMurtry, the bookkeeper, came into his office and contemptuously slapped a check on his desk. She was a red-headed, scrawny woman in her fifties, and the only one at Wendell Harlowe Associates who did not like John. For one thing, she thought his books were cynical, iconoclastic, immoral, and at times even downright *dirty*. Secondly, she thought he was grossly overpaid.

She focused her bloodshot eyes on him briefly, then walked out without speaking. Sharon was a weekend alcoholic, and it had been one hell of a weekend. In spite of his antipathy, he sympathized with the hangover she must have.

He hurried to his desk to look at the check. $10,000.00. Ten thousand and No/100 Dollars. Signed, Wendell Harlowe. The signature was a bit shaky, but it was Wendell's all right. He put on his jacket, stuck the check in his billfold, and left the office.

At the bank things were moving slowly. A number of the tellers seemed to be absent, and he noticed that two of the vice presidents were perspiring away as substitutes, counting cash with rusty fingers. John chose one of these lines to wait in. His was going to be a rather large transaction, and it would be handy and time-saving to have a vice president teller.

Three cigarettes and a half hour brought him up to the counter.

"Mr. Trampelli," he said.

The harassed banker looked at him more closely. "Oh, Mr. Tate. How are you?"

"About as well as could be expected. I want to cash this. I'll take it in hundreds." He scribbled his endorsement on the back.

Trampelli looked at the check. "Holy smackeral. Ten G's. You want it *all* in *hundreds*?"

Tate nodded.

"You wouldn't consider a cashier's check for nine, and the rest in cash?"

"Uh uh. I want all cash."

Trampelli shrugged. Strange things were happening today. "Hang on. I'll have to round up some hundreds." He went away shaking his head.

Fifteen minutes later John left with a stack of one-hundred dollar bills too thick to fold in his wallet. He had put a rubber band around them and slipped the packet into his inside jacket pocket.

Next on the schedule was a good lunch. He walked to Lexington Avenue and started uptown. Between 44th and 46th Streets he noticed that the pros were still out and in business, not yet ready for Jesus, he gathered. He had passed them all many times on his way to lunch. There was the dark-haired fat girl who hovered near the entrance to a seedy hotel. Twenty feet on was the leaning post of a black girl with tremendous breasts and legs like stilts. Further on stood the Spanish type. Honey-colored skin, gleaming black hair and lips painted shiny red. No hips. Bad case of buck teeth, made even more dramatic by her bright plastic lips.

Of the some eight regulars who worked the two-block stretch, there was only one who even vaguely aroused him. She was a blonde with very fair skin and almost white hair, young, and too improbably pretty to be walking the streets. He reflected that perhaps she was terribly stupid, though she looked bright enough. Probably the first thing every customer said to her was, "How did a nice girl like you—?"

Today she was wearing a blue shirt, unbuttoned enough to show her firm, unblemished breasts right to the point where the cloth concealed the nipples, a tight miniskirt, and four-inch platform sandals.

She smiled, showing very white, regular teeth.

He smiled back, slowing his pace. Should he? No, he decided, and continued on. He was in no mood for quick relief in a grimy flophouse. Besides, some of these girls worked with pretty rough pimps. He might be suddenly relieved of his ten thousand. Then a new thought reinforced his decision. She might well be a decoy lady cop. She looked far too good to be a street walker. A high-priced call girl, maybe, but not a pavement pounder.

The Four Seasons resembled Grand Central during a

power failure. Not a chance without a reservation. He couldn't even get through the crowd to the maitre d'. Being smaller, Brussels was worse. People with reservations were clustered on the sidewalk, unable to even get in. At Cote Basque, he showed the headwaiter a crumpled twenty quickly, but with no success.

"I'm sorry sir, I'd like to accommodate you, but— *im*-possible."

Laurent was the same. They were all trying to operate with considerably reduced staffs.

He ended up on a stool at Zum Zum. The German waitresses, he noted, were all present and hustling about with their usual determined efficiency. He ordered a weisswurst platter and a stein of beer. Hardly a meal to celebrate his new-found riches. He could have done as well at the Overseas Press Club and maybe heard some inside scuttlebutt too. He polished off the weisswurst, sauerkraut and hot potato salad morosely, then ordered strawberry shortcake with vanilla ice cream on it. Ordinarily he never ate desserts.

Back on the sidewalk he stood for a moment watching the crowds amble by. Stuffed and depressed, the strawberry shortcake and beer combination giving him mild indigestion, he strolled to Park Avenue and started back downtown to the office.

The Mercedes-Benz showroom caught his eye. He wandered in and looked around idly. No salesmen seemed to be on duty.

The manager finally came out of his office. "May I help you? We're a bit shorthanded today."

"How much is that one?" Tate asked, pointing to a maroon sedan.

The manager walked over and peered nearsightedly at the price listing pasted on the rear window. "Ninety-one hundred. With tax, ninety-seven thirty-seven.'' He sniffed. ''You understand, this is a previously owned automobile.''

''I'll take it. How soon can I have it?''

The manager looked startled. He glanced at his watch. ''With a cashier's check I guess you could have it about 4:30. If there's no foul-up at the license bureau.'' He coughed lightly. ''Of course you'll have to arrange insurance coverage.''

They went into the office and Tate waited while the manager wrote up the sale. He called his insurance agent, who strangely enough was at his desk at Allstate, and gave him the registration number and other details.

''Now,'' said the manager, looking up, ''I'll require a deposit until you come back for the car.''

Tate pulled out his stack of one-hundred dollar bills. He counted out ninety-eight of them. ''Might as well take care of the whole thing.''

The manager looked at the bills suspiciously. ''This is rather unusual. That is—''

''Look, I just got these from the bank. They're perfectly okay.'' Tate glanced at his watch. ''You've got plenty of time to take them to the bank and make sure they're not counterfeit. Well before I pick up the car.''

The manager reddened. ''I didn't mean to imply—''

Tate smiled. ''I'm not offended. Everything is a little crazy today, right? I've always wanted a Mercedes. Now that I have one, I'm naturally anxious to take possession of it as quickly as possible.''

The manager stood up. ''Of course.'' He gave Tate his receipt and sixty-three dollars change.

Tate walked slowly back to his office, feeling a little guilty about the Mercedes. He had meant to give Ginny half of the ten thousand. Still, she would enjoy the Mercedes, he rationalized, and after he finished the

damned gold bullet campaign, maybe they might drive
up to Maine. She'd like that. And if she wanted to buy
herself something special, like a mink coat, they could
take the money from the savings account. A mink coat?
Under the circumstances, that was definitely out. Well,
there were probably a lot of things she might like.
Anyway the car would get them around in modest
comfort and luxury.

Back at his typewriter he began work on the newspaper ads. By now the whole project had begun to
disgust him, and he was sorry that he had spent most of
the bonus. His thoughts kept wandering to the moment
when it would be necessary to take the capsule. His
inner conviction had been that while he was afraid of
pain, he was not afraid of dying. Yet a sense of gigantic
loss kept sweeping over him in nauseating waves. No
time for writing the book that would firmly establish
him as a major writer. Not even the continuity of
family, not even the tiny immortality of his strain being
added to the progression of generation piled on generation. How could a brain so complex, with so many
millions of memories and ideas and visual images—
visual images so startling in clarity and intensity that
they were more real than John himself—how could this
brain cease to exist? He shrugged. It was just a matter of
it ceasing to exist a few years earlier than expected.
Why was it so hard to accept the inevitability of death?

When he finished three ads he took them into the Art
Department, which was empty except for the art direc-
tor, Hank McIntosh. A handsome, boyish looking man
in his thirties, and admittedly gay, McIntosh sat with
his three-inch platform heeled boots cocked on his
desk. His slacks were so tight he could have used a
codpiece, and his baby-blue shirt with ruffles was immaculately ironed.

"Three smashers for you, Hank," said John. "Big rush."

The boots moved slowly to the floor. "I'm not rushing any fucking layouts. I don't even have any goddamned board man."

"Anytime within the next half hour will be okay."

"Aren't you *aware* that the fucking world is coming to an end?"

"I am. Take a couple of Valium or something. No need to dwell on it."

McIntosh threw the copy on the floor. "I'll dwell on it as much as I fucking well want to."

"Now Hank. Wendell's in a big hurry to get these into production."

McIntosh bent to pick up the copy. Wendell Harlowe confused him. When Wendell finished giving McIntosh directions, McIntosh still didn't have a glimmer of what Wendell wanted done. He depended on John to interpret. If he didn't cooperate, he would be facing a session with Wendell. This he would go to almost any lengths to avoid.

He read the copy, and then pondered John's notes on the suggested layout treatment. "My God. You mean we've got to produce ads for that *ghastly* pill? You make me want to *throw up*."

"I feel a bit that way myself Hank. Try not to throw up on the layouts."

He returned to his office, took the television copy from his file cabinet and put it on Harlowe's desk, relieved that Harlowe wasn't there. Otherwise they'd have to spend an hour chewing over the copy while Wendell rolled each sentence around in his actor's voice, testing for bugs John had already eliminated.

It was ten minutes of four, and he had contributed enough garbage for one day. He slipped on his jacket, left the building and strolled uptown to the Mercedes-Benz showroom.

The maroon beauty was ready for him. He walked around it, admiring it from every angle. The manager stood by looking depressed and tired. John paused at the back, his eyes glazing over as he looked at the shiny new license plate.

"What the hell kind of sick joke is this?" he yelled. The plate read DED-123.

The manager jumped. "What do you mean?"

"The license plate. DED-123."

The manager examined the plate carefully. "It's not DED. It's DEO."

"Oh." So it was.

"I'm afraid our nerves are a bit edgy, Mr. Tate."

"Not at all, not at all," said John, ducking and sliding into the driver's seat. He started the motor and felt a small thrill listening to the powerful but quiet purr. He put it in gear and rolled slowly out the parking bay to the street, admiring the wood-grained instrument panel and noting that there was only 41,280 miles on the odometer.

VII

The man whose house was half-covered with redwood-grained aluminum siding had tears in his eyes. He was a chubby five-foot-seven, and had closely cropped but curly black hair.

He blinked his misty eyes. "I figured you guys wouldn't come back. I said to my wife Teresa, I said Teresa, them hippie types will never come back. They couldn't care less."

"We wouldn't let you down, Mr. Carlucci," said Jack Tate. "Hell, nobody wants his house half crapped up this way." Three members of the four-man crew had shown up. They could finish the job in two or three more days.

"I'm telling you, Teresa cried like her heart was breaking."

"Don't you worry, Mr. Carlucci," said Tony, the subcontractor. "You're going to have one hell of a beautiful house in two-three days."

"Teresa said to me, we gotta die like *this*! Listen, it broke my heart."

He hurried into the house, surreptitiously brushing his eyes with the back of his hand.

In a few minutes Teresa came out with a platter of rolls and a pot of coffee. She was as plump as her husband and just about as tall.

They stopped work and gathered around.

"God bless you. You're true gentlemen," she said.

Jack accepted a roll and a cup of coffee, a little embarrassed. "We figured it was only right to finish the job. Of course, we probably won't be starting any new ones. At least, I don't think so." He looked at Tony.

Tony shook his head. "I don't think we'll be starting no new ones."

They went back to work in high spirits, cutting and nailing up the siding with great care to assure perfect fit and alignment. The job was going so fast there was even time for kidding around. At one point they removed the ladder and left Tony clinging to the roof with his chest and arms, his legs and rear end dangling over.

"Put the ladder back, you goddamned mother fuckers!" he yelled.

They hurriedly put the ladder back, not wanting Mrs. Carlucci to hear and be shocked by his language.

At the end of the day, they were invited into the house. Carlucci ushered them to the dining room, where the table was crowded with food and drink. On it was a bottle of Seagram's Seven Crown, bottles of ginger ale and Seven-Up for mixers, a plastic picnic hamper filled with ice cubes and cans of Budweiser, platters of Italian bread, rolls, cakes, pastries, cold meats and cheeses and antipasto with olives, artichoke hearts, and anchovies.

"Man, you got enough here for an army," said Ed, the third member of the crew.

"Eat," said Mrs. Carlucci. "Enjoy yourself." She was shy and a bit tongue-tied.

"First we drink," said Carlucci. He put ice cubes in four tumblers, poured about two inches of Seagram's into each glass, then offered the mixers. Tony took Seven-Up, Ed ginger ale, and Jack said he'd drink his on the rocks.

"Oh, a tough guy. Likes his whiskey straight," said Carlucci. He topped off his own drink with ginger ale, and lifted his glass. "Now I wanna propose a toast.

Here's to a bunch of great guys that got pride in their work.''

They stood smiling self-consciously while he took a swallow.

Jack lifted his glass. ''Let me toast our host and his very lovely wife. Here's to Mr. and Mrs. Carlucci, a couple of real decent human beings.''

Jack had liked Carlucci from the first day on the job. Carlucci had taken them into the house and showed them where the bathroom was. ''You gotta use the john, here it is. You want ice-water, go in the kitchen. There's a gallon jug in the refrigerator. You want coffee, just ask Mrs. Carlucci. She'll make you some.'' Most people they worked for didn't want them to set foot in the house. Maybe they thought people putting up aluminum siding didn't have kidneys or bowels. If you asked to use the bathroom they looked at you like you were maybe going to leave syphilis germs around or infest the place with cockroaches. With types like that you held it until you were busting, then got in the truck and drove to a filling station. It was a damned nuisance.

The others lifted their glasses. ''Yeah man! Here's to the Carluccis!'' said Ed.

Now the Carluccis stood smiling self-consciously.

After two more stiff helpings of Seagram's the atmosphere relaxed. Even Mrs. Carlucci, who had sipped only a glass of red wine, seemed tipsily at ease. They sat around the table, sprawling comfortably, drinking, smoking and eating.

''What you guys think?'' asked Carlucci. ''You think this sun business is *real*?''

Ed popped open another can of beer. ''It seems like a—a impossibility.''

''Maybe His Holiness will figure it out,'' said Jack.

He had noticed a bleeding-heart-of-Christ picture in the living room, and there was a big crucifix in the dining room.

Mrs. Carlucci crossed herself.

"Aaaauh, he's more confused than the rest of us," said Carlucci. "I lost a lot of confidence in that guy already."

"Yeah, well—" said Jack. He himself had lost a lot of confidence in the *Well of Resplendent Aurae* and most of the other facets of the Church of Empirical Mysticism. He and Chris had first tried being Seventh Day Adventists, but it hadn't worked out.

"I think—" said Tony, leaving the words hanging. The others waited. Finally he shrugged helplessly and went back to eating.

"I tell you one thing," said Carlucci. "Them blacks are gonna make trouble. I'm glad those fu—" He stopped, glancing at Mrs. Carlucci quickly. "I'm glad them bleeding-heart innalectuals fell on their asses outlawing guns. I'm keeping my shotgun and my carbine oiled and loaded. I tell you, we're gonna be fightin' for our lives before this is over."

Jack drained off a can of beer. "Geeze, I hope not. It seems so, so damned futile."

Carlucci shook his head slowly. "Mark what Carlucci told you, boy. Get yourself a gun and keep the fu— keep the damned thing loaded."

VIII

Old Archibald sat in his small office smoking cigarettes and wondering why he had bothered to come in to New York. He shared a suite with five other lawyers, which solved the telephone answering and secretarial problems at reasonable expense. Today, however, the place was virtually empty. Only Mrs. Ruben, a legal secretary in her late fifties, had come in. She was seated at the receptionist's desk taking calls and working the small Key Chief switchboard.

"Mr. Tate," she said, "Judge Blaufeld on three-eight."

"Arch, how are you?" asked Blaufeld, his deep voice so sincere it sounded like a real question. Archibald and Marcus Blaufeld had been at Columbia Law School together, and had been friends for almost fifty years.

"All right, I guess. You?"

"Swamped. I'll have to make it brief. I've been asked to chair a committee to coordinate—well, to try to straighten out a situation that may get out of hand. The mayor, the police commissioner, the borough presidents, and various other worthies are on it. I'd like to have you with us."

Archibald cleared his throat softly. "What's the purpose of the committee, Marcus?"

There was a pause. "It's a bit hard to pin down, but, well we can see a number of serious problems brewing in connection with the, ah, terminal situation we're in. Someone's got to try to cope with them, and we seem to be elected."

"I see."

"Will you serve?"

"Why not?" It was something to do.

"Good. I was hoping you would. I have a lot of confidence in your, ah, diplomacy. And brother, are we going to need it!"

"Hmmm."

"We're meeting at two-thirty today. The Wilton room of the Hilton."

"All right. By the way, what's the name of the committee?"

Blaufeld grunted. "GNYCCS, The Greater New York Committee to Coordinate the Situation. No doubt it will shortly be known as GYNECOCCYX."

Replacing the phone, Archibald left the office and strolled over to Charlie Brown's in the Pan Am Building, where he occassionally lunched. He was wryly amused at Blaufeld's request. They couldn't let the world end simply, of course. There would have to be a committee involved to screw it up. He shrugged. There were, he supposed, many practical problems relating to the logistics of world-ending which would demand attention.

The bar was packed, one end crowded with boisterous shouters drinking with heavy-handed gaiety, the other end tightly threaded with morose, silent men who sipped their martinis in quiet depression. Archibald worked his way past the manic section and took his place among the downhearted. He drank two martinis, smoked four cigarettes, and then went to the dimly lit restaurant for a steak and kidney pie and a tall ale.

The meeting room seemed overly large for a committee, but as members entered, some singly and some in groups, it filled rapidly. About fifty chairs stood in rows facing the speaker's table, which was occuppied by Mayor Pellman Schapiro, Major-General Francis Tolan, representing the governor, Police Commissioner Wallace Reagan, and Judge Blaufeld. Seated in the first row were Councilman Harrison Ricketts, the black leader, the borough presidents of Manhattan, Queens, Bronx, Staten Island and Brooklyn, and Councilman Juan Ramiriz, spokesman for the Spanish speaking minority. In the second row were the county executives from Westchester, Putnam, Rockland, Nassau and Suffolk Counties. Assorted political leaders from New Jersey and Connecticut filled the seats next to and behind the county executives.

Here and there Archibald recognized other civic leaders such as Dwight Denton, the newspaper publisher, Chalmers Tuckett, the commissioner of parks, and a religious contingent which included a distinguished rabbi, a representative from the Archidiocese of New York, and Buck Bramble, the noted Protestant evangelist. Several prominent labor leaders were also present.

Archibald slipped into an empty seat next to Vincent Caruso, the Westchester county executive.

"How goes it, Vinnie?" he asked, turning in his seat to shake hands. Archibald had supported Caruso in the Democratic Primary and in his subsequent election.

Caruso said, "Great. I need another committee like I need a case of shingles. *Committee*. This is a mob scene."

Archibald nodded. "I'm surprised to see Bramble here. I thought he was praying with the President."

"That was at breakfast."

Archibald recalled that he had heard a rebroadcast of some of Bramble's remarks. He had switched off the radio when Bramble said, "We must accept with humility and understanding the fact that God's game-plan calls for phasing out the planet Earth." Archibald

had muttered dryly, 'What the hell kind of shafting are
we meek getting? We're supposed to inherit the earth.
It's going to be in pretty damaged condition if you ask
me.' Had he kept the radio on, Bramble might also have
mentioned the game-plan for phasing out Mercury,
Venus, Mars, Jupiter, Saturn, Uranus, Neptune and
Pluto. Mercury and Venus had already become brief
stars, and were now clouds of gas.

Mayor Schapiro called the meeting to order and
thanked all those present who had agreed to serve, with
particular thanks to Judge Blaufeld. He dwelt for a
short time on the qualifications of this eminent jurist,
then turned the meeting over to Blaufeld.

Blaufeld pulled the microphone closer and cleared
his throat, a sound which when amplified resembled an
old DC-3 taking off. "As you can see, we have quite a
large committee, and you are probably wondering how
we can function efficiently with this unwieldy number
of participants. Let me assure you that we intend here
only to outline the problems we face. Following this
we'll break up into subcommittees to tackle the nitty-
gritty.

"Our primary problems are maintenance of transport
and vital services. A quick survey has indicated that we
are not in too bad shape in this area. Yet. Today has
been only a little worse than the Monday following a
holiday weekend. However, we recognize that this
situation could deteriorate rapidly. Habit dies hard, and
many people probably came to work today because
they didn't quite know what else to do with themselves.
Next week, or even tomorrow, may be a different story.

"The president's coordinating committee will, of
course, deal with interstate transport of essential goods,
and interstate maintenance of power and other vital
services. Our concern will be with distribution and

maintenance of local services in the New York metropolitan area.''

Harrison Ricketts stood up. "Mr. Chairman.''

Blaufeld glanced in his direction. "Mr. Ricketts, if you will kindly allow me to finish outlining our objectives and priorities, we'll then open the floor for brief comments before dividing up into subcommittees.''

Ricketts remained standing. "Mr. Chairman. You got your priorities all wrong, man. You better get that luxury scrip out to my people up in Harlem in a big, big hurry. Otherwise you won't have to wait for the sun to burn New York to the ground. You talk about essential goods. Up there, essential goods are going to be new cars, fine clothes, caviar and champagne. And man, you don't give it to them in a hurry, they going to take it. They been cheated by Whitey long enough.''

Blaufeld kept his temper. "This is one of the matters we're here to deal with. That is, if you will allow us to get on with it.''

Ricketts sat down.

"As luck would have it, we're not in bad shape on the luxury front. There are probably more mink coats here in New York than any other city in the country. A quick check indicates that current inventories of new cars, including imports, exceed five hundred thousand. There are close to a million color television sets, several hundred thousand stereos, about a million square yards of top-quality carpet, and so on.''

Ricketts yelled, "Get it out to my people. They want it *now,* not two months from now!''

Juan Ramiriz stood up. "Mr. Chairman. My people are not so much concerned with mink coats.'' He glanced at Ricketts, his lips curling upward in a pained smile. "If a man must die, he should be allowed to die with honor. How can we die with honor in our hovels

infested with rats, cockroaches, bedbugs, lice and de-
caying garbage which is never picked up?''

Blaufeld cleared his throat. ''Yes, well, this will be
dealt with.''

Obviously disconcerted by the thought of having to
provide new housing for possibly two million blacks
and Puerto Ricans, Blaufeld finished his opening
statement in a rambling, somewhat disjointed manner,
and hurried to read his list of subcommittee appoint-
ments.

Archibald was surprised to find that he had been
appointed to the executive subcommittee. On it were
Judge Blaufeld, the mayor, the police commissioner,
Major-General Tolan, Carey O'Farrel, a prominent
labor leader, Dwight Denton, the publisher, Juan
Ramiriz and Harrison Ricketts.

The subcommittees adjourned to smaller meeting
rooms. The nine men of the executive subcommittee
assembled around a conference table, and Blaufeld
introduced those who were not already well-
acquainted. Archibald knew the mayor, the general,
and Dwight Denton well enough to be recognized by
them; the other members glanced at him curiously.

''I wanted Archibald Tate on this committee for
several reasons,'' said Blaufeld. ''First of all, he's a
fine lawyer and one of the most able diplomats I have
ever had the pleasure of knowing. Anticipating the
tensions under which we shall be working, I think we'll
be grateful for his conciliatory talents. Secondly, I
think he can act as liaison with the county executives.
Archibald lives in Westchester, and is familiar with
suburban problems.''

Archibald bowed his head modestly. With all this
talk of his being an able diplomat, they might be misled
into thinking he was a doyen of the State Department.
What Blaufeld had meant was that he was an able

negotiator. He focused his attention back on Blaufeld.

"The executive subcommittee will function primarily as a coordinating and liaison agency. Our job will be to coordinate the works of GNYCCS subcommittees and to maintain liaison with the State and Federal coordinating committees."

Harrison Ricketts interrupted. "All this coordinating is mighty fine, Mr. Chairman, but the big question is, when we going to get those Cadillacs rolling up to 125th Street?" He held up his hand to ward off Blaufeld's impatience. "You gentlemen know me as a moderate, and believe me, I'm trying to remain a moderate. But I think you also know we got some fire-eating militants up there like Ahmid Dak. They *looking* for trouble."

Blaufeld clipped the end from a long cigar. "The printing presses are rolling, Mr. Ricketts. The vouchers will be ready for distribution Wednesday, possibly even tomorrow."

"How these vouchers work?"

"The vouchers will be good for ten thousand dollars worth of luxury goods. These items must be selected from a specific list. Every family with an annual income under fifteen thousand will be entitled to ten thousand dollars in luxury vouchers."

"What about the young people away from their families?"

"Unmarried singles will receive five thousand in vouchers." Blaufeld stuck the cigar in his mouth and lit it. "Also, each family with an annual income of under ten thousand will receive three hundred dollars a week in food vouchers. Singles will get a hundred and fifty." He puffed the cigar, staring through the smoke at Ricketts. "Fair enough?"

Ricketts shrugged. "We'll see. Let's hope so, man. As you say, the world's got trouble enough—"

General Tolan played the piano idly on the table top with one hand. "To be on the safe side, I've asked the governor to give me a couple of regiments of the National Guard."

"I don't want any goddamned National Guard in my city," said Mayor Schapiro.

Commissioner Reagan nodded. "Absolutely the last resort, General."

"Count me as also opposed to bringing in the National Guard," said Dwight Denton.

Carey O'Farrel, the labor leader, slapped the table disgustedly. "You bleeding-heart liberals better come out of your dream worlds. You better let the General get those troops in here in a hurry. The blacks start any rampages, about a million of my people in Queens and Brooklyn are going to be taking those shotguns out of the closets and you're going to have open war. We're sick to death of violence and muggings."

"What you mean is they're creaming in their pants to get at us. They can't wait to use those shotguns," said Ricketts. "They aren't sick of violence, they're *looking* for it. They been pettin' those shotguns for years, sayin' 'just you wait, baby, you gonna have your chance to blow a hole in some black man's guts.' Violence! You white honkeys got more violence in your little finger than the black man's got in his whole body."

Judge Blaufeld, having no gavel, rapped the table briskly with a heavy-bottomed water tumbler. "Please gentlemen, this type of exchange will get us nowhere."

"Let's hope there'll be no need for troops," said Archibald. "Remember, people—and I include a lot of whites—are going to be pretty busy living it up with these new-found riches." As he spoke, however, he wondered how long the kids, black, white and brown, would be diverted by their new toys.

IX

The supermarket in the Green Valley Shopping Center, which was located some two miles from the Tate house, was only mildly crowded. Word had spread quickly that nothing was being given away.

"I don't think we'll get much of that food scrip up here, Mrs. Tate," said the manager. "Nobody up here's eligible." He paused to light a cigarette. "Except my clerks, and they steal that much every week already." Then he forced a big laugh and slapped the counter behind his check-cashing window.

Chris was pale and had a distraught look about her that worried Ginny. She decided to limit her shopping to a quick trip through the aisles to pick up a few things that were actually needed. Then there was a long wait. Only two of the check-out aisles were open.

Chris was making little whimpering noises, hardly audible, but managed to hold herself together until they got back to the old station wagon. Then she burst into tears and became hysterical.

"Don't you see, I've got to get this thing out of me! It's not my baby!" She broke off, sobbing unintelligibly, then screamed, "It's a monster. It's eating my insides out. It's a futile, hopeless, deformed little bloodsucker. And it's growing. God, it's growing so fast. It's pushing right up to my throat!"

Ginny tried to soothe her. "I'm going to drive you right to Dr. Howard. Try to be calm."

Chris bent over, holding her face in her hands, her shoulders shaking.

Ginny started the motor, backed up, and raced out of the parking lot.

"Sit up honey, please. If I have to stop suddenly you'll crack you head on the instrument panel."

"I don't *care!*"

"Dr. Howard will take care of everything. You'll see."

Chris raised her head. "Will Dr. Howard give me back my beautiful baby? That's what it was, you know. Now it's a *monster.*"

"I know dear."

"How do you know?"

Ginny applied the brakes, almost skidding around a sharp curve. "I've had three children. They were all beautiful." Then she began to cry, and could hardly see the road.

Dr. Howard's waiting room was filled with nervous, depressed looking patients, but when the receptionist saw the condition the two Tate women were in she led them immediately to one of the small examining rooms.

For about ten minutes they sat intermittently smoking and crying until Dr. Howard came in. His hair had fallen over one eye, and he was looking both harassed and preoccupied.

"Now girls, what's this all about?" He stared at Chris, who was sobbing wildly. "Now Chris, this isn't going to do your baby any good."

Chris shrieked.

How could the man be so stupid, Ginny asked herself, tears rolling down her cheeks. "Surely you can understand, Doctor—"

Howard nodded, aware of and embarrased by his gaffe, and quickly prepared a hypodermic. He swabbed Chris's arm, making soothing noises, and quickly injected a sedative.

The nurse, who had been standing by, handed him another hypodermic. "Ginny, I think you can use a quick fix too," he said, with a pained smile.

Ginny shook her head. "If you have a five-grain Valium—"

He handed the hypodermic back to the nurse. "Right. Valium coming up." He turned to the nurse. "Thelma—" She left, nodding.

It suddenly occurred to Ginny that Duncan Howard had been a friend for more than twenty years. For five minutes he had been a total stranger.

The nurse returned with a pill and a glass of water.

Ginny popped the pill into her mouth and took a swallow of water. "Duncan, I'm sorry, I—"

He patted her arm. "I understand."

"Chris needs to have an abortion. Right away."

"Hmmm."

Chris sat with a vaguely glazed look, the drug taking effect.

"Hell, Ginny . . . From a practical point of view, of course, obviously—"

He stood up. "I'll ask Thelma to check some of the better clinics. I expect there'll be quite a few gals lining up." He walked briskly to the corridor. "Sit and relax. Both of you. You'll feel better soon."

When they got back to the house, Chris was so drowsy she could barely walk. Ginny got her upstairs and into bed.

Returning to the kitchen she emptied the grocery bags, wondering whether the frozen items had defrosted too much. She held several vegetable packets out for dinner and dumped the rest in the freezer. To hell with it.

The putt-putt of a small car in the driveway sent her to one of the dining room windows. It was the Boynton's white Volkswagen. The Boyntons had a white Cadillac, a white Buick station wagon, and a white Volkswagen. All of Mr. Boynton's other cars were black. He was an undertaker.

Billy and Heather Boynton got out. Billy opened the front end and lifted out two suitcases and an open cardboard box jammed with rock records. Heather filled her arms with a pile of clothes on hangers.

Ginny hurried around through the living room and met them at the front door.

"Heather is moving in with me," said Billy. "I hope you don't mind. If you do, we'll go somewhere else."

Heather watched Ginny warily, her mouth slightly open, her full lower lip giving the impression of a faint pout. She was an exceptionally pretty girl with gleaming chestnut hair billowing down her back, startling blue eyes widely spaced, and a sprinking of tiny freckles bridging her small but well-shaped nose.

"I—does Heather's mother—?"

"Mother says it's all right."

"Heather, you're only fifteen!"

"Sixteen. I'll be sixteen day after tomorrow."

Billy turned away. "Come on," he said to Heather, "we can find some kind of pad down in Greenwich Village. Lots of kids down there."

"Wait," said Ginny. "You might as well stay. If it's all right with Heather's mother and father."

"My father doesn't know about it yet."

"Oh. Well, come in anyway." Better here than in a *pad* shooting heroin or angel dust or something. Didn't anyone care anymore about contributing to the delinquency of a minor? When Jack had brought Chris home they had been frightened that Chris's parents might have put him in prison. She had been four months short of eighteen. Now a sixteen-year-old.

Considering the situation, she supposed Heather and Billy had a right to some happiness. If this was what would bring them happiness. Who knew?

Billy clumped up the stairs with the suitcases. Heather followed, carrying the clothes on hangers and looking at the Tate house with new interest. It was now her home.

Ginny watched them, half-frightened, yet telling herself, why shouldn't they play at being married for three months if this was what they wanted? She hurried to the kitchen and dug frantically around in the cabinet containing coffee, tea, flour, sugar and spices until she found her container of Valium tablets. She swallowed one with a few sips of water, hoping it would combine with the pill she had taken in the doctor's office and act swiftly, before she started screaming.

The youngest, Billy had the smallest room. About ten by thirteen, it had one large window facing the wooded area in the back of the house. It contained a maple bed, a small desk, a bureau, a record player and FM radio in its own stand with his record collection underneath, and boxes of additional records on the floor nearby. Posters quilted the walls and the back of the door. He had put down his own carpeting of orange glue-down squares.

"I like your carpet," said Heather.

He smiled. "Not as elegant as the Boynton mansion." He thought of the silky white shag, about two inches thick, in Heather's bedroom.

"Who cares?"

"I don't if you don't."

"I don't."

He hung her clothes in his closet, pushing his own roughly to one end. "Will you miss your family?"

She shook her head. "They're only ten minutes

away. Anyway, Daddy's awfully grumpy. He says the situation is making a mockery of his entire life's work.''

He found a place for her box of records against the wall. ''I guess we could all say that.'' He pulled open one of the bureau drawers and looked at the contents. ''But I can see how he might feel sort of overwhelmed.''

''Oh, you know how parents are. They think *their* problems are the only ones that are important.''

He continued staring into the drawer absentmindedly. ''Later I'll clear out some of these drawers for your stuff.''

''Okay.''

''Would you like a cup of tea? I think I'll have one.''

''Okay.'' She switched on the FM radio and rock immediately came vibrating through the two large speakers. Then she flopped down on the bed, cocking her white sneakers up on the footboard. She was wearing faded jeans and a yellow T-shirt. Bra-less, her rather full breasts pressed against the taut cloth showing a faint outline of her nipples.

He paused for a moment at the door staring at her. ''I'll be right back.''

''Okay.''

In the kitchen he ran water into the blackened copper-bottomed kettle and put it on the stove. Ginny stood staring out the window, her back to him.

''I'm making tea for Heather and myself. Do you want a cup?''

She turned, her face softening. It was the first considerate word she had heard from Billy in weeks. ''No, I'll have a cup of coffee. Would you like me to make sandwiches for you?''

He went to the bottom of the steps and yelled, ''Heather, do you want a sandwich?''

"No thanks," drifted down the steps faintly.

He went back to the kitchen. "No sandwiches, thanks."

"Billy, I hope—"

"Mom. Would you please call me *Bill*? I'm not a *little boy*."

She turned her head away, her eyes filling. "I was just going to say, I hope you and Heather will be—be happy." She went back to staring out the window, blurry-eyed.

He came over and touched her shoulder. "Mom. I'm sorry, I—thanks. Mom, you don't really mind calling me *Bill*, do you?"

She turned and clutched him briefly. "No, of course not."

Whistling softly, he set out three cups and saucers, putting tea bags in two and a teaspoon of freeze-dried coffee in the other.

The cups long empty, Billy and Heather lay on the bed listening to soft, plaintive, folk music. A small ceramic ashtray overflowing with cigarette butts rested on the floor beside them. He pulled her closer, her lips pressing against the side of her slender neck, his hands stroking her back gently.

He could smell just a trace of scented soap on her skin. Through the wide-open window came the stronger odor of fresh cut grass from next door, where the neighbor's power mower had finally ceased its clatter. Was it his turn, or Jack's, to do theirs? Maybe his father would get irritated and cut it himself.

Billy and Heather had laid this way many times, but now it was for real, he told himself. And she was probably a virgin. At least, she said she was. Actually he was too, though he pretended otherwise, even to himself. Having lied his way into X-rated films several

times down in New York, he felt thoroughly experienced. In his imagination he had done all those things
again and again, all the many variations of position and
foreplay required to make a girl ecstatic. Heather had
been entered in the front and the rear, she had been
licked and sucked and titilated with his tongue until she
was trembling and panting with passion.

He tugged at her T-shirt, pulling it upward.

"Are we going to do it *now*?" she whispered.

"Ummmm."

"Wouldn't it be better to wait until *tonight*?"

"Uh-uh."

He continued his efforts with the T-shirt. She lifted
her arms and helped him pull it over her head.

Feeling the softness of her breasts, he bent over and
kissed her nipples. They had stiffened, and tilted
slightly upward. He ran his tongue over them until she
stopped him.

"It tickles," she whispered.

He unbuttoned her jeans and began pulling them
downward. Her hips were wide, and they were men's
jeans, creating a temporary stalemate.

"How in hell do you ever get these things off?"

She wriggled, helping him. The tugging and scraping brought several small cries of pain. Her shorts came
along with the jeans. He threw them both on the chair
with her T-shirt, then bent over and kissed her body,
starting at her shoulders and working downward.

When he reached her triangle she giggled and pushed
his head away. "That tickles."

The neighbor's power mower started up again.
"Damn," he said under his breath. He reached over
and turned up the volume of the folk music. Then,
sitting up, he kicked off his sandals and undressed
quickly, throwing his own clothes on the floor.

He stretched out facing her and again pulled her

tightly against him, running his hand down her back, stroking her buttocks and working his fingers in between them, probing gently. She tightened her legs and he stopped. He kissed her hard, his lips parted, thrusting his tongue into contact with hers. They remained locked in this position for a while until she twisted her head away.

"What's the matter?"

"I can't breathe."

"Can't you breathe through your nose?"

She sighed, "I don't know. It just seems like I'm smothering."

He pulled away and brought his hand around to her front, where his fingers found her pubic hair and explored further. She tightened her thighs again, becoming rigid.

"Heather," he whispered, "they say girls don't enjoy it the first couple of times, but after that—"

She put her arms around his neck and snuggled closer. "I know." She kissed him, putting her tongue in his mouth this time.

The excitement suddenly became unbearable and he lost control, throbbing against her soft stomach.

"For Christ's sake. Goddamn it!"

She giggled.

He found some Kleenex and wiped her stomach dry. Then he reached for the pack of Marlboros on the FM radio, shook one out and lit it.

"We'll have to wait a little while."

"Light one for me."

He handed her his cigarette and lit another for himself."

"It may even hurt a little," he said.

"I know."

"If you want to wait until tonight—"

The power mower suddenly became quiet, bringing

relief from the barely conscious irritation of its metallic roar.

They crushed out their cigarettes and again lay pressed together, relaxed and waiting. Only a few minutes went by before he found himself ready.

"Ouch! That hurts!" She arched her back, gasping.

"Shall I stop?"

"No."

"Oh!" Her fingers dug into his shoulder.

"I'll stop."

"No."

Afterwards she lay in his arms, listless and depressed. "Is that all there is to it?" she asked.

"I told you you wouldn't enjoy it the first couple of times."

"You were so right."

"I'm sorry."

She kissed him. "Don't be."

Now he was depressed. The real thing was quite a letdown. Still, it would be better when Heather began to enjoy it. But what if she didn't? Maybe she was frigid.

He got up wearily and pulled on his clothes.

"You're hurt."

He shook his head. "Everything'll be mellow, you'll see."

The Boyntons' white Cadillac pulled into the driveway. Lawrence Boynton wrenched open the door and got our hurriedly. He was wearing a plaid sport jacket and looked more like a plump, jolly real estate salesman than an undertaker.

He trotted to the front door and impatiently rang the door chimes.

Ginny answered the door.

"Mrs. Tate?"

She nodded, looking past him at the white Cadillac. "You're probably Mr. Boynton."

"I am," he said, tight-lipped. "I understand my daughter is here."

She stood aside for him to enter. "She is. But before you make a scene—"

"I'm not here to make a scene. I just want to talk to my daughter."

"Before you talk to your daughter, will you sit down a minute?"

He looked suspiciously around, as though expecting to find Heather hiding behind a chair.

"Please sit down. I'd like to tell you about the situation before you speak to her."

He sat down on the edge of the sofa, his hands resting on his knees. "What is there to tell? She's moved out to live with your son. I won't tolerate it. She's only fifteen."

"Sixteen day after tomorrow."

"Well—" He grimaced. "Some *Sweet Sixteen* party. We were going to have a bunch of people out to the country club. Her friends, your son, some of our friends—"

She nodded. "I let them stay here because they were going to run away otherwise. Would you rather have her here, playing at being married, or down in Greenwich Village, playing at being married? And living in some rat-infested slum, associating with addicts and other unsavory types, and perhaps getting gang-raped and killed? Or becoming an addict herself?"

Boynton paled under his light tan. "Surely—"

"Mr. Boynton, you can't keep a teen-ager under lock and key. If she decides to run away, who's going to stop her? There are literally millions of kids wandering the country. How hard do you think the police are going to look? Especially with the situation being what it is?"

"But I want her with *us*. We're going *together*."

Ginny remained silent, staring at him. Was that all he could think about, their little pill-taking party?

"In all honesty, Mr. Boynton, don't you think the kids have a right to try for a taste of the life they're being cheated out of?"

"But, my God—"

"She's only a child?"

He nodded. "That's it. She's only a child!"

"Girls grow up very quickly at that age. She's certainly more mature than Billy. And think of it this way. If she finds that she can't cope with it, and she's unhappy, home is only ten minutes away. Suppose that happens to her in San Francisco, or Chicago, or even down in New York? Is she going to come home, or drift off with some other boy? Or boys?"

He sat chewing his lower lip, agonies of doubt wrinkling his forehead.

Ginny stood up. "I'll call her."

"Wait—"

She sat down.

"They must get married immediately. I won't have her going to meet her Maker wallowing in—in sin."

He was perspiring, and his eyes rolled upward cautiously. The Maker was obviously pretty damned angry already.

Ginny, who had done considerable soul-searching, couldn't imagine a god with any interest in human beings cruel enough to allow the things that had already happened in the world, much less the thing that was in store for it. However, she wouldn't patronize anyone else's belief.

"I suspect we could talk them around to it," she said.

He tugged at his collar, now embarrassed. "Would

you—could you talk to them? I—I don't trust myself.''

Good old Ginny. Receptacle for all troubles, all problems.

She nodded. "All right, I'll do the best I can?''

He stood up. "Thank you. I think I'd better go home. I don't feel at all well.''

He walked to the door, his shoulders hunched, no longer the jolly, self-confident salesman. Without the plaid jacket, he could very well be an undertaker. Ginny felt sorry for him. But then Ginny felt sorry for everyone. One day she'd start feeling sorry for herself, and then the family would be in real trouble.

Marcia Louise came home to pack. With Jeff.

Ginny rushed into the master bedroom and slammed the door. Flinging herself face-down on the bed, she lay beating the pillow weakly with her clenched fists. Where was John? He was never there when she needed him. All day she had been accepting responsibility, making decisions without any help. And John and Jack had both stayed away all day, probably getting drunk or something. Damn them!

The phone rang. She rolled over and picked up the bedroom extension. It was Thelma, Dr. Howard's nurse. They had checked a number of reputable clinics. All were swamped with demands for immediate operations. The earliest date they could arrange was a trifle over a month away.

"Would it be possible to speak to Duncan please?'' Ginny asked, deliberately using Howard's first name. Thelma sometimes became rather officious.

"Dr. Howard's with a patient. But hold on, I'll see.''

She waited five minutes until Howard came on.

"Duncan,'' she said, her voice higher with panic,

"I'm afraid Chris will have a nervous breakdown if she has to wait a *month*."

"It's that bad?"

"Couldn't you do it yourself? I mean, it's a very simple thing, isn't it?"

He coughed gently. "I suppose I could. But I'd really prefer—Let me see if I can persuade Josh Friedman to—" He explained that there were new techniques that made the process much more foolproof. Friedman was a gynecologist and therefore—

The age of specialization. Soon there wouldn't be any more general practitioners such as Duncan Howard. Soon there wouldn't be any more—She shuddered.

She got up and went downstairs. She wondered if a drink on top of the Valium would make her sick? Was it one of those tranquilizers you could drink with? Or couldn't drink with? Suddenly she didn't really care whether she was sick or not. She found the Scotch and poured several ounces into a squat Old-Fashioned glass, then went to the kitchen and added two ice cubes.

Upstairs the kids were moving around noisily. Separating the voices, it appeard that Billy and Heather were helping Marcy pack. She could picture Jeff standing there, smiling foolishly. He wouldn't be helping with the packing. Jeff never acted. He was acted upon. If there were a future to worry about, she would oppose a relationship between them vehemently. Under the circumstances, she supposed there was no point. John would be furious. Or devastated. Marcy and he had a very special relationship. He adored her. She was his only daughter.

The maroon Mercedes pulled up in the driveway. John Tate got out and walked around it, looking for dust.

Ginny stood on the small entranceway porch, holding her glass of whisky.

"How do you like it?"

"What?"

"The car. Can't you see it's a *Mercedes*."

"Oh. It's all right, I guess."

"What's the matter?"

"Where have you *been* all day, damnit?"

He paused to light a cigarette. "At the office. Where else would I be?"

She took a long swallow. Why hadn't she thought of calling him at the office?

He came up to the porch and put his arm around her waist. "What's the matter?"

"Matter! Chris is going out of her mind. Heather Boynton has moved in with Billy, and Marcy is packing to go live with Jeff." It sounded like one of those summaries of soap operas which precede the current episode.

"Oh."

"And Heather's father was here giving me fits. She's only fifteen."

He had been about to say, "But Marcy's only nineteen."

He took the glass from her. "May I?" He took a couple of long swallows.

"So Marcy's leaving us."

She nodded, taking the glass.

"Jeff's no husband for Marcy, he's—"

"Feckless."

"A nice kid, but—"

She took another big swallow. Unaccustomed to this sort of drinking, she knew she would be very drunk if she kept it up.

"Well, you might say it's only a temporary arrangement," she said.

He studied the concrete slab of porch disconsolately.

Badly discolored, it needed a coat of porch and deck paint. But did that work on concrete?

"Do you think they'll be happy together?"

Ginny shrugged. "She can always come home if she isn't." At least there would be no unpleasant surprises. Marcy had been swiping her birth control pills for some time.

He pulled her closer. "I'm sorry I wasn't home. I can see you needed me."

Suddenly things seemed not so bad, but the Scotch came welling up in her throat. She turned and rushed to the downstairs bathroom.

He hovered outside the bathroom door, asking if he could help.

"No, I'm all right. I'll go lie down."

She carefully wiped the toilet bowl and the tile floor where some had missed, washed her mouth out with Lavoris, and then went upstairs to bed. John followed her anxiously.

"Sure you're all right?"

"Sure. I just shouldn't have taken the drink right on top of two Valiums." She turned over and shut her eyes.

He closed the door quietly, then went down the hall to Marcy's room. Conversation came to a rattling halt when he appeared in the doorway. Four pairs of young eyes stared at him with suspicion.

"Marcy, can you come out here a minute? I want to talk to you privately."

Marcy, who had been sitting on her bed smoking, crushed out her cigarette and got up reluctantly. She came slowly out into the hall. He led her about twenty feet away.

"Now Daddy, please don't start—"

She wouldn't look at him. He took her by the shoulders and gently turned her to face him. "Marcy, are you sure this is what you want?"

"Yes." Her eyes were focused on his chest.

"This is what will make you happy?"

"Yes."

"Look at me."

She raised her eyes. "Yes, Daddy, I want to be with Jeff."

He stared at her, hating the thought of her leaving, of her sleeping with feckless Jeff, of her not being there to love. "I'm just afraid you won't be happy."

She smiled. "I'll be happy."

"If you're not, will you promise to come home?"

"Sure."

"Remember, your room will always be waiting for you."

"Yes, Daddy."

He bent over and kissed her. "Okay, dear," he said, trying to keep the huskiness out of his voice. He turned away. "Good luck."

"Thank you. It'll be all right, Daddy." She hurried back to Jeff.

He went slowly downstairs, one step at a time, grasping the banister lightly. It seemed such a damned permanent separation. Yet Jeff lived only a few houses down the road, and Marcy would probably be in and out of her own home frequently, if for no other reason than to get spending money. There was no reason to expect Jeff's father to finance this unasked for addition to his family.

Then there was his *new* daughter, Heather. Boynton, that poor bastard, was probably frantic.

He poured himself a big drink and sipped it. The warm anesthesia of Scotch flowed through him, and he could feel his stomach unknotting. Lighting a cigarette, he reached over and flicked on the television set.

A panel of scientists appeared. They were discussing the *situation*. One, a pebble-faced man with a Salvador Dali moustache, maintained that they could create a thermonuclear explosion powerful enough to deflect the world into an orbit that would bypass the sun's deadly cone of destruction.

"Doubtful," said another, who had bushy eyebrows that tilted up at the outer edges. The screen flashed his name just below the conference table. Dr. Harvey Michailmas, Chairman of the Atomic Energy Commission. "Of course, our committee is exploring every possibility. Our present reading is negative. All we could do with the combined nuclear capacity of the US, the Soviet Union, France, China and Israel, is make a new Grand Canyon somewhere. That's like setting off a firecracker compared to the power we need to change the earth's orbit.

"Our committee is considering numerous suggestions, most of them impractical in the time-frame available. One, which we may just be able to carry out—and this, I would say, has perhaps one chance in a thousand of succeeding—involves—" He paused and scratched his chin. "How shall I simplify these highly technical matters for the listener, or viewer, I should say? Let me put it this way. We drill two or three thousand holes. As large in diameter and as deep as we can go in the time allowed. Hopefully two or three thousand feet. We concentrate these holes in a circular area about five hundred miles in diameter. We shall in effect be creating several thousand gigantic but crude rocket cannons. We coordinate them by the split second to all go off at once, and who knows?" He shrugged, smiling apologetically.

"Is there enough equipment to drill all those deep holes that fast?" asked the moderator.

"Ah, gentlemen, that's one of our gravest problems," said Michailmas, shaking his head sadly.

"How about rocket fuel? Is there enough?"

"That's another serious problem. You see, we referred this matter to the Committee for Assessment of Rocket Fuel Supplies. Dr. Malcolm Jones, the Chairman, ah, ah, did away with himself early this morning. Ah, no doubt we shall have to get a new chairman."

John Tate banged his glass down on the coffee table and yelled, "Well get off your ass and *do it*, damnit! Don't just sit around talking!"

The panel ignored him.

"What about space ships?" asked a lady panelist. whose credentials were not displayed. "Can't we at least try to move some of the young people to another planet?"

Dr. Michailmas sighed deeply. "Alas, if we only had another fifty years. Unfortunately our technology hasn't progressed this far. You must realize that it would be necessary for this space ship to leave our own solar system. Our planets are being destroyed one by one. Now to get to a planet outside that might support life, our ship would have to travel a minimum of a thousand years. We'd need to provide a life support system capable of sustaining these emigrants for thirty generations. We do not yet have this capability."

A depressed silence followed. Even the moderator was stumped.

Dr. Michailmas looked around, smiling shyly. "I must say we do plan to launch a very large space ship—and this we can do—and it may offer some small consolation. There will be no human beings on this ship. It will, however, be a repository of all the human knowledge and art we can cram into it—priceless human artifacts; microfilm of all the greatest works of literature, science, history, philosophy in every language; tapes and videotapes and film of the world's greatest music, drama, and motion pictures; color film showing the finest works of art and architecture. These treasures and many other examples of human culture will be sent winging toward the planet Orizon. They'll arrive there approximately a thousand years from now. We hope that eventually intelligent beings will find and preserve, even profit by and learn from our priceless human heritage.''

Another silence fell on the group. It was a fairly small consolation.

John reached over and switched off the set. He would drink alone with his own gloomy thoughts. He drained his glass, then poured another two inches of Glenlivet. They'd never include microfilm of *his* four books in the space ship. Yet, if they only would! There was so much in them that most of the critics had missed. Missed or dismissed as banal, without looking for deeper implications. Surely they would include a number of twentieth century writers. Why not John Tate? If only as an example of an excellent minor writer? How much space would a tiny microfilm of his four volumes take? No more than a roll an inch or two in diameter, probably. Even if they would take just one volume—

He hefted his glass thoughtfully and took another long drink. Norman Mailer and Saul Bellow and the other big names would hog all the space. He reached for the cigarettes and lit another. No more fear and guilt and other such crap about lighting a cigarette. Another very small consolation.

Wasn't anyone going to prepare dinner? The silence of the house, usually noisy with voices and music, was vaguely unsettling. He stood up and looked around the empty living room uncertainly, then climbed the steps to prowl the second floor. Ginny, fast asleep. Chris, fast asleep. Billy and Heather, door closed and absolute quiet within. Marcy's room, empty. Gone with feckless Jeff. Jack still out with his aluminum siding. In a bar with the boys getting drunk, do doubt. Archibald? He had called Willard Cohn with some story about having to serve on a committee.

He stared down the seedy looking corridor, the dark green carpet threadbare, the walls in need of paint. There was his colorful Mexican serape hanging over one section. Billy had dug it out and tacked it up. When you looked closely, there were small moth holes dotting it. How did they get there? Who let the moths eat up his serape? It had once covered the studio couch in his pre-Ginny one-room apartment in the city. A lot of memories were wrapped in that old serape. A lot of memories were wrapped in this old wreck of a house. Everything from ecstasy to stark terror, from manic, joyous hopes to deep, paralyzing depression.

Stark terror? That was overdoing it, wasn't it? No. Sheer, stark terror. Ginny hemorrhaging with a miscarriage while the ambulance went to the wrong address. The middle of the night phone calls from the police. Jack had been picked up. It was serious. Billy had been picked up. It was serious. When would a call come saying Marcia Louise had been picked up? What the hell were they, the Jukes family or something? The drug thing. Absolutely incomprehensible to his generation.

Better the serape memories. He fingered the stiff material idly. He thought back on all the sweet young female bottoms that had warmed those rainbow-hued stripes, and on Mexico, where he'd bought the thing. The intoxicating thin air of Mexico City came back to him, and the relaxed sunny days of writing, of interviewing Mexican politicians, of prowling the cantinas with young Mexican intellectuals. Nights of talk and tequila, of beer and rum, all gloriously cheap then. Guitars and singing and shy young teen-age whores from the thatched roof shacks of remote country villages, girls who had never had shoes on before coming to the city.

John also recalled the millionaire's yachts off Acapulco. It had been considered part of the conversational one-up-manship to be invited aboard one. He'd never made it. He sneered at the idea anyway. When friends in the small, inexpensive hotel near the Morning Beach came back with excited stories of caviar, champagne and other rich delights, he noted that those invited were always attractive girls or couples consisting of an appetizing wife and a nondescript husband. So there you had it. Why should he, John Tate, pander to a millionaire's nooky hunt?

His reverie shattered, John walked down the steps slowly and sauntered out to the Mercedes. One side of it gleamed beautifully in the dim light from the porch. He got in and drove, making his way cautiously through the small Village of Green Valley, then east to Rye. Outside Rye he picked up the New England Turnpike. On the wide, high speed thruway his speedometer climbed steadily. Sixty, seventy, seventy-five, eighty, eighty-five, ninety. He had never driven this fast before.

A big beige Cadillac smoked past him in the center lane, going, he estimated, at least a hundred and twenty. Sirens shrieked. Two state patrol cars roared by chasing the Cadillac. He slowed, thinking one of the patrol cars might be after him.

On the next curve ahead, the Cadillac veered left, out of control. Brakes screaming and rubber burning, it rolled over. And over, and over, and over. Ripping metal screeched in spine-chilling torment. Bouncing hard on the concrete, the five-thousand-pound projectile rang out with the sound of a hundred garbage cans being thrown on the road all at once. It finally came to rest on the center grass verge, on its side, one wheel still spinning, the top partially collapsed. The horn, shorted by the impact, set up a loud, steady moan, like a man in pain at the mike of a rock amplifier.

Braking, John passed the smoking wreck with sick horror. He pulled over, some fifty yards beyond it, and stopped. The squad cars, overshooting the Cadillac, U-turned by crossing the grass verge and hurried back to the accident on the Westbound side. John ran back on foot.

The driver was beyond help. Snugly fastened in with seat belt and shoulder harness, he had been neatly decapitated. The stub of his throat was a dark red fountain gushing in a gradually diminishing arc. Next to him a young woman lay screaming, caught in the tangle of crushed metal.

They sweated in the headlights of the squad cars trying to pry her loose. John held one of the pieces of jagged metal back with a crowbar while the Highway Patrolmen gently disentangled what was left of her and laid it on the ground. She stopped screaming and died. Almost half of her torso, from shoulder to hip, had been torn away.

The horn continued to moan from the big smoking amp.

"Christ, how do you shut that damned thing off?"

The other cop reached under the sprung, crumpled hood and yanked wires loose until it stopped.

"I wonder where the fuck his head is?" he asked.

A few feet away on the ground the head lay staring at them. Its wig, dislocated by the fall, had pulled mostly off. The bald pate was a big ostrich egg hiding in the dark grass.

John hurried into the darkness beyond the headlights

and threw up. His hands felt sticky with blood, though actually it was only sweat and grime from the crowbar. The squad car men had handled the girl's body, not he. He found his handkerchief and wiped his face and hands carefully, then walked on to the Mercedes.

He drove slowly to the next exit and left the turnpike. How many more crazy people would be out killing themselves tonight? It was unbelievable. Fifty thousand torn-up bodies a year. Every year. Fifty thousand giddy idiot dolls ripped apart, spilling blood, brains and viscera on the highways, flinging heads, arms and legs onto the grass. Before, he had been mildly amazed at these statistics. Now he'd seen the carnage in full color, the countryside littered with human parts, a gigantic open-air slaughterhouse. It was even more insane than the *situation*. And he was an idiot too, like the headless slab in the Cadillac.

X

They began distributing the luxury scrip on Wednesday. The State Employment office in the Village was crowded, and lines stretched out onto Main Street. No one had thought a rich community such as Green Valley would have many families earning less than fifteen thousand dollars a year. They had forgotten about the old people squeezing by on retirement incomes, and the young people, like Jack Tate, married, but living at home.

The volunteer ambulance corps had a frantic morning. Three heart attacks and two strokes erupted among the waiting senior citizens. Hardly had they rushed on to the hospital when another would fall. The under-twenty-fives, who made up at least a third of the applicants, were asked to give way to the oldsters, so that they could be processed more quickly. Peculiarly, the old folks were more excited than the young, and the strain was too much for them.

Late in the afternoon Jack Tate made it to the counter. He proved his identity with his driver's license, and payroll vouchers established his income. He was able to leave quickly with a thick stack of scrip, all in one-hundred denominations. Hurrying to the Chevrolet showroom, he bought the last Corvette they had in the lot, a used sky-blue number with white upholstery, tape deck and AM-FM radio. It had been driven twenty two thousand miles. He was able to get it for five thousand, complete with a one-year guarantee. He decided to give the other fifty bills to Chris, who was going the next

morning to Dr. Friedman for her abortion. He hoped
the money would cheer her up, and wondered idly what
she would spend it on.

Leaving the showroom on foot, since it was too late
to get plates for the Corvette that day, he found a booth
and telephoned Carlucci. He wasn't at home. Jack
explained to Mrs. Carlucci why they hadn't been there.
He assured her that the crew would return the next day
to finish the siding. Mrs. Carlucci said she knew Mr.
Carlucci would understand. He too had been downtown
all day collecting his ten thousand dollars.

Relieved that the Carluccis were not disheartened,
Jack went to the Red Devil Coffee Shoppe, Texas
Frankfurters with Chili Bean Sauce, and ordered two
franks and coffee to make up for the lunch he had
missed waiting in line.

He munched the spicy hot dog, wondering whether
buying the 'vette had been the right decision. He had
had to move fast. In another five minutes there
wouldn't have even been the used one available. He
already had a fine guitar, one of the best money could
buy. Six hundred dollars, saved over many months. He
could use a better amp, but what the hell.

The guitar lessons were probably shot anyway. Was
there any point or hope in continuing? Would Harold
Harold close up? Maybe he could get back into a group.

The old group had broken up when Jack and the bass
guitar player had left town for college. Spending three
years plodding through a two-year junior college in
Florida, Jack had at least learned more about music
than rock. He now played the piano, and had some
feeling for classical music and jazz. He had delighted
John by giving him a Bartok album for Father's Day.
Bartok was not one of John Tate's favorite composers,
but he played the record over and over to reassure
himself of Jack's approaching maturity.

When Jack got home he found Chris lying on the bed, her face blank. She was wearing faded jeans and the inevitable T-shirt. He noticed that the soles of her bare feet were shades of gray and black, except for the pink insteps. She wore her shoes until the soles fell off, then padded around barefoot. Eventually Jack took her over to Korvettes to buy another pair or two.

Slightly larger than Billy's, their bedroom had two windows, with a view only of the driveway and tall evergreens screening the neighbor's garage. It was crowded with possessions, mostly Jack's—a three-quarters size bed, the big amp, three guitars and three cases, never together; one three-hundred-dollar folk guitar, the six-hundred-dollar electric, and a less expensive bass electric; boxes of records, record player and radio, and old dresser with wet glass rings on the faded wood, an oversize green footlocker in gray-white and two armless upholstered chairs that had been in Wendell Harlow Associates' reception room until Wendell decided the place needed new furniture. Empty wine bottles and homemade candles of varied colors and shapes lined the window sills.

It was the room Jack had grown up in. Gradually crib, diapers and big cuddly toys had given way to baseball gloves, model cars, trumpet and Junior High School Band uniform, then to rock posters, pot, records, guitars. It was not a proper room for a wife, but more, he thought, like a cubbyhole for a couple of kids camping together in a tent.

"Hi," he said, "here's your half of the money. I bought a 'vette with mine." He put the stack of bills on their small dresser. Then staring in the mirror, he began combing his beard idly.

Her silence made him turn. "Aren't you glad to get the money? What are you going to buy with it?"

"I don't know. You buy something."

"I already bought a Corvette."

"Buy another guitar. Or another amp. Or some goddamned thing." Her voice was soft, but carried an undertone of hostility.

"What's the matter?"

"Who cares?"

He went over and sat on the bed, looking down at her. "You're upset about the abortion."

She shook her head. "Why should I be upset about the stupid abortion?"

He stroked her hair. "Of course you are. I'm sorry as hell. And I can see how you resent me now. Because I wanted it so I could keep up my damned guitar lessons."

She turned her head away.

"Remember, I didn't fuck up the sun. That wasn't me, right? I always wanted to have children. But later."

"Why? You'd always have your guitars. Why would you ever want children?"

He stopped stroking her hair. "Oh, now it's my guitar you resent."

"Oh no. How could I resent a guitar?"

"Chris!"

They were silent for a while.

"Your appointment with Dr. Friedman is eight in the morning?"

"Why?"

"I've got to go to the Carluccis to finish off that job. But I want to be sure you're okay. So I guess I'd better call Tony and tell him I won't be showing up till afternoon.

"Don't put yourself through changes on my acount."

"Chris, *please*!"

"There's nothing to it. They just stick something up

inside me and it goes suck-suck-suck, and, *slurp,* out comes Junior. Then, into the garbage can with him.''

He sighed deeply, wondering how she could be so unreasonable. It was hard, but it was obviously better than carrying a Junior who would never have a chance to be born. You'd think that with less than three months to go, she'd want to find some happiness, or at least, some tranquility. But then women were naturally unreasonable. He had seen it often enough in his mother and Marcy. Some days they actually didn't seem to know which end was up.

He began stroking her hair again. ''How would you like to get in the old 'vette and drive to California?''

She shook her head, pushing his hand away. ''Don't.''

''How about Quebec? Or even Mexico City?''

''I don't want to drive anywhere in your damned Corvette.''

He got up and went to the dresser and stood, leaning against it. ''You're sore about my buying the Corvette?''

''Oh, for God's sake will you shut up and leave me alone?''

''We could go for a trip in the van, but then you know it would probably conk out.''

''Oh *God*.''

''You used to love to go on trips.''

He went to the kitchen and made himself a peanut butter and jelly sandwich and ate it moodily.

XI

John Tate had finished his shower and was drying himself when Ginny came into the bathroom. He stepped aside while she opened the laundry hamper and spilled dirty clothes on the floor. Bending to pick up an armful, she noticed the abrasion and the blue-black bruises on his right arm where the "IN" basked had crashed in powerful fury.

"What happened to your arm?"

"Oh, that. I ah, I was helping Marilyn get something heavy off the shelf in the mail room. It fell on me."

"*What* fell on you?"

"The mimeograph machine."

She stared at him, holding the armful of clothes bundled against her. A sock dropped to the tile floor. "And is that why she bit you? Because you let the mimeograph machine fall?"

He looked down. The teeth marks on the inside of his left forearm were still discernible. In this light.

"You won't believe it, so I suppose I shouldn't even try to explain." He rubbed his leg vigorously with the towel.

"Try."

The back of his neck where his longish hair rested was still wet. He dabbed at it self-consciously. "We were just fooling around, joking. She bit me. I don't think she meant to bite as hard as she did. It was nothing, just playful. She's a crazy girl."

"Is she the one who works in the massage parlor?"

He nodded. "Look, she's just a kid. Hardly older

than Marcy. It was just a goofy impulse she had.''

"Just out of the blue, she bit you?''

He thought hard, his face warm. "We were kidding around. She said I was a dirty old man. I gave her a slap on the rear. She grabbed my arm and bit.''

"Right through your shirt?''

"My sleeves were rolled up.''

She dumped the clothes on the floor and began pulling his shirts from the pile and holding them up. "I haven't seen any of your shirts with the sleeves rolled up.''

"For Christ's sake, I didn't *leave* them rolled up.''

"The creases would still show.''

He finished drying and reached for his clean underwear. "Well, if you can't find them, evidently they *don't* show.''

She scooped the clothes back up and left, slamming the door.

He combed his hair, then shook up the can of Rise and lathered his face. The lie he had told her was not really a lie. Nothing more serious emotionally than the tussle he had described had really happened. It had been purely a solo physical act, about on a par with a bowel movement or masturbation. But you couldn't expect a woman to understand this kind of reasoning. On the other hand, would he understand it if the positions were reversed. Suppose she'd had a quick roll in the hay with Vito, the curly headed, handsome postman? That, it's true, would upset him. Not because of emotional involvement, but just simple jealousy and worry that she might have enoyed it more with Vito than with him. After all, Vito was twenty years younger. Perhaps that was the crux of it. He hadn't really enjoyed the connection with Marilyn, and even if the violence that had followed had not taken place, he would not have sought a replay. Especially with Marilyn always yapping about money. A purely commercial transaction. Why should anyone take that any more seriously than a slap on the rear?

At breakfast Ginny said, "I'm thinking of leaving."

He put his coffee cup down with a hard clank. "Leaving?"

"I'll see Chris through her *operation*. Then I'm going."

"Why? Where?"

She turned her head. "Everything seems sort of pointless now. I want to get away by myself where I can think."

He reached for her hand. "Dear, what is this? Surely that silly business of the bite—"

She pulled her hand away, than found a cigarette and lit it. "No, it isn't that. I just feel that I don't really have anything here. Never have had anything. I'm just a slave that everyone depends on for creature comforts." She puffed on her cigarette furiously. "Well, the children all have mates now. Let *them* take care of each other."

"You have me."

"*You*."

He turned away, hurt.

"I don't think I've ever really had *you*. You're the stranger who writes books in his spare time."

He put down his knife and fork, leaving his breakfast of eggs and bacon congealing on the plate, and lit a cigarette.

"Aren't you going to finish your breakfast?"

"No, I feel a little sick."

She got up, snatched his plate from the table, took it to the garbage container and noisily scraped the bacon and eggs into the bag.

"I really don't know how I can stand being without you," he said, aware that he had made her angry by not eating his breakfast, though for God's sake how could she expect him to have any appetite?

"You can write a book about a tragic man whose wife has left him."

He shook his head sadly. "That was very cruel."

She turned away and stood staring out the back window.

He went over and grasped her shoulders. "Look Ginny, I love you very much. I know things haven't been easy for you. But my God, we've been together *twenty-two years*—"

"Twenty-two years of nothing," she muttered.

He dropped his hands. "If that's the way you feel—"

She turned, keeping her face averted. "Oh, I don't know. I really just don't know. I'm going down to Sarasota to see Mother and Dad. I'd have to do that anyway."

"We could drive down together in the Mercedes."

"I don't want to go with you. I want to be alone. I want to think about what to do with my last two and a half months. Surely there's *something* for me—"

He went back to the table and crushed out his cigarette, which was about to topple from the ashtray. "Perhaps if I had been a William Styron or a Saul Bellow, you'd think less contemptuously of my writing. If you were the rich Mrs. Tate, wife of the famous author, you probably wouldn't mind the hours I've spent writing in my spare time."

"That has nothing to do with it."

"You never had much confidence in my writing, did you?"

"Oh for Christ's sake!"

"Don't think I haven't sensed your contempt underneath."

"That is *not* true!" She hurried from the room,
holding her head.

He went to his study and dug into a bottom file
drawer where he kept extra copies of his novels. Pick-
ing out fresh copies of each of his four books, he
slipped them into a heavy clasp envelope, pausing first
to admire the jackets and riffle the pages for a glance at
a sentence here and there.

What the hell did she know about writing? They were
fine books. She should have been proud of them.
Twenty-two years of nothing. Three children. All the
heartaches and happiness that this alone implied. The
trips they had made together to Europe and Nova Scotia
and Quebec and Cape Cod and Maine.

He sat down, holding the envelope on his lap, de-
feated, unable to think about what he should do next.
She had become a stranger to him. The familiar facade
had fallen away, exposing an evil within. For there
must truly be evil in her if she could live with him for
twenty-two years and despise his writing. It was as
though he had turned to her and cursed the three children she had borne. Certainly more blood, sweat, tears
and agony had gone into those four books than she had
suffered in bearing Jack, Marcy and Bill. In fact,
Marcy and Bill almost delivered themselves enroute to
the hospital. As for what had happened after, he had
worked as hard at being a good father to them as she had
at being a good mother. She had been a very good
mother. To be fair, perhaps a slightly better mother
than he had been a father, but then mothers had more
time for it, not chained to the routine of earning a
living.

But how could a man understand anything when a

burned out star *no larger than a grain of dust* could weigh a million billion tons, and plunge through the earth, knocking down trees for twenty miles in all directions, go right through as though the earth were made of sheerest gossamer, and exit in the Arctic to continue its fierce passage through space? If a grain of dust could weigh a million billion tons, then what was man but a shadow? A small collection of gases, water and tissue paper.

He stood up, placed the envelope on his desk, then began a search for the Manhattan telephone directory. There was one underneath something somewhere. Sweating, he finnally found it and turned to the M's. Microfilm Corp., Microfilm Jackets, Inc., Microfilm Unlimited, Micrographics—

XII

Judge Blaufeld called an emergency meeting of the executive subcommittee of the Greater New York Committee to Coordinate the Situation. An armed mob of young blacks had been roaming Harlem. For two days they had been collecting cars and crashing them through the railing of the Hellgate Bridge into the water below. These water-logged wrecks were becoming a threat to ships passing under the bridge. Not only was the channel becoming clogged, but one car had crashed onto the deck of a freighter, partially destroying a container load of Scotch.

The meeting was held in a conference room adjoining the mayor's office. After the opening amenities were completed, everyone stared at Harrison Ricketts.

The black man shifted uncomfortably in his chair. "Don't everybody look at me. I warned you."

Judge Blaufeld said, "But what more do they want? We assigned a batallion of people up there to get the luxury scrip out in a hurry. We waived all the red-tape. I think everyone in Harlem must have ten thousand dollars by now."

"True." Ricketts unpeeled a big cigar and lit it. "But the black man finds that whenever he gets anything from Whitey, there's a great big worm in the apple so he can't eat much of it without throwing up."

"Just what do you mean?" asked the Mayor.

"Everybody up there wants new cars, right?"

"I suppose so."

"The black man takes his scrip and buys a new car.

Then he can't get plates because he hasn't got money for insurance. Then even if he digs up the money somehow, he still can't get insurance because the insurance companies think us black people are unreliable. Nine out of ten of my people who have *paid* for cars can't drive the goddamned things out of the showroom. How long do you think they going to stand for this shit?''

A moment of bewildered silence followed.

Archibald cleared his throat. ''General Tolan, it would seem that the state could make some sort of accommodation here. Guarantee the insurance, or even provide it free?''

General Tolan's plump jaw jutted briefly. ''The governor's working on it.''

''How long he going to work on it?'' asked Ricketts.

Tolan moved his lips in and out. ''There are many complications. We can't have a lot of maniacs who don't know how to drive roaring around killing everybody. Most of those people trying to get insurance don't even have driver's licenses.''

Ricketts looked at Blaufeld. ''You see what I mean? You fucking bureaucrats got yourself so tied up, you just like the Ordnance clerks at Pearl Harbor. The Japs blowing the ass off the Americans, and they can't get ammunition because they don't have no proper requisition.''

One or two polite laughs rippled over the silence that had settled in.

''Are you saying, Mr. Ricketts,'' asked Police Commissioner Reagan, ''that we should turn people who can't drive loose in these lethal boxes? A ton or two of metal that can go a hundred miles an hour? Would you like to take responsibility for the carnage that will certainly take place?''

"Even when they have licenses they drive like fucking maniacs," said Carey O'Farrel.

"I think we can do without that kind of comment," said Archibald. He lit a cigarette. "It would seem that what we need is a crash program in Driver's Ed up there. Learning to drive isn't all that complicated. I expect a lot of the young people already know how, even though they don't have licenses. I know my grandchildren somehow managed it. They were accomplished drivers long before they were eligible to apply for a license."

The mayor looked at Reagan. "How about that, Commissioner? Shouldn't you give this distinguished member of the bar a ticket?"

Reagan smiled. "The Driver's Ed program makes sense. If they'll cooperate."

"You do it fast, they'll cooperate. You going to take two months to get it set up, forget it," said Ricketts.

"I think the police should move in and train these people around the clock. Use the volunteer police and other civilian volunteers. We should aim to put several thousand people up there *immediately*," said Dwight Denton.

Judge Blaufeld asked, "How about that, General? If we take care of the license problem, will you see that the State takes care of the insurance problem?"

"Well—"

"General, when it comes to the insurance, I agree with Mr. Ricketts. You're throwing up red tape comparable to the Ordnance clerks at Pearl Harbor. In the situation we're in, what the hell difference does the money involved mean? I personally will be glad to guarantee the insurance companies all the money they want as fast as we can print it."

There was a light sprinkle of laughter, then silence as they waited for Tolan to answer.

Tolan's big fat face had reddened. He sat chewing his lower lip. Finally he shrugged and said, "I suppose we can make some kind of arrangement." As the former president of one of the nation's largest insurance companies, it was a bitter pill for him to swallow.

Judge Blaufeld said, "Thank you, General. Can we depend on speedy action? Such as right now?"

"I'll speak to the governor."

"The State Motor Vehicle Bureau should begin issuing plates without further delay."

"I'll do what I can, Judge."

Mayor Schapiro asked, "What does that mean, General?"

"It means, Mayor, that I am not the governor. I can only recommend."

The mayor lit a cigarette with an irritable flick of his lighter. He would have called the governor himself, but they had not spoken to each other for seven years. "I want an immediate answer on this. If we can't get action, I'll instruct Commissioner Reagan to take steps to correct the situation."

"Such as?"

"We'll announce that no car driven in the five boroughs requires plates, and that no arrests will be made in this connection."

"That would be anarchy."

"This is no time for red tape, damnit."

Dwight Denton said, "I support the mayor's position with regard to plates. I believe, however, that each driver should be required to have a driver's license. The police must continue to enforce this law."

Glancing at his watch, Judge Blaufeld hurriedly appointed Dwight Denton and Commissioner Reagan to set up a committee to expedite the massive Driver's Ed program. He then announced that he had to attend another committee meeting, and closed the session.

Archibald wandered out of the building and over to Broadway where he stood trying to decide how to get uptown. Subway service was sporadic, and he had a horror of being trapped underground in a long delay. Cabs were scarce, but preferable. He started uptown, walking slowly and keeping an eye out for cruising taxis.

A big red Cadillac pulled over and double parked just ahead of him. Juan Ramiriz hopped out and hurried over.

"Mr. Tate."

"Hello Mr. Ramiriz."

"The executive committee meeting is *over*?"

"I'm afraid it is."

"I'm so sorry I'm late."

"Well—"

"I was attending another committee meeting."

"Are you going back uptown by any chance? I've been looking for a cab, but—"

Ramariz smiled. "Most assuredly. May I offer you a ride? You will be kind enough to brief me on what happened at the meeting?"

Nodding, Archibald followed him and climbed into the Cadillac, noting its new-car smell and immaculate appearance.

Ramariz put the car in gear and moved off. "How do you like my beautiful automobile? My magnificent gift from the Federal Government?"

"You qualified for the luxury scrip?"

"But certainly. I am not politician long enough to be rich from graft."

Archibald fumbled for his package of cigarettes and offered them to Ramiriz. "I think you're the kind of man who will never wish to be rich from graft."

"Thank you," said Ramiriz, taking one. "Unfortunately, there will be no time for me to be tempted."

Archibald smiled weakly. Lighting his own cigarette, he speculated that it was perhaps the height of irony that even the approaching world's end would not markedly change politics.

"So tell me, my friend, what transpired at the executive committee meeting?"

"Very little, actually." Archibald gave him a quick summary of the hoped-for solution to the license plate problem.

Ramariz nodded, puffing his cigarette. "So. Good. My compatriots have also been complaining."

They rode along in silence for a while.

"Mr. Tate, you are in this country for a long time, eh?"

"About seventy-five years."

Ramariz gave him a quick glance. "Ha. No, I mean your family is here many generations, yes? You are what they call WASP."

"Not in the implied sense of being a bigot, I hope."

Ramiriz cut sharply in front of another car, honking loudly.

"What is wrong with being proud of family? I am proud of family. We are pure Castilian."

If pure Castilians had high cheekbones and Indian eyes, then Ramiriz was pure Castilian.

Archibald crushed out his cigarette in the shiny, spotless ashtray. "I'm not proud of it, or ashamed of it. It's such a vague term."

"Why do you say this?"

"Being Protestant, especially if you're not religious, is purely a negative thing, meaning you're neither Catholic nor Jew. As for the Anglo-Saxon thing, that's patently ridiculous. The Anglo-Saxon tribes settled in Britain in the fifth and sixth centuries. Can you picture the changes that took place over the next thousand years? The Tates, I believe, were Huguenots who fled from France to England in the sixteenth century. As for being white—'' The old man snorted.

''Then you're not a real WASP?''

Archibald glanced out the window. They were nearing the Grand Central area. ''Oh, I guess if the label has any meaning at all, it applies to me. I can't take it very seriously.''

They were at 42nd Street and Park Avenue, and Archibald asked to be let off. They parted, shaking hands. Ramiriz was still puzzled.

Archibald was closer to John's office than his own. Lonely, and with no plans for the rest of the day, he decided to stop in. They might have lunch together if John was not already committed.

John had spent a frantic two hours arranging for his books to be micro-filmed. The first place he tried was crowded with authors who had the same idea. When he spotted Jerome Botsford in line with two large shopping bags crammed with his paperback science-fiction novels, he left in disgust. At the second place the line was shorter, but even more discouraging. The woman ahead of him had a large pin-ribboned box containing love letters, and ahead of her was a beefy man carrying his high school yearbook, which he was showing her, the pages open to photographs of himself and other members of the football team.

While he was waiting, Gregory Marsh came up behind him with a large, heavy bundle. Marsh was a chubby-faced writer, almost as wide as he was tall. They had met on occasion at the Overseas Press Club. Surely Marsh didn't think his tepid imitations of Hemingway were for posterity?

''Ah, great minds run in the same channels, I see,'' Marsh said to him. He even quipped in clichés.

''Hello,'' said John, eyeing Marsh's huge bundle. It

easily contained fifteen or twenty volumes. "You expect to put your entire output aboard?"

Marsh smiled. "Well, I've had several best-sellers, you know." Unlike John A. Tate, he implied.

His best-sellers were full of paper characters not quite as credible as Jerome Botsford's Martians.

"Of course, quality will be considered," said John. None of the reviewers who counted took Marsh seriously.

"Quality is what the public buys, my friend. Don't you agree?"

"Sometimes."

Marsh put his bundle on the floor and fumbled in his pocket for his pipe. "Don't be bitter. We can't all write best-sellers. Actually I think your novels, though esoteric, are fairly good. I wish I could hold out some hope for your getting aboard." He shook his head sadly.

John juggled his small package and lit a cigarette. He was about to say, "You may get aboard if your mother is on the selection committee," but decided against it. Their chances were probably no better than the man's with the high school yearbook. "Thanks, you're very kind," he said.

Marsh stuffed his pipe, listening hard for a sarcasm which he couldn't detect. John had suddenly felt sorry for them both, and his reply was totally sincere.

"I'd even be willing to leave out one or two of my lesser works to give you a chance," said Marsh. "You can mention that in your letter, if you wish."

That was really too much. John nodded with what he hoped would be interpreted as a cynical smile. Why should he even talk to the idiot? He glanced at his watch impatiently, then turned his attention to those in the line ahead.

When it finally came his turn, he argued with the clerk with a folded-up one-hundred-dollar bill, and managed to get the delivery time reduced from four weeks to one.

He hurried back to the office and spent the rest of the morning writing ads for the gold bullet. It was heavy going. He was deeply depressed about Ginny, and found it hard to concentrate. He was finally finishing up when his father appeared in the doorway.

"Am I intruding?" asked Archibald.

"Not at all. I was about to call you." He had wanted to talk to Archibald about Ginny. They had a very warm relationship, better than most fathers and daughters, and Archibald's thoughts might be helpful. In any event, he had to let him know about the dislocation in the household, as they would have to forage for their meals.

"Are you free for lunch?"

"Fine."

On their way out, Wendell Harlow, who could be overbearingly exuberant at times, swept them up and insisted that they accompany him to a luncheon of the Magazine Publisher's Association. Archibald was insatiably curious about business groups, and seemed pleased with the invitation. John was not. He was in no mood for speeches and the mediocre food which would certainly follow, but Archibald's attitude left him no choice.

It was far worse than he expected. The fruit cup was cloyingly sweet, the soup as tasty as the water in a hot shower, the beef dry and overdone. Then all the magazine space salesmen got up and sang to the tune of "God Bless America,"

> God Bless the medium
> It's number one

We'll stand beside it
And guide it
Till our jobs—all our jobs—
   have been done.

XIII

Chris lost her baby with little discomfort, not much more than having a corn removed.

Jack who had been waiting nervously, was allowed to go into the small examining room where she lay resting.

"The doctor says you're okay."

"Yes." She avoided looking at him.

"He says you'll have to stay here for a couple of hours. Then you can go home and take it easy for a few days."

She didn't answer.

"I'm still on your shit-list, I guess."

"No."

"You act like it."

"I'm tired."

He sat on the edge of the plastic covered couch and put his hand on her cheek. She twisted her face away.

"Why don't you go finish your work at the Carluccis. Ginny is going to take me home."

He took his hand away and reached for a cigarette. Maybe it would be better for her to be with Ginny. Women understood each other, he supposed, at a time like this. Anyway, it was obvious that his presence was not only not comforting, but even irritating.

He lit the cigarette. "Sure there's nothing I can do?"

"You can quit blowing smoke in my face."

He stood up quickly. "Okay, I'll see you at home."

The Green Valley Chevrolet Motors lot was clogged.

Tractor trailers piled high with new cars fought each other for unloading space. In the showroom, each of the three salesmen had a long line waiting. They were giving out numbers, like the shopping center bakery on Sunday mornings.

In spite of the confusion, Jack managed to collect his Corvette, though he had to put on the new plates himself. The car was not as pristine as it had seemed the day before. There was a faint mark of scraped paint on one rear fender, and mud had caked on two of the wire wheels. He opened the hood. The engine looked new and clean enough.

Pulling out of the lot, he noticed two brand new Corvettes on one of the trailers, and felt vaguely cheated. Oh well, for two and a half months, what difference did it make? It was still a cosmic set of wheels, something he had wanted to own for a long time.

He made it to the Carluccis in minutes, shifting up and down the gear range with growing expertise, and floating the rear end around corners like a professional.

Carlucci had a Lincoln Continental, Tony a Buick Riviera, and Ed a big Ford LTD. They stood around for half an hour comparing cars, admiring, and praising the virtues of each man's choice.

When they finally turned to the aluminum siding, they found there was little left to be done. They worked slowly, somehow reluctant to finish the job and leave.

"I hate not having nothing to do," said Tony.

"Fuck off while you can," said Ed. "I hear they're going to draft us guys from twenty to thirty to fill in on them essential jobs. Like maybe helping the cops or running a subway train."

Jack finished cutting a piece of aluminum. He laid the cutters down, then stretched and closed his fingers, working the cramp out. "Say, that sounds pretty interesting. I wouldn't mind driving a subway train."

"I'd rather be an auxiliary cop. Not so goddamned noisy," said Tony.

"He wants to be a vice cop and screw all the hookers free," said Ed.

"Hey, man, now you're talking," said Tony.

"Actually, we'll probably get put to work unloading heavy cases of food at some goddamned supermarket," said Jack.

Tony said, "You're a fucking pissimest." He gave Jack a playful shove. "You hear that? I just made up a word. It means you're a gloomy bastard and you piss me off."

Even though they dawdled, the job virtually finished itself before it was quite two o'clock. Jack tacked a small aluminum horsehoe up under the eaves for luck, pointing it out to Carlucci. It was a goodwill, public relations gimmick his father had suggested, and it almost always pleased their customers. A pleased customer tells his friends, and you get more jobs through word-of-mouth advertising.

The Carluccis walked around the house admiring it from every angle. They, too, were subdued, however, and inwardly at a loss now that the big moment had finally come.

"You fellows want a drink?" Carlucci asked.

"Too early in the day for me, Ted," said Tony. "I really hung one on last night."

"Me too," said Ed.

"My wife's sick. I promised to be home early," said Jack.

Carlucci turned to him. "I hope it ain't nothing serious?"

Jack shook his head. "Naw, she'll be okay."

Carlucci gave Tony his check for the final payment, then handed each of them a twenty-dollar bill.

"Aw, you didn't have to do that, Ted," said Jack.

Carlucci extended a forefinger and poked him in the ribs. "You gonna need a lot of gas for that thing."

Jack smiled, eyeing Carlucci's big Lincoln Continental. "That's no Volkswagen you got. What do you get, three miles to the gallon?"

Carlucci nodded. "You ain't just a woofin'. Seven, eight, ten, with luck."

They stood around for another five minutes, self-consciously aware that this was more than a casual parting. They had gone through knowledge of a final disaster together, and this parting was also final and irrevocable. They were not only saying good-bye to the Carluccis, but to each other.

"You fellows drop by and see us. We can always round up some booze," said Carlucci.

Mrs. Carlucci wept a little and shook hands with them all.

Driving home, Jack's mind wandered abrasively over his wounds. Chris was through with him. He knew it. It was as clear as one of Mrs. Carlucci's windows, and it hurt like a cigarette being ground out on his liver. Why? Everything had been fine, then boom. Suddenly he had become dog shit. His loving little wife, who curled up in his arms every night, clinging to him like a sleepy child, no longer loved him, sneered at his guitar, and turned away when he wanted to comfort her. She hated him. She hated his music. Yet he could have sworn that it excited her more than it did him. She literally vibrated to it, almost in the way she vibrated to their love-making. He couldn't watch her when he was

playing because he became too aroused to concentrate.
Her face said he was making love to her with the guitar.
So how could it possibly have been an act? The truth
was, she had flipped. That was the only answer.

And the aluminum siding job. Why should he miss
it? He had hated the goddamned boring work, and the
painfully boring people he shared it with all day, five or
six lousy days a week. It was only a tiresome way of
paying for his guitar lessons, a penance offered to his
parents. They didn't mind his living with them free as
long as he was working. But when he was not working,
and not in school, they began to talk threateningly, and
he always felt he was in imminent danger of being
thrown out on his ass.

He pulled into the small parking lot adjoining
Dominick's Bar and went in. He hadn't wanted to drink
with Tony, Ed and the Carluccis, but he desperately
needed a prop. He felt dizzy, as though he was already
tilting into oblivion.

The narrow, shadowy room was so quiet Jack could
hear his wrist watch ticking. Dominick, lean faced and
gap-toothed, had his elbows on the bar and was studying a racing sheet in the dim light. The only other
customer was Louise Reedy, a girl Jack had known in
high school. She had long hair, dyed blonde and dark-
ening at the roots, big breasts, shapely legs and a
scrubbed-clean but petulant face. She was strictly a
very bad scene. She had been in trouble with the cops
from age fourteen on. They had finally nabbed her
selling heroin, but as a juvenile addict she was allowed
to go through the local rehabilitation program. Then,
having successfully kicked the habit, she immediately
got herself three years probation by getting drunk and
holding up a filling station. In a stocking mask and
waving her uncle's shotgun. She was sipping a beer.

"Well, if it isn't old Jack Tut," she said.

"Tate."

"I always thought of you as Tut-tut."

Jack turned to Dominick. "Dom, gimmee a double Imperial on the rocks."

Dom abandoned his handicapping slowly, creasing the newsprint with his thumbnail to mark his place.

As he poured the double shot over the ice, Louise edged closer. "Gimmee a sip."

Dom put his hand over the glass. "You don't drink *no* hard liquor in my bar Louise."

She sat down on the next stool. "Oh, fuck off, will you, I'm talking to Jack."

Dom took his hand away and said to Jack. "Give her any and I throw you both out on your ass."

Jack said, "You heard him, Louise."

"You chicken of poor old Dom?"

Jack smiled. "It's his bar." He winked at Dom. "Besides, he's got a sawed-off baseball bat back there."

Dom went back to his racing sheet. "You goddamned right I have."

"You afraid of a crappy baseball bat?"

"Yep."

"He hasn't got strength enough to hurt anybody with it. When he swats a fly, the fly gets up and kicks him in the balls."

"You have a vivid imagination," said Jack. He sipped his drink, then lit a Marlboro.

"Gimmee one of those." She turned to Dom. "Hey Dom, is it okay if I smoke one of Jack's cigarettes?"

Dom ignored her.

Jack flipped up his Zippo lid and lit her cigarette. "So what are you doing these days, Louise?" He knew her aunt and uncle had moved to California. Probably fled, actually to get away from their bad news niece.

"I was working in Edgeford, but I got fired."

"Doing what?"

"Waitressing. Gimple's Coffee Shop."

Jack nodded. "I know the place." Edgeford was a sizable town about four miles away. Industrial. A lot of blacks.

"I just got laid off, actually. Business has been lousy."

"You live in Edgeford?"

"Yeah."

"Where?"

"You know the Red Strobe Bar?"

"Yeah."

"I got a room over the Red Strobe Bar."

Jack took a big swallow of his drink. "That's a pretty crummy neighborhood."

"Yeah." She drank some beer. "That's what I keep telling them down at Welfare. I don't mind the neighborhood so much, it's the noise."

"You on welfare?"

"What else?"

"I thought your family had a lot of money."

She took another one of his cigarettes. "Naw, all front."

"I remember your uncle had a pretty swift little Triumph he used to go blasting around in."

She shook her head. "Yeah. My aunt used to call it his hollow Triumph."

He laughed, then drained his drink. "Well, I've got to shove off. See you."

She caught his arm as he was turning. "Come over and see me. You can listen to my record, the *Songs of the Humpback Whale*."

"The *what*?"

"The *Songs of the Humpback Whale*. I'll bet you didn't even know whales could sing."

He stared at her. "You mean these are really whales singing?"

"Sure."

"You're kidding."

She held up her right hand. "Swear to God."

He put a dollar and a half on the counter in front of Dom. "Maybe I will."

She leaned over and whispered, "Bring a bottle."

He waved his hand at her and hurried out.

When he got home the first thing he noticed was that his van was missing from its regular parking spot near the road. Nobody but nobody drove that van but Jack. It was tricky to handle—you had to have the split-second timing of a jet fighter pilot to keep from grinding all the teeth off when you shifted gears.

He hurried into the house yelling, "Where the fuck's my van?"

Heather Boynton was sprawled on a sofa in the living room, and seemed to be the only one at home.

"Chris took it."

"Chris? She can't drive the van. My God, in her condition she might even get a hemorrhage."

"She wasn't driving it."

The enormity of the insult stunned him. Who would dare drive his van without his permission? "Who? Who was driving it?" he asked, his voice belligerent and loud.

"She left you a note. It's in your room."

"Who was driving it, damnit?"

Heather just stared at him, curious, but half-frightened.

He turned and ran up the steps, leaping them two and three at a time.

The note was propped on the dresser, a hairbrush holding one end of it against a framed photograph of Ginny.

"Dear Jack, I have taken the van and am going away with Tommy Fitzhugh. You said we each owned half of everything we have. You have the Corvette, so I'm taking the van. I also took half of the money you left on the dresser. The rest is in the top drawer. All my love, Chris."

He sank down on the bed, holding the note and staring off into space. How could she take the *van*? He had practically built it from the wheels up. He had cut the steel sides and put in the jalousie windows, installed insulation and wood-grained paneling, built the platform for the bed, bought material for Ginny to make curtains. He and Jeff had even put in a rebuilt engine. Three days of back-breaking work. The transmission, clutch, brakes, muffler, and countless other parts had been replaced in hours of sweaty frustration and fighting with rusty, frozen bolts and other unyielding metal.

The van had been their home for months. It had taken them across the country to San Francisco. To New Orleans, Houston, Santa Fe, Miami, Tampa, and even to Rapid City, South Dakota.

How could she let Tommy Fitzhugh drive the van? The gear box would drop out before they made it to the Jersey Turnpike.

He stretched out on the bed, still holding the note. What did she mean, "all my love"? Didn't she have any for Tommy Fitzhugh? Was it routine, like "sincerely"? No, she wanted to tell him she still loved him. And hated him. Nothing could wound him more grievously than her running off with another man in his van. She meant to crucify him.

He got up creakily, tossed the note on the dresser,

and went downstairs to his father's liquor cabinet. There were several bottles of Glenlivet, two of Jack Daniels, and one of Wild Turkey. Unobtrusive in the back, there was a bottle of Seagrams Seven Crown for the occasional peasant who, like Jack, preferred a blend. He lifted the Seagrams bottle out carefully and broke the seal.

Heather came to stand in the doorway. "I'm sorry about Chris," she said.

"That's okay."

"Is there anything I can do?"

He stared at her, puzzled. In his confused state the words registered literally. What could Heather Boynton do for him when his heart was torn into bleeding shreds?

"I mean, can I fix you something to eat or something?"

He shook his head. "No, thanks."

"Maybe you want to talk about it to somebody?"

He forced a smile. Not to a little high school teenybopper, that was for sure. But she meant well. "Thanks. But I don't feel like talking."

"Well—I'm sorry."

He nodded, filling a tall glass with ice cubes. Clutching the bottle and the glass, he said, "I just want to be by myself and try to figure it out."

"Yeah."

He trudged back upstairs to his room. He was surprised she hadn't taken the record player or his best guitar. Neither would have been any more cruel than taking the van.

He put the bottle and glass on the footlocker, stacked some records on the turntable and flicked it on, then propped himself against pillows at one end of the bed. The first record dropped, and seconds later music leapt out louder than his mood could tolerate. He lowered the sound, then filled the ice-tea glass with whiskey, noticing that the level of the bottle dropped sharply.

Lifting the glass, he took small swallows of the strong, not yet diluted whiskey, and wished he had some pot. He had just about given it up. It was such a hassle to get. And expensive. And there was always the chance of getting busted. More trouble than it was worth, really.

He tried to think about Chris, but his mind only wandered in circles, toying with memories of their life together and then sinking into gloomy defeat. The future was shot to hell anyway. What the hell difference did it make? If she wanted to spend the time with that twit Tommy, to hell with her.

It was the *situation* that had broken them. The baby that couldn't be. But who could argue with a fucking solar upheaval? The curious thing about it was that she wanted something more than he could give her for those last two months. What could Twit Tommy give her?

And why shouldn't he want the same? Wasn't there something more than she could give him? But what? Everything he wanted was now impossible. He'd never be playing the guitar for a couple of hundred thousand kids, driving them out of their minds with his great soul-blasting, mind-blowing performance. And face it, that vision had kept him going, kept him practicing two hours a day, kept him driving all the way to New York twice a week for lessons when he was so damned tired from cutting aluminum siding that he could hardly hold the damned steering wheel.

The drink gradually became watery. Dregs curled past the ice cubes, some missing his mouth and dribbling down his chin. He put the glass on the footlocker, leaned back against the pillows and went to sleep.

When he woke, the room was completely dark. He fumbled for the lamp button, then glanced bleary-eyed at his watch. Eight o'clock. The whiskey had knocked him out faster than Seconal, but he knew that now he would not sleep the rest of the night.

It was going to be a long night.

Yawning, he made his way slowly downstairs. The house was dark except for a light in his father's study.

John was sitting at his desk, his elbow propping a hand that shaded and covered his eyes.

"Where's Mom?"

Without looking up, John said, "She's gone down to Sarasota to see your grandparents."

"Oh, yeah?"

"Yeah."

"I wondered why nobody woke me for dinner. When's she coming back?"

John dropped his hand, as though suddenly aware that he was being impolite. "I'm not sure exactly. Maybe in a few days. In the meantime we'll have to hustle our own meals. Sort of every man for himself. Canned soup, TV dinners, that sort of thing."

"Oh sure, that's okay." He hoped his father wouldn't mention Chris. He didn't want to talk about Chris with anyone. "Well, I guess I'll grab a hamburger at McDonalds'."

John nodded, shading his eyes again.

On impulse Jack hurried back upstairs and collected the quart of Seagrams. He carried it out to the Corvette and slipped it in the glove compartment.

He didn't want to see any of his friends. They were Chris's friends too, and talk about her leaving him couldn't be avoided.

Starting the motor, he faced up to the impulse which had sent him upstairs to get whiskey. Bad news Louise Reedy. Why not? He was an outcast too. Chris had cast him out, humiliating him by running away with a pill-popping pothead, a guy whose mind was as empty and as interesting as a box of cornflakes taking up more room that it should in the garbage can. And he really wanted to hear the songs of the humpbacked whales. He had a vision of a chorus of friendly whales singing their hearts out, the ocean waves lazily lifting and dropping them in time with the rhythm, an occasional geyser ascending above them to accentuate a high note. The image penetrated his depression with a feeling that was almost delight.

The seedy entrance to the rooms above the Red Strobe Bar was a wooden door flaking ancient green paint. It opened to a small hall with four mailboxes. A flight of uncarpeted wooden steps led precipitously upward. The box marked *Reedy* had the number "100" on it. The other three bore the numbers, "101, 102" and "103."

He trudged up the steep steps and rapped on the first door, which had "100" stenciled in faded white.

"Who's there?" asked Louise through the closed door.

"It's me. Jack Tate."

"You can't come in. I'm reading."

Jack shifted the bottle to his other hand and reached for his cigarettes. "You invited me over to listen to the songs of the humpbacked whales."

There was a silence, then she asked, "Did you bring a bottle?"

"Yeah."

The door opened and Louise examined him in the dim light, her eyes dropping to the bottle almost immediately. She was wearing a knee-length flowered cotton wrap, her big breasts straining the thin material.

"Well, come in. I guess I can read some other time."

The room was small, but it had all the facilities of a one-room apartment. Sink, small four-burner stove, and a tiny refrigerator. There was a studio couch bed, an upholstered lounge chair with a cheap floor lamp hovering over it, two straight chairs, two small bookcases, and a long, much used coffee table. Only the lamp next to the one comfortable chair was burning. Another light came from the miniature bathroom, in which he could see a shower stall of unpainted metal.

A huge volume lay opened on the coffee table, a magnifying glass resting on one page. "What are you reading?" he asked.

She closed the hall door. "I'm reading every word in the English language."

He put the bottle of Seagrams on the coffee table and lit the cigarette he had been holding. "Why?"

"Because I happen to want to."

"Okay." He sat down and looked at the big volume. It was part of the two-volume edition of the Oxford English Dictionary which contained the complete text of the thirteen-volume set. Just about every word in the English language all right. But you had to use a magnifying glass to read it.

"I'll bet you don't know what *androgynous means*."

He picked up the magnifying glass.

"Don't cheat!"

He put the glass down. "Okay, what does *androgynous* mean?"

"It means you're a hermaphrodite and have the sex organs of both male and female."

He nodded. "Oh yeah. I know what hermaphrodite means."

"I wish I was a hermaphrodite and could make love to myself," she said.

He smiled. "I don't think they can, actually." He picked up the glass again and studied the page. "Is this where you're up to, *androgynous*?"

"Umm."

"You've got a way to go."

"Yeah."

"Did you get your luxury scrip?"

"Yeah. The food allowance scrip too."

"What are you going to buy?"

She glanced at the bottle. "I was thinking maybe a little house on a lake. But I doubt I could find one for five thousand. Not around here anyway." She went across the room to the kitchen area to get two glasses and some ice cubes from the refrigerator. "I can't figure why liquor isn't allowed on the scrip," she said over her shoulder. "They ought to *give* the fucking stuff away."

"Yeah."

She brought the glasses back filled with ice cubes, and poured them both large drinks. "I bought some caviar and a lot of other crap like that. You want some?"

"Maybe later."

"It gets pretty noisy here later. Right now the beasts are quiet, Later, it's like being over a fucking zoo at feeding time."

He lifted his drink. "What's that got to do with eating caviar?"

"At the zoo you eat Cracker Jack. I always eat Cracker Jack." She collapsed on the couch next to him, then straightened up, and like a schoolgirl reciting, chanted, "When the lions start roaring and the elephants are rumbling and grumbling and the hyenas are screeching and screaming, it's Cracker Jack time." She reached for her drink, and took a long swallow. "I got Cracker Jack. *And* balloons."

"You're kidding."

She blinked her long lashes at him. "I have *lots* of balloons. When the zoo gets noisy I'll give you one to play with.'' She flipped open the box of Marlboros he had put on the coffee table, put one in her mouth and waited until he lit it. ''Sometimes I fill them up with water and drop them out the window. When the drunks start rolling home.''

He smiled. ''That sounds like it might be sort of irritating to the drunks. Don't any of them ever come up here and clobber you?''

''Some of them yell at me. I yell back.'' She tipped her glass up, draining it. ''I yell, 'I've got a shotgun pointed right at you, and I'm going to blow your ass off!' They usually leave pretty fast, to get out of range.''

He laughed. This Louise was really far out.

''Men don't mind running from a crazy chick. If I were a man they'd have to come up and make a big deal out of it.''

''Yeah.''

''So maybe you better not drop any water balloons.''

His glass was now empty, too. He poured them both some more Seagrams. ''I hadn't planned to. I want to hear the humpback whales sing.''

She touched his arm. ''You're gonna be disappointed.''

''Why?''

''You got a Walt Disney picture in your mind. Some nice jolly whales singing 'Asleep in the Deep.' Right?''

''Hmmm.''

''These are not *nice* whales. You should forget about them. They're weird.''

''Still—''

''I'll show you my shotgun.'' She pushed herself to her feet and went to a closet. Opening it, she reached inside and brought out a shiny new shotgun. She turned, raised it to her shoulder and pointed it right at him. "Now you bastard, I'm going to blow your ass off!"

Staring at the little black hole at the end of the barrel, his first impulse was panic. She *was* a crazy chick, and she might just blow his brains out. Then a sort of resignation flooded him, aided by the growing but anesthetic feeling of well-being the Seagrams sent coursing through his veins and arteries. If she was crazy enough to shoot him, what the hell, who cared?

Cocking an eyebrow, he said, "You're aiming a little high for the ass." He picked up his drink calmly and took a swallow. Then he lit a cigarette, ignoring the gun which was still pointed unwaveringly at his head.

She lowered the barrel. "Man, you're really laid back. Everybody else I've done that to really sweated it. I mean they just about crapped in their pants."

"You shouldn't scare people that way."

"Why shouldn't I? People scare *me?*"

He settled back and closed his eyes. It was a pretty frightening world all right. Muffled rock music was beginning to drift up through the floor.

In a moment he felt her settle beside him on the couch, very close. She ran her fingers over his beard lightly. "You have a very silky beard."

He opened his eyes. "Yeah."

"Most men want to fuck. I suppose you do, too."

He glanced at her. Her eyes were looking past him. "If you do. If you're sure it won't scare you."

She twisted a tuft of his beard. "You being sarcastic?"

He caught her hand. "No, I'm not being sarcastic. People are scared of different things. Maybe you've got some hang-ups about screwing."

She stood up and, untying her cotton wrapper, slipped it off. "Oh I've got hang-ups all right." She reached around and unfastened her brassiere, freeing her two plump grapefruits. "My father raped me when I was twelve, so you can imagine what kind of hang-ups *I've* got." She stepped out of her white nylon shorts and tossed them on one of the straight chairs. "It wasn't the screwing that scared the wits out of me. He held his hand over my mouth to keep me from screaming. I couldn't breathe. I thought I was going to die." She brushed her hair away from her face with the back of her hand. "With his weight on top of me, and that big hand over my mouth, I really thought I was going to die."

Jack shifted umcomfortably. "You poor kid," he muttered. "I don't know how a man could do such a monstrous thing."

She stood with her legs slightly apart, hands on her hips, looming over him naked, a big-breasted Venus. "It was really my fault. I crawled into his bed one night."

Jack reached for his drink.

"My mother ran off with another guy, Dad was completely shot. He drank and drank, and he wouldn't go to work." She bent to pick a cigarette from the package. "Being a dim-brain, I thought I could take her place. I tried to cook and clean and do everything to please him." She straightened up and lit the cigarette, inhaling deeply. "It wasn't enough. He was still drinking and not going to work. I thought we were going to starve. So one night I slipped into his bed naked. I knew what husbands wanted. But I didn't know it hurt so much." She touched his beard again. "If I hadn't been an idiot, it wouldn't have happened."

His face was hot. He buried it in the cool flesh of her stomach.

She stood, letting him hold her for a moment, then pulled away and went back to the closet. He had a few seconds of wild fear. Was she going for the shotgun?

She squatted in the doorway, searching, then found what she was looking for. She returned, holding a plastic-wrapped package containing three bottles. Ripping it open with her thumbnail, she handed him one of the bottles.

He read the label. "*Rapture of Love. The sensuously flavored body lotion. Orange Ecstacy.*"

"Which do you like best, *Raspberry Rapture, Cherry Joy,* or *Orange Ecstacy*?" she asked.

He looked them over carefully. "I don't know. Which one do you like?"

She pushed her hair back again. "*You're* the one who has to lick the goddamned stuff."

"I lick it?"

"Sure. You rub it on me, then you lick it off."

He looked at the bottles again. "What are you supposed to be, a damned lollypop?"

She picked up one and handed it to him. "Here, Raspberry Rapture me."

He unscrewed the cap, tilted some of the liquid into his palm, and began applying it to her stomach like suntan lotion.

"If you want *rapture,* you better put some on my tits, and down here." She pointed to her crotch.

He tilted more liquid into his hand and gently rubbed it on her breasts. Then he slapped some on her thighs, and patted his wet palm through her pubic hair. The strong fruity odor permeated the air, reminding him of a cheap candy store.

She moaned and groaned while he licked her breasts.

"Does it really feel all that good, or are you putting me on?" he asked.

She smiled at him, her hair covering half of her face. "It feels nice, but—"

"You're faking a little."

She nodded.

He went back to licking dutifully.

The sweet, fruity taste did not appeal to him. In fact, it even made him a little nauseous on top of all that whiskey on an empty stomach. However, her wriggling and gasping and nakedness kept him aroused. When he finally decided he could hold off no longer, she stopped him.

"I have to be on top," she said, pushing him away. "Ever since my father, I can't stand anybody on top. I'm afraid I'll be smothered."

He sighed and turned on his back.

It was over so quickly and with so little feeling on his part, hardly more than a slight tingle running from his spine to the end of his penis, that he lay wondering if he had even finished. Orgasms varied in intensity, of course—some had every nerve in his body screaming with delight, others weren't even in the same league— but he had never experienced one so mild. She continued pumping away like a man, but after a while gave up without finishing.

"You didn't like it." she whispered.

"Sure I did. It was great." He hugged her. Poor kid. What a life she had had.

"You didn't like it."

He stroked her back. "It was just that I'm not used to doing it that way. A man can't control the situation when he's in that position. I mean, it sort of forces him into a passive role."

"But it's the only way I can do it."

He kissed her. "Don't worry about it. It's not all that important."

She sat up and lit a cigarette, then got up and went to the closet, smoke trailing over her shoulder.

He wished she would stay away from that closet with the shotgun in it. He should really check it to see whether it was loaded, but to show that sort of common-sense apprehension would destroy his image.

Squatting, she began to pull out freshly wrapped packages and large paper bags. She piled them neatly on the floor, and then began tearing them open. She had been shopping with her luxury scrip.

She threw her cigarette in the sink, then brought her treasures to him one by one to admire. An Audubon wild song bird whistle, an ice bucket shaped like a driver's helmet, a spherical lamp filled with exploding colored fibers, a Black Forest cuckoo clock, a paper-weight sculpture of a stick man pushing a huge boulder, an Australian back-scrubber, a life-size stuffed beagle, a set of handwoven bamboo plates, a ceramic cow creamer, a Wedgwood loving cup with a wreath and George Washington in profile, an Accutron watch, and a large hammock of handwoven all cotton twill with durable aged oak stretchers.

He tried to comment enthusiastically on each purchase.

"Man you really spent up a storm," he said when they finished examining the hammock, which she wanted to install across a corner of the room.

"Yeah. Well, I'm not really going to buy any house on a lake. What's the use?"

They took turns blowing wild bird calls, which were a bit hard to hear because of the increasing noise from the Red Strobe. Abandoning Audubon, they plugged in the spherical lamp and watched the thousands of tiny fibers whirl about in a fluid kaleidoscope of colors.

The noise from below increased. She was right. Exactly as a zoo must be at feeding time. Or maybe more like wild animals trapped in a forest fire.

He put on his jeans. "Let's get out of here and get something to eat."

She was hanging the Black Forest cuckoo clock.

"Why don't we eat caviar here?"

The bird came out and cuckooed ten times. She jumped up and down delightedly, her breasts jiggling.

"I feel more like pizza and beer."

"Okay." She opened a small box and took out her Accutron watch, and slipped the expansion bracelet over her hand.

"Is that all you're going to wear?" he asked, grinning.

The apartment was becoming unbearably hot. And if the animals below were in a forest fire, was it only his imagination, or did he smell smoke?

"Do you smell smoke?"

She tilted her head back, sniffing. "Yeah. Of course, we've been smoking a lot."

"Not that kind of smoke."

He walked around the room sniffing. It seemed heavier near the hall door. He opened it, then closed it quickly as a gray cloud rolled in. He had glimpsed a wall of flame moving up the steps.

Coughing, he yelled, "The damned place is on fire!"

He ran to the window. "Come on, we've got to get out of here!"

She was hurrying around trying to gather up her treasures.

"Drop that stuff. We've got to get out!" He banged at the screen with the palm of his hand. "Come over here, damnit, we've got to go out this window!"

The screen was stuck. From the location of the hinges, it should have swung outward from the bottom. The wood had probably swelled, he thought, as he raised his foot and kicked at it with his bare heel. It held, bruising his foot.

Flames were eating at the edges of the hall door, and

heavy smoke began seeping in around the top. The
floor felt hot, and he wondered if fire was burning
under them too.

Louise rushed up holding the shotgun. "Out of the
way," she yelled, sticking the muzzle against the lower
wooden frame of the screen.

She pulled the trigger. The yellow flash was uncomfortably close, and the deafening explosion sent him
leaping to one side, his ears ringing. The bottom half of
the screen disappeared.

Suffocating with smoke, he yelled, "Now climb out,
damnit!"

He looked past her. The floor over near the hall door
was on fire. More smoke was pouring in. You could be
overcome by smoke and die. He moved quickly to the
window and leaned out, gasping. Through teary eyes
he could see that they were directly above the canopied
entrance to the Red Strobe.

He pulled his head back in and yelled to her, "Come
on!" She was back trying to gather up her things. He
ran to her and knocked them out of her hands. "You've
got to go out the window *now!*" He grabbed her arm
and yanked her across the room to the window. If he left
her she might die trying to rescue her damned cuckoo
clock.

"The English language, save the English language!" she screamed. She bent over and grabbed the
shotgun from the floor where she had dropped it.

He pushed her head through the window. "Climb
out, damn you! The canopy's right below!"

She lay the shotgun on the window sill, and striding
it, pushing the tattered remnants of the screen away
from her face, climbed out and lowered her feet to the
wooden canopy roof. Then she grabbed the gun.

"Get the English language or I'll blow your ass off!" she screamed.

Well, he now knew the gun was loaded, that was for sure.

He turned and groped through the smoke-filled room. One of the huge volumes was on the coffee table, the other in a bookcase near the door. The floor was burning almost underneath it. He swam through the thick smoke, now more black than gray, the floor stinging his bare feet like hot pavement on a summer day. He grasped the heavy book and staggered toward the coffee table for the other one.

Gagging and coughing, he cradled them both in his arms like a stack of logs and managed to get to the window. He handed them to her and climbed out. They scrambled to the end of the canopy, which was only about eight feet high. He lowered himself over the edge and dropped to the pavement. She handed him the dictionaries and the gun, one article at a time, then awkwardly let her legs drop over the side. He dropped the books, laid the gun down carefully, and reached to clasp his arms around her hips. He eased her to the ground. She was still wearing nothing but her new Accutron watch, and in spite of the smoke, still reeked of *Raspberry Rapture*.

Couples stumbling out of the Red Strobe brushed past them, too frantic to notice her.

The whole block of old frame buildings on their side of the street seemed to be burning. People, both blacks and whites, were milling around in the street yelling and shoving. Some were laughing, and a few were crying.

A fire engine came around the corner clanging and shrieking. He could hear other sirens in the distance.

A black man in the middle of the street yelled, "Look at that white chick! She's bare-assed naked!"

Jack picked up the shotgun quickly, cradling it like all the deputy sheriffs he had ever seen on the television.

Across the street a gang of kids were filling bottles with gasoline.

Luckily the Corvette was parked up a side street in the opposite direction.

"We better get the hell out of here," he said, reaching for her arm. She jerked away, bending to pick up the dictionaries.

"Come on. My car's up this way."

"Carry one of these, damnit, they're heavy," she said.

He took one volume, tucking it under his other arm, and they hurried away from the fire to the dark side street. The Corvette was still intact. He unlocked it quickly, got her into the passenger seat, then dumped the books and the shotgun in the back.

She began to cry. "All my beautiful things are burning. Burning to a *crisp*! I don't even have any *clothes*."

He comforted her. "Don't worry, you can buy all those things again. I have plenty of scrip left."

"It's not the same," she sobbed.

"They'll be even nicer."

"No!"

"Do you think I should go back to help? There may be other people trapped in those buildings," said Jack.

She wiped her eyes with the back of her hand. "The firemen are there. They wouldn't let you go in anyway."

It had been a quixotic impulse that didn't make sense, he admitted to himself. Here he was, barefoot and half-naked. What could he do to help? Probably get in the way. Thank God he'd put on his jeans, with his wallet and car keys in them. Otherwise they'd have both had to walk home naked. He turned the key and started the engine.

At the house he asked her to wait in the car while he went in to get a blanket. She said to hell with that, and followed him in, clutching the English language to her big, soft bosom.

In the hall, they met John.

"Dad, this is, ah, Louise Reedy. We were in a fire."

She put the books on the floor and offered her hand.

John shook hands, trying to keep his eyes on her face.

XIV

Judge Blaufeld's chambers were warm and stuffy. A large blue-black bottle fly circled Archibald's head buzzing annoyingly. Archibald lit a Marlboro, hoping the smoke would drive it into orbit somewhere else, preferably around Carey O'Farrel. The Greater New York Committee to Coordinate the Situation was now having emergency meetings almost every day. Since the judge was sitting regularly, it became necessary to hold the sessions in the room behind his courtroom.

At this session a strangely subdued Harrison Ricketts presented a visitor. He was a young man with skin the color of light chocolate, a scraggly goatee, and a big ball of Afro hair.

"Mr. Chairman," said Ricketts, "I think you and the other members of the committee know—," he paused, "—or *know of* Mr. Ahmid Dak. 'I'm afraid today that Mr. Dak is more representative of the mood of our people than I am." He pulled a white handkerchief from his pocket and wiped his face. "I am therefore going to propose that he replace me on this committee. I offer my resignation so that this substitution can take place."

Judge Blaufeld tugged at his collar nervously. There had been fires in Harlem, Queens and Brooklyn, and unbelievably, even up in Westchester, but the situation was still under control. It would be a disaster to lose a moderate spokesman for the blacks, and he was aware of the complete intransigence of Ahmid Dak.

"Let me suggest that we simply add Mr. Dak to the

committee," he said. "I'm sure we can benefit by your continued counsel."

Ricketts shrugged. Archibald decided he wasn't subdued, he was frightened.

"I'll leave that up to Mr. Dak," said Ricketts.

Dak smiled, spreading his long brown fingers on the conference table. "Whatta I care? Harrison here just another white man." He glanced around the table, counting faces. "You got seven against me. Might as well make it eight."

Judge Blaufeld leaned forward. "Mr. Dak, we are not against you. All we want is to let this poor, beleaguered old planet die in peace."

Dak snickered. "You want us blacks to go peacefully. Like we marching off to jail for stealing five dollars. How much did you pay for your seat on the bench, judge? I understand the going price in New York is forty thousand. You been around a long time, so I guess you maybe got it cheaper. Twenty thousand?"

Blaufeld reddened. During the awkward silence while he struggled to control himself, Archibald said, "Mr. Dak, this sort of abrasive name-calling will get us nowhere. I've known Judge Blaufeld for about fifty years. I would stake my life on it that he has never given or taken a dishonest penny. What's the point of trading insults?"

Dak smiled. "How many hundred-dollar-a-plate dinners you been to in the last fifty years, judge?"

"Don't be ridiculous," said Blaufeld.

"Who ridiculous?"

"There's no law that says a judge can't support the political party of his choice. I did it before I was a judge, and I damned well will continue to do it."

"You saying white men in politics don't steal us

blind? Man, you can't pick up the paper without reading about somebody getting caught paying off.''

Archibald said, ''The fact that you read about it in the paper should indicate to you that society disapproves strongly.''

Ahmid Dak laughed. ''Yeah. A big shot whitey gets a trial and a suspended sentence. The black man steals twenty dollars, gets sent to prison for ten years.''

''Mr. Dak,'' Commissioner Reagan interrupted, ''People of any race react differently to crimes of violence as opposed to graft. When you mug a man and send him to the hospital for months, no amount of money can pay for what he suffers. The twenty dollars taken from his wallet has no bearing on the matter.''

''Don't give me that horseshit,'' Sak yelled. ''A black man slips into somebody's apartment and steals a fucking five-dollar radio without hurting *anybody*, he gets ten years!''

Archibald crushed out his cigarette impatiently. ''Mr. Dak, I think we are all aware of the injustices suffered by the black man. While we may share some collective guilt as whites, I believe most of us here individually have done what we could to right these wrongs. But now we have little time left. No major changes are really possible. We're trying to buy tranquility. What's the price, Mr. Dak?''

Dak fingered his goatee. ''Maybe there's no price, Mr., uh—''

''Tate.''

''Mr. Tate.'' He gave the name sarcastic emphasis. ''Maybe we just sort of propose to go out fighting. Maybe we don't want tranquility. Maybe we say, 'take your tranquil pill and stuff it right up your pink asshole.' ''

''You want a fight, we'll give it to you,'' said Carey O'Farrel.

Dak grinned at him. "You gonna lead a lynch party, you soft white tub of lard? Maybe we string *you* up, and cut *your* balls off."

O'Farrel half rose in his seat. Commissioner Reagon caught his arm, tugging him down gently.

"If there's no price, why are you here?" asked Archibald.

Dak tipped his chair back. "Just curious, maybe. Anyway, folks don't think Harrison been getting the message across. They asked me to come."

Major-General Tolan cleared his throat. "What's the message, Mr. Dak?"

Dak thought for a few seconds, his glance flitting from face to face. "Maybe you honkies think the fires we been having been set by the Black Revolutionary Guerrilla Movement. Well, you wrong. When we set a fire, baby, you gonna *know* it. You gonna know it because you gonna burn too."

Juan Ramiriz, who had been listening silently, a half-bewildered look on his face, said, "Mr. Dak, why you want to stir up trouble just for malice? If we had any future, this I could understand. With what we face, there's nothing left but to implore our beloved Savior and the Holy Virgin Mary for compassion."

"Fuck the Holy Virgin Mary," yelled Dak.

Tolan, Reagan and O'Farrel stood up almost simultaneously.

Judge Blaufeld said hurriedly, "Gentlemen, please sit down. Mr. Dak is being deliberately offensive to incite you. He'd like nothing better than for one of you to punch him in the nose."

Reagan said, "I do not intend to stay in this room and hear the Holy Mother blasphemed."

"Me either," said Carey O'Farrel. "Anymore crap from this monkey and I'm gonna take him outside and kick his ass all the way back to Harlem."

Dak stood up. "You fat crook! You touch me, I cut your fucking liver out, even through all the blubber."

Blaufeld yelled, "Gentlemen! Sit down, damnit!"

The four men sat down, glowering.

Dwight Denton, the newspaper publisher, said, "Mr. Dak, if the BRGM isn't setting those fires, who is?"

Dak twisted his mouth down. "That's for me to know, and you to find out, baby."

Denton turned to Harrison Ricketts. "Can you throw any light on this problem, Mr. Ricketts?"

Ricketts said, "Sure I can. Not that it'll do any good."

"I'm sure we'd all appreciate your enlightening us."

Ricketts straightened his shoulders, his face uncertain. "You been giving away all this luxury scrip, right? Everybody getting himself a big car, stereo set, motor boat, diamond ring, fancy clothes. Who's getting nuthin? I'll tell you who's getting nuthin'. The same one's who usually cause trouble. The kids fifteen, sixteen, seventeen. They got no jobs, no money, and ain't nobody giving them no Cadillac."

Denton rubbed his chin. "Aren't they able to share their parent's good fortune?"

Ricketts said, "Man, the kids I'm talking about, they so alienated, they don't even admit they *got* parents."

Archibald lit another cigarette. "He has a good point."

"Yes," said Denton, "he has. We should have thought of it."

Mayor Schapiro, who had spent the meeting quietly smoking his cigar and scribbling an occasional note, said, "Maybe we need to get some of the loot out to these kids in a hurry. A special issue of scrip or something."

Judge Blaufeld's clerk came in and told him the jury had reached a verdict.

Blaufeld glanced at his watch. "I've been thinking the same. As long as we're printing money—" He cleared his throat. "We don't have to worry about inflation, do we?"

Denton laughed politely. "Detroit, Philadelphia and other cities with potentially tense racial situations are probably having the same problems. We should ask the governor to get on to Washington about this immediately."

Blaufeld quickly appointed himself a committee of one to call the governor, and adjourned the meeting. He had reached the conclusion that General Tolan was a complete ass, and useless for liaison with the State. Tolan had dallied so long on the license plate situation that Blaufeld had had to call the governor himself. They had settled the matter in five minutes.

XV

Heather found Louise a pair of jeans in Ginny's closet. They were too big around the waist, but then Heather's were far too tight. The shirt was easier. All Ginny's shirts fit reasonably well. Heather contributed a pair of sandals. Louise had accepted her help with stolid indifference.

John, whose hurt preoccupation had left him only half-attentive, came out of his study to see what was going on. Voices in the kitchen, and the smell of pizza in the oven, reminded him that he had not eaten for hours.

He was relieved to see that Louise was now clothed. If Ginny came home and found her wandering around naked, she'd be furious. But then Ginny probably wouldn't come home.

"Hi, Dad," said Jack. "We're defrosting a couple of frozen pizas." The girls smiled self-consciously but said nothing. As newcomers to the household they were unsure of John's attitudes. And he wasn't an ordinary father, he was an *author*, which meant he was probably a little crazy.

"Is there any of that Gallo Burgundy around? It's not bad," asked Jack.

John nodded. "I think there's a half-gallon here somewhere." He bent, opening doors to the lower cabinets, and found it.

Louise said, "I read your last book."

"You did?"

"Yeah. I liked it."

"Thank you." He lifted the half-gallon of wine onto the long counter. "What did you like about it?"

She thought about it, stumped. "Well, the people, they seemed—" She paused, then blurted, "You used a lot of words I don't know. I have dictionaries now, with every word in the English language."

In spite of the shock of seeing her naked with his son, he had noticed and recognized the two volumes. "I think you'll find all the words I used in an ordinary dictionary. But then you didn't buy it just to look up the words in my book, I'm sure."

"They cost seventy-five dollars."

He had joined the Book-of-the-Month Club for the fourth time to get the set for fifteen dollars plus shipping charges.

"Well, I'm sure you'll enjoy having them."

Jack said, "She better. I almost got my tail burned off saving them."

John got four glasses from the cabinet. "That's touching. I'm proud of you."

"She was waving her shotgun at me."

John smiled, glancing at Louise with new interest. He uncapped the wine and poured it. "Where's Billy?"

"He's asleep," said Heather.

"Call him *Bill*. He's a married man now," said Jack.

They looked at Heather. She blushed. "I'd like to read one of your books, Mr. Tate," she said.

His spirits rose a little. Perhaps a quarter of an inch. It was nice to have some attention from these pretty young girls. His books were probably meaningless to them, and would win him few Brownie points, but still it was flattering.

He looked at her, smiling. "That's nice of you. Hope you won't be bored." He reached for his cigarettes. "I think Bill has copies in his room. If he doesn't, you can take one from my study." He had given them all an inscribed copy of each book, and they had dutifully read them, and had made a point of discussing different sections to prove that they had. Having read from time to time of writers whose children had never read their father's books, he appreciated their loyalty.

The two big pizzas were ready, and Jack took them out of the oven. He cut them into wedges with a big serrated knife and put them on the kitchen table.

Hungrier than he expected to be, John crushed out his cigarette and took one of the slices. They drank wine and ate in silence.

Jack said, "Well Louise, tomorrow we'll go shopping. Buy you some clothes and replace your cuckoo clock. And other things."

"Where am I going to sleep?"

Jack glanced uneasily at his father. He didn't dare offer Marcy's room. John would want it kept vacant, hoping Marcy would move back. "You can stay in my room if you want. Or if you don't want, I guess Dad wouldn't mind you sleeping on the studio couch in his study."

John's eyebrows lifted. He hated anyone using his study. It was his private retreat from the noise and harassment and domestic worries. It was like telling an addict you were going to cut off his supply for a few days. He cleared his throat. "Well, since your mother's away, it might be simpler for her to have our room. I can sleep in the study."

Louise glanced at Jack. "I'll stay in your room."

He had expected her to say that. He was both pleased and annoyed. He was lonely, bitter, and he hoped Chris would come home and see how quickly she had been replaced. On the other hand, Louise was unpredictable, and would probably bug hell out of him.

But he managed a smile, and said, "That's fine with me."

John refilled his wine glass and stood up, taking the glass with him. "Well kids, thanks for the pizza. I think I'll go back and do some work. Or read." Work? What a silly thing to say. She was going to sleep in Jack's room. His sanctuary was safe. *Jack's* room?

"Where's Chris?"

Jack looked down at the table top. "She went away with Tommy Fitzhugh. And I don't want to discuss it."

"Oh." He stared at his son tenderly. The Tate men weren't doing very well with their women. "I'm sorry."

"Don't be."

"Well—" He walked to the door slowly, careful not to spill the wine. He had filled the glass too full. "See you later," he said, his voice trailing off.

He went to his study and switched on the radio, sat down and sipped the wine.

The announcer was interviewing Dr. Harvey Michailmas, the Atomic Energy chairman, on the progress of the project to rocket-propel the earth into an orbit that would miss the sun's deadly searchlight of 26,000,000-degree rays.

"Yes, yes," said Dr. Michailmas. "I would say progress is most encouraging. Mind you, I don't want to get your hopes up. It's still what you might call a very long shot. At least we now know that we can bore all the holes we need in time. This was an exceedingly grave problem, you know."

"I understand this *Subterrene* method melts holes in the earth just like butter," said the announcer.

Dr. Michailmas laughed. "How apt. You have described it perfectly. Melts like butter. Actually better than butter. The heat is so intense, earth and rocks are fused into high-density glass, giving us nice smooth walls for our rocket motor barrels."

"Would you tell us about this process, Dr. Michailmas?"

Michailmas coughed nervously. "Ah yes. Well, it's highly technical. I think it will be sufficient to say that we use heat in excess of 2200 degrees Fahrenheit in a probe. We simply lower this probe into the earth. To use your expression, the earth melts like butter. The probe melts rock and earth at the rate of about twenty feet per second. So you see we can make a hole two thousand feet deep and ten feet in diameter in a hundred seconds. Less than two minutes."

"Fantastic."

"Indeed."

"Absolutely fantastic."

"Actually the process is not new. It was developed a number of years ago. In 1973 to be exact. For much smaller holes, of course."

"Incredible."

"Yes."

"So there's a chance we may yet escape this awful holocaust."

Michailmas sighed so loudly that it made a statical sound. "Do you want me to be honest with you?"

"No. Give us hope."

"Well, I'm sorry, but there is hope, of course. But you must remember that we've never done this before. We have no idea whether it will work."

"You had never put a man on the moon before, but you did."

"*I* didn't."

"I mean you astrophysicists."

"Thank you."

"So why not?"

"My dear boy, there isn't a single doubt in my mind that we couldn't solve this problem if we had sufficient time. Ah, *time. That time may cease and midnight never come.*"

"That's beautiful, Dr. Michailmas."

"I expect Swinburne thought so."

"I'm sure you physicists are working with all possible speed?"

Michailmas chuckled. "Ah yes, it's full steam ahead and don't spare the horses. We have a bit of a stake in this situation too, you know."

John switched off the radio in disgust, then drained the glass of wine. Fucking idiots.

He took the wine glass to the kitchen and left it on the drainboard. Filling a small pitcher with water, he selected an old fashioned glass and carried both back to his study. He opened a fresh bottle of Glenlivet, filled half the glass with Scotch, and topped it off with water.

He flipped on the radio again, turning the selector to another station.

"—murder. Today officials of the Soviet Union announced that Russia will also launch a culture space ship. It will be filled with the greatest examples of literature, science, art and philosophy of the Communist bloc countries. In commenting, Premier Borrosilov said, 'While the United States will undoubtedly include the Soviet Union's great artists of the past, such as Dostoevski and Tolstoy, we suspect that they may not find space to include adequate representation of the true cultural greatness of the socialist countries.' The Soviet space ship will also travel to the planet Orizon.

"President Fargo has announced the appointment of Dr. Rattigan Derwent, the eminent critic, as chairman of the Committee of Arts and Sciences which will choose the world's cultural treasures to be included in America's space ship. "It's an impossible task," commented Derwent, "but we'll do the best we can."

"Three youths this morning gang-raped a seventy-five year old woman in the hallway of her Bronx apartment, then threw her nude body out a sixth floor window. In falling, she was caught in a tangle of clothes lines and hanged. One fireman was injured in retrieving the body when wet sheets, flapping in a high wind, almost knocked him from the extension ladder. Clinging by one hand, he sustained a dislocated shoulder. He was treated at Morrisania Hospital and released. Two of the youths are being held, and the identity of the third is known.

"Four youths were today charged with pouring gasoline over a camel in the Central Park Zoo and—"

He quickly snapped off the set, utterly disgusted.

Rattigan Derwent. If he remembered correctly, Derwent had dealt kindly with all of his books but the second. He went to his small metal filing cabinet and found the four folders containing review clippings. Shuffling through them he located Derwent's review of each book. Number one, thoroughly positive. Number two, definitely negative. Number three, half and half. Number four, at least three quarters favorable with a couple of nasty cracks here and there.

So perhaps there was hope. He took a long drink, savoring the thought of a group of super-humans, a thousand years from now, poring over his books with pleasure and approval.

He took another drink, then picked up a book and tried to read. It was a book on environmental planning, and he read almost ten pages before remembering that it was now completely irrelevant.

The front door chimes sounded. He jumped up and hurried to the front of the house. He was so lonely even a visit from the police would be welcome. Or even a vacuum cleaner salesman. He'd buy one. Glancing at his watch he noticed that it was two A.M., certainly too late for a salesman. About right for the police. Maybe they wanted Billy. He'd make a nasty fight this time. Even go to the Civil Liberties Union.

Switching on the porch light, he could see the callers through the small window in the door. Two blacks. A man and a woman. The woman's face looked familiar. He opened the door cautiously.

"Hi," said the young woman.

"Fran!" He stared, puzzled at her big ball of Afro hair. "How'd you grow all that hair so fast?"

Smiling, she pulled off her Afro wig and let her own straight black hair fall down over her shoulders.

"Oh, that's the way you do it."

"You know my husband, Terry, don't you John?"

"Sure. Come on in." He shook hands with Terry, who was a tall, bespectacled light-brown Negro immaculately dressed in a glen plaid Brooks Brothers suit, a white shirt and conservative dark red tie. Fran Carter was an artist employed by Wendell Harlow Associates. John had worked with her for several years. Darker than her husband, Fran's features were more white than black. With her lively eyes, comparatively thin lips and small, turned-up nose, she could have been a black colleen transformed by some whimsical leprechaun.

He led them back to his study.

"Can I make you a drink?"

"*I* could sure use one," said Terry.

John got additional glasses and a tray of ice cubes from the kitchen. "Trouble?"

John poured Scotch over the ice cubes, serving Fran first. She accepted it, looking uncomfortable.

"Thanks. John, we've been trying to find somewhere to sleep for hours. The last place we tried was the Rye Town Hilton, and I remembered you lived only a couple of miles away." She sipped her drink awkwardly. "So I wonder if you can put us up for the night? We can even sleep on the floor somewhere—"

John handed Terry a glass. "Of course you can stay here. Glad to have you."

"Thanks. We're really exhausted."

"No problem. What happened?"

Terry said, "Everything, man. Our neighborhood's gone crazy. Everybody either stoned or drunk and mean as cat shit. They burned the building next to ours this afternoon."

"The hotels are all sold out. They're getting refugees from all over," said Fran.

John shook his head sympathetically.

"I said to Terry, we've got to get the hell out. New wall-to-wall carpeting or not." Fran sipped her drink quickly, then reached in her bag for cigarettes. "So we just packed what we could get in the car and left."

John lifted his own drink. "You were wise to get out."

"We sure hated to leave all that new furniture. But what the hell—" said Terry.

"Well, we have plenty of space. My wife's away, so you two can have our room. I'll sleep here in my study."

Fran waved her glass. "Now look, we don't want to inconvenience you. We can just curl up on a sofa or something."

John shook his head. "No inconvenience at all. Have you eaten? We can throw together something if you're hungry."

Terry yawned. "All I want to do is hit the sack. Any sack."

This started John and Fran yawning.

John led them upstairs, got fresh sheets from the linen closet for them, collected his bathrobe and other things he might need, and left them sleepily making up the beds.

Back in his study he contemplated the sleepless night ahead with even greater depression. He had smoked far too much all day, and he was feverishly wide awake. If the *nice* neighborhood in Queens that Fran and Terry lived in was in that sort of turmoil, how soon would this mindless cruelty invade Green Valley? Edgeford was only four miles away, and there had already been fires there. Was Ginny safe in Sarasota? He took two Seconal capsules. On the top of the whiskey, they might knock him out.

XVI

As a wedding gift Heather Boynton's father presented the bride and groom a Carousel slide projector and a box of 1700 slides depicting the complete Old Testament in color pictures. He assumed Heather and Bill were now bride and groom, and they did nothing to contradict this impression, though they had not yet gotten around to the actual marriage. He made them promise to go through the whole series.

Heather set the projector up in their small bedroom, removing two large posters to make a screen of the white wall.

"You don't really plan to go through the whole set? Seventeen *hundred* slides?" asked Bill.

Heather began loading the Carousel. "When I make a promise, I keep it."

He flung himself on the bed. Flicking on the FM radio, he muttered, "Jeeze."

"Look at it this way, at ten slides a minute, it's only about three hours."

"Oh, shit," he said it quietly, in a tone of neutral discouragement.

She looked at him, hands on hips. "What else is there to do anyway? We've done nothing but make love for days. And I'm getting so sore I can hardly walk."

He rolled over. "Oh, come on."

"I mean it."

"Oh, shit."

"All you do is pounce on me. Every hour on the hour." She turned off the light and fiddled with the projector, focusing it.

"I thought you enjoyed it."

"Well I do. But we can't do it *all* the time."

Adam and Eve in the Garden of Eden bounced on the wall, steadied, and came into focus.

"I wanna luv, I wanna luv, I wanna luv," bawled the radio.

"I don't think you dig it at all," said Bill, trying to speak above the noise of the radio. "You're probably frigid."

"That's a *lie*."

On the wall a big snake was having a conference with Eve.

"I wanna luv, told her—"

"Shit, you never moan or groan or anything."

She left the projector, bent over and kissed him. "Let's don't quarrel. You know I love you."

"I wanna luv, I wanna luv, I wanna luv."

"You can make love to me any time you want to. I'm not really sore." She went back to the projector.

Eve offered Adam an apple. He looked vaguely annoyed, and might have been asking, "What's this? Where are my bacon and eggs?"

Bill sat up. "Oh the hell with it."

"I tole her, I tole her, I tole her, I wanna luv."

An angel with a flaming sword escorted Adam and Eve from the garden. Eve was hanging her head in shame, but Adam appeared to be blandly unconcerned, even a little smug.

Bill jumped up. "Oh, shit. You look at these damned things. I'll be back later."

He hurried from the room, closing the door with a sharp thump.

He found the keys to the station wagon where Ginny usually kept them, tucked back among her herbs and Valium tablets. At seventeen, with only a limited license, he was not supposed to drive at night without an adult in the car, but he'd changed the birth date. So far, no cop had noticed it on the frequent occasions when Bill was stopped for checks. The forgery was a fairly skillful job.

He revved the engine up and backed out of the driveway with it roaring, his feet hard on both the brake and the accelerator.

Dominick's was a drag. No one there but three skin heads humped over the far end of the bar.

"Gimme a rye and ginger, Dom," said Bill.

Dominick came over, taking his time. "Lemme see that license again. I could swear to God you ain't eighteen."

Bill reluctantly pulled out his wallet and handed Dominick the much worn license. Dominick studied it in the dim light, then sighing, tossed it back on the bar. He dumped ice cubes in a glass, poured a shot of Calvert, then filled the glass with ginger ale.

The men at the end of the bar were looking at Bill and snickering.

The Edgeford-Green Valley area had more than the ethnic tensions caused by black-white friction. In Edgeford, practically anyone not black was second generation blue collar. Italian-Americans predominated, though Hispanics, Poles and offspring of other immigrant groups made up a sizable percentage. The first generation sons of these families tended to be ultra-conservative, super-patriotic, and displayed bumper strips on their cars reading "BRING BACK CAPITAL PUNISHMENT" and "SUPPORT YOUR LOCAL POLICE." In Green Valley, bumper stickers were more likely to read, "I BRAKE FOR ANIMALS" and "STOP NUCLEAR POLLUTION." The second and third generation natives, now more affluent, had moved to Green Valley and other more rural areas nearby. These sons wore their hair collar-length

and "styled," and were indistinguishable from their
peers among Protestants, Jewish and Irish Catholic
neighbors, though some Italian-Americans made a
show of ethnic loyalty by pasting Italian flag stickers on
their cars.

In lower schools the Green Valleyites and the
Edgefordites saw little of each other. In their teens,
they came together in Green Valley High School,
which served the whole area. The Edgefordites out-
numbered the Green Valleyites five to one. Not only
was Edgeford's population much greater, but many of
the Green Valley families sent their sons and daughters
to private schools.

In high school the "skin heads" dominated all
sports, the band, the drum majorettes and every other
extracurricular activity. As a result, the Green Valleyites took little part in school activities, hurrying
home to their own neighborhood social life as soon as
classes finished for the day.

The Green Valleyites, with their styled, blown-dry,
collar-length hair which sometimes even covered their
ears, were regarded by the Edgefordites as fags, bleeding hearts and in many instances, atheistic commies.

The three Edgefordites leaning against Dominick's
bar were in their mid-twenties and had been out of high
school for a long time. Bill did not know them.

One of them, tall, with a big nose and a scar on his
right cheek made up of raggedly healed stitch marks,
looked down the bar at Bill and said to his friends,
"Some chick. Not much ass on her, but I wouldn't
mind running my cock through her hair." The other
two laughed.

"How about it, Doll? Buy you a drink?" he called to
Bill.

Bill muttered, "Get lost." There were three of them
against one, and he wouldn't stand much of a chance.

Dom was pretty handy with that baseball bat, and he was reasonably safe, he supposed, as long as he stayed in the bar.

Dom said, "Cut it out, Tony. I don't want no trouble."

Tony ignored him. "Hey, Doll, will you take it in the ass? I wouldn't ask, but you look like you got a big, flabby, loose cunt to me."

Bill took a swallow of his drink, studying the bottles behind the bar.

"I'll give you five bucks to take it in the ass."

Tony staggered the few paces to where Bill was sitting and draped an arm around his shoulders. "How about it, Doll? You got sexy hair. Like I said, I got an impulse to run my cock through it."

Bill knocked his arm away. "Fuck off, will you?"

Tony grabbed a fist full of Bill's shirt. "Who you shovin'?" He jerked Bill off the stool.

Doubling his fist, Bill threw a short, but hard punch into Tony's stomach. Tony bent over with a small gasp, but straightened up quickly and slammed a fist in the direction of Bill's face. The blow glanced off one cheek, jolting him.

Dominick hurriedly dived for his sawed-off baseball bat. Leaning across the bar, he shoved it between them. "Leave the kid alone, Tony. You're heavier than him, you're older than him, and I don't like your fucking foul-mouthed way of talking."

Tony pushed the bat aside contemptuously. "You wanna come outside and finish this, Doll?" he asked Bill, between teeth that were bared and almost clenched.

Bill backed up a little. "No, you dumb fucking ape. I don't want to come outside so you and your shithead friends can work me over."

Tony moved around him quickly, giving him a hard

goose in the rear, yelling, "Wu, wu, wu, *WU*!" in a high falsetto. Then he half-danced, half-staggered back to his friends, who were laughing loudly.

Bill climbed back on his stool, his temper rising murderously. How much put-down could a man take? If there weren't three of them, he'd kill the son-of-a-bitch.

He fumbled for his cigarettes and lit a Marlboro, trying to control his agitation. If he left, they would probably follow him out. All he could do was sit there and take it, wait until they got tired and left. If he could get hold of Dominick's bat, he could lay all three of the bastards out. But Dominick had put it back under the bar. And traditionally, he would not let anybody touch it. He glanced around the room, looking for some kind of weapon. One of the wooden chairs? Too heavy and awkward. He might get one of them with a chair, but the other two would kill him in the meantime.

He drained his drink. "Gimme a refill, Dom."

Dom picked up his glass. "Why don't you go home before you get your ass beaten off?"

Bill leaned across the bar, ready to mention his fears to Dominick in a low voice, when pride stopped him. Instead, he muttered, "To hell with them. I'm meeting my brother here."

The lie about meeting his brother was wishful thinking. He would call Jack and ask him to come over and lend support. But the telephone booth was located on the way to the men's room, in a narrow hall in the back of the bar. If he went there they could jump him as easily as outside. In fact, there was a back door, and they could hustle him right out into the backyard.

Dominick shrugged and quickly put together another rye and ginger ale. Sliding it over, he said in a low voice, "Tony is one mean son-of-a-bitch when he's loaded. He can take you *and* your brother. And kick your father in the ass with his left foot while he's doing it."

"You're scaring the shit out of me," said Bill.

Dominick grinned. "Better scared than scarred."

Bill's mood changed. There was nothing to be ashamed of in being afraid of a character like Tony. He leaned over the bar again. "To tell the truth, I'm afraid if I leave they'll follow me out."

His mouth tight, Dominick nodded. "How 'bout I call you a cab?"

Bill lifted his new drink. The cab would pull up right in front of the door. He could be in it, with the door locked, in ten seconds. "Yeah. That'd be fine. Thanks."

Dominick dialed the two local cab companies, speaking in a low growl.

He turned back to Bill. "Nobody available. They'll call when they have one free to see if you still want it."

Bill took a long swallow. "Okay. Thanks."

Tony and his friends slid off their stools and sauntered to the front of the bar. As they passed, Tony patted Bill's hip and said, "Come on with us, Doll. We got a bottle in the car."

"Thanks. I'm waiting for my uncle, who's a cop," said Bill.

Tony continued on to where Dominick was standing. He pulled out a wad of bills. "Four Calverts each. That's twelve at seventy-five cents. Eighty dollars."

Dominick said, "If it was twelve, it would be nine dollars. Only it was *five* Calverts each. Fifteen. Eleven twenty-five."

Tony slapped a ten dollar bill on the bar. "Come on you fucking crook! We only had four apiece!"

Dominick's baseball bat came out again. "Who you calling a crook, you fucking dumb-assed Polack? Get up another dollar and a quarter."

Tony grabbed at the bat. "Don't wave that stick at me you fucking cross-eyed Wop! I'll break it across your ass!"

Dominick evaded his grab, and started around the end of the bar.

One of Tony's friends hurriedly threw a dollar and a quarter on the bar. "Come on, let's blow this dump. Maybe it was five."

The other friend moved in and they each took one of Tony's arms, hustling him out. Tony made some show of struggling to get at Dominick, but he wasn't really trying. When the door slammed, Bill slowly let out the breath he had been holding.

Dominick returned to his position behind the bar. "That bastard ain't welcome here no more. He comes again, I'm gonna throw his ass right out."

"Yeah. He's poison."

"You're fucking right." He reached under the bar and brought up a note pad. "You think I don't keep a tally? Look at that, five each."

Bill glanced at the pad. Scribbled on the top was, "Tony Urrachek & pty," with the fifteen drinks indicated by three groups of four vertical marks, each crossed by a slanting line. Under it was "Tate," with two marks.

"Yeah," said Bill. "They had fifteen drinks all right."

Dominick threw the pad back under the counter. "Well, now you got no problem."

"Yeah. Well, I think I'll stick around a while. Be sure they aren't waiting for me."

Dominick nodded, moved down the bar and picked up his *Daily News*.

Bill smoked three more Marlboros, had another drink, and wondered whether it would be safe to leave. He estimated that a half hour had passed. Probably okay. Surely they wouldn't hang around in the dark for a half hour?

He put three dollars on the bar and wandered to the door.

"Hey, you got change coming," said Dominick.

"Keep it."

"You don't have to give me no tip."

Bill waved his hand. "You can gimmee one on the house sometime." He had never heard Dominick turn down a tip before.

Outside, he looked around cautiously. No one in sight. He moved slowly along the sidewalk to the side of the building facing the parking lot. The lot was flooded by bright moonlight and a mercury vapor lamp as well. He stood for a couple minutes, his eyes searching every corner and shadow around the four cars still parked there. He remained absolutely still, looking and listening for movement, ready to run back to the bar if he saw anyone.

He finally decided they had gone. He trotted to the station wagon, opened the door and quickly looked in the front and back. Empty. He slid into the front seat and fumbled with the ignition key.

There was a quick thudding of feet on the asphalt. The passenger side door jerked open. A figure dived in. Before Bill could move, the door on his own side flew open and Tony gave him a hard shove to the center of the seat, climbing in and slamming the door. "Move over, you fucking fag," he said.

While Tony was rattling the starter, Bill reached across the other man and managed to unlatch the passenger side door. He was trying to fight his way out when an arm from the rear encircled his neck and pinned him tightly, his head arched over the back of the seat. The pressure on his throat was so great his breath was cut off, and he began to struggle wildly in panic, thrashing his legs and arms and gagging.

Tony had gunned the motor, backed up, and shot out of the lot without stopping at the street entrance, ignoring Bill's flailing arms.

Then he glanced at Bill. "Don't strangle the son-of-a-bitch."

The pressure eased enough for him to breathe. He stopped struggling, afraid that if he kept it up the hold on his throat would tighten.

With his head pulled back, Bill could see only the shadowy ceiling. What were they going to do? He was going to get the shit kicked out of him. But once he got out of the car, he could fight back. Maybe run like hell.

After five or ten minutes of driving fast and silently over smooth concrete, Tony made a sharp turn and the wagon began to bounce over pot holes.

"Christsake slow down, you almost put me through the fucking roof," said the voice on his right.

The arm around Bill's neck withdrew. The man in the back needed both arms to hang on. Bill could now see straight ahead, but nothing but the dark shapes of trees were visible in the headlight beams. From the condition of the road, they might be in the wooded area back of the Taggert Country Club. The further they got from the highway, the less chance he'd have of being heard or helped. On impulse he snatched at the ignition keys, and with a quick flip of hand and wrist, got the key out of the lock and threw the ring out the open window on Tony's side. The engine exploded a few times, then died. Tony stepped on the brake.

He sat there, his arms on the steering wheel. "Now why the fuck did you do that?"

"What happened?" asked the voice from the back seat.

Tony turned his head. "This mother grabbed the ignition key and threw it out the window."

The man on Bill's right popped open the glove compartment and felt around. "No flashlight."

"Even with a fucking flashlight you'd never find 'em," said Tony.

"You know how to jump it?"

"Naw. You know?"

"Naw."

"Maybe we oughta kick her ass back there until *she* finds 'em," said the voice behind Bill.

"Oh, shit, this is as good a place as any," said Tony. He jerked the door handle and moved to get out, grabbing Bill's arm to pull him along towards the door. "Come on, Doll. You got work to do. You gonna give us all blow jobs. Free." He gave a big tug and yanked Bill off the seat and sprawling onto the broken blacktop. "We was gonna pay you, but since you was so fucking smart with them keys—" He gave Bill a sharp kick in the ribs. "On your knees, you fucking fag. You got three big ones to eat."

Bill tried to scramble to his feet, but was grabbed and thrown down by the other two, who had climbed out quickly. They dragged him around the front of the wagon to the side of the road. The toe of a work book lashed out, catching him in the jaw. Lights exploded in his head, and for a few seconds he didn't know where he was.

"On your knees, you fucking fag," he heard someone repeat in the distance. Then he felt his arm being twisted behind his back. The pain was unbearable. "On your knees, or I'll break your fucking arm."

He struggled painfully to a kneeling position, only half-conscious of what was expected of him.

Tony unzipped his slacks. The sharp, rank odor of unwashed male crotch invaded the warm night air.

"All right, Doll, get sucking. You know you love it."

Bill stared at the rough, dark ground, still confused. Perspiration dripped from his forehead. They expected *him* to put *that* in his mouth? They were out of their fucking minds.

A hard kick in the rear almost knocked him over. "Get sucking, you goddamned fag!"

He shook his head groggily. "No. Not a fag."

Another boot caught him in the ribs.

"No!"

He tried to struggle to his feet, but was grabbed and thrown down again.

"Pull her pants off," said Tony. "If she won't suck, she'll fuck."

Bill struggled wildly as they tried to pull his jeans down. One of them sat on his chest, pinning his arms to the ground. Another held his thrashing feet, while the third fought to unpeel his tight pants. They succeeded finally in getting the jeans and his shorts down to his ankles.

"Pull them all the way off, you fuck-up," said Tony.

They had to tear off his loafers to get the jeans past his feet.

Tony settled heavily between his legs. "Get your fucking ass out of my way, Vito."

Vito, who had been sitting on Bill's chest, moved aside. Partly free, Bill twisted to one side and lashed at Tony's face with his fist. It connected, but without much power. Tony's fist came back and drove into Bill's jaw, hitting the same place where the kick had landed. Lights again went on and off. He felt Tony's hands under his buttocks, lifting him slightly. After a moment of fumbling, there was an excruciating pain, like a railroad spike being driven into his body. He let out a short, high-pitched scream, and made a tortured

effort to fight Tony off and roll away. A boot caught
him in the side of the head.

After the third one finished, someone stood over him
and pissed on him. He covered his face with his arm and
tried to turn his head away as the warm, foul-smelling
liquid splashed on him. Above the roaring in his head
he heard someone say, ''Fucking crazy fag, throwing
the keys away. Now we gotta walk ten fucking miles.''

He lay there for sometime after they left, battered
and half-conscious. When he breathed, sharp pains
shot through his chest.

Finally his mind cleared a little. He struggled to his
knees and crawled a few paces, hurting in so many
places that he wasn't sure he could stand up. He had
reached the back of the station wagon, and leaning
against the rear fender, was able to push himself up to
his feet. Trembling, and holding himself upright with
his hands flat against the car, he crept forward to the
front passenger door. He managed to open it and get to
the glove compartment. There was a box of Anacin
there, he knew. He finally found it after pulling a few
old maps and other bits of debris to the floor. It took
him a long time to open the tin. He got three of the pills
into his mouth and chewed them, trying to bring up
enough saliva to swallow the bitter, sour paste. Eventually it went down.

He eased himself onto the seat and lay down carefully. He lay there for a long time, hearing nothing but
the occasional creaking of the trees in the wind, and the
rustling of small animals in the brush.

The clouds which had been hiding the moon moved,
and the old road was bathed in its light. It entered the
station wagon, bright in his eyes after the almost complete darkness. He sat up, his pains still there but more
bearable now that the Anacin had had time to work. He
remembered that there was a spare ignition key in a

little magnetic metal box attached to the underside of the right front fender. His mother was always misplacing her key, and he had bought it and attached it in a fit of caution. It had never been used. He hoped it was still there.

He got out, still shaky. The key was there. He crept around to the driver's side and fitted it into the ignition lock. Then he searched the ground painfully for his jeans and loafers. The moonlight was a help, and he found them quickly. He had to go back and lean against the wagon to get the jeans on. The loafers were easier; he just had to step into them.

The station wagon had power steering, but it hurt like hell to step on the brake. Groaning, he backed up, turned around and drove home.

The old house was completely dark. Everyone was either asleep or out.

He made his way slowly to the downstairs shower, stripped and stood under the hot water for a long time, scrubbing himself from head to toe, and shampooing his hair vigorously. Every movement hurt. He was almost in agony the whole time, but he had to do it. He had been defiled in a way that he couldn't live with, and if he scrubbed for two weeks he still wouldn't be clean.

Drying himself, he noticed that blood was still trickling down the back of his legs. He wadded up a thick pad of toilet paper and stuck it between his buttocks. Then he climbed the stairs painfully to his room.

The projector was dark, and Heather was asleep. Moving quietly he found a clean pair of jeans, a shirt, and put them on in the hall, leaning against the wall. He padded barefoot to Jack's room and eased the door open. In the light from the hall he could see that it was empty. He switched on the light. He looked around the room quickly, then went to the closet. Louise's shotgun was propped in one corner. He lifted it out, looking it over carefully and checking the magazine. It was an automatic, and loaded. He pumped a shell into the chamber.

He turned out the light and carried the gun downstairs. There was only one Urrachek in the local telephone directory. He dialed the number. A voice answered, fuzzy with sleep.

"Lemmee speak to Tony."

"You want Tony? Tony don't live here."

"Where does he live?"

"He lives—" The voice was that of an old man, and he had to think a minute. "He lives at Mrs. Lavega's."

"Is that the big white house with a parking lot? On the corner of Main and . . ." He let his voice trail off, hoping the old man would tell him what he wanted to know.

"Main and Elm," he volunteered.

"Yeah, that's it. I think I've seen Tony's car there. It's a Chevy, isn't it?"

The old man coughed. "The last time I seen him he had a white Pontiac."

"Oh, right, a Pontiac. Okay, thanks." Bill replaced the handset.

He found his loafers, and limping, carried the shotgun out to the station wagon.

Lavega's had a wide front porch, and had been someone's elegant Victorian mansion many years ago. He drove slowly past, turned the corner and went one block beyond Main Street, turned again and parked in front of a house that probably backed up to Lavega's property.

Cradling the shotgun, he walked slowly back to the Lavega parking lot. There were five cars in it, but no white Pontiac.

He limped around, looking for a hiding place. A thick clump of rhododendron near the corner of the porch provided an ideal post. Sitting in them he could see the parking lot and both approaches to the house, one walk leading to the front door, the other to a side door.

He sat in the soft dirt, the heavy, slick leaves brushing his face, thinking about the moment of confrontation. He wouldn't talk to the slimy bastard, just blast. No, he *would* say something. He wanted to be damned sure Tony knew who was giving it to him. He'd say— His mind went blank. "All right you son-of-a-bitch, this is *Doll*, and I'm going to blow you to hell." He shrugged, sending twinges of pain through his chest. That would do as well as anything, he supposed.

After a while he began to wonder if Tony was coming home at all. Might have passed out somewhere. His back and arms and legs hurt, his face itched intolerably from the leaves brushing it, and his chest hurt if he breathed more than shallowly. Maybe a rib had broken and pierced his lung. No, if that had happened, he'd be spitting up blood. He was dizzy, and when he looked at the full moon overhead, it seemed to move a little, first to one side, then to another. Maybe he was concussed from the blows on the head.

The white Pontiac finally roared into the parking lot, coming to a halt with a loud screech of brakes.

Bill raised himself to one knee to see through the bushes better.

Tony flung open the door, and holding onto the frame, climbed unsteadily out. He closed the door, not latching it all the way. Staggering slightly, he headed in the direction of the front door.

When he was about twenty feet away, Bill stepped out of the bushes. Pointing the gun from the hip, he said, "All right, hold it, Tony. This is *Doll*, and I'm ready to blow the shit out of you."

Tony stopped, bewildered. He looked at the gun,

then up to Bill's long hair and white face. Recognition dawned, and even in the moonlight Bill could see sweat shiny on his face.

"You ain't gonna shoot a guy for fucking around when he's drunk? Man, I was drunk. I'm still drunk."

"Sure."

"Man, I didn't mean you no harm."

"Sure."

"You can't kill a man for being drunk." His voice was shaking.

"Too fucking bad about you being drunk."

He moved towards Bill, raising one arm piteously. "Look—"

Bill lifted the gun to his shoulder. "Hold it."

Tony stopped.

"Who were the two guys with you? Vito somebody and the other guy."

"Who?" Tony knew what he wanted, but stalled instinctively.

"The names. Vito and the other guy. I'll give you ten seconds, counting to myself. Then I blast your guts all over the sidewalk. You won't even know when it's coming." Bill spoke slowly and distinctly.

"Vito Frumenti and S-s-s-sal Livo." Tony began to stutter.

"Salivo?"

"Salvatore Livo."

Bill felt wetness again trickling down his leg, then almost bent over in agony when excruciating cramps stabbed his lower abdomen, and razor cuts of pain slashed his anal region. He groaned, leaning forward. The gun tilted upward, and his finger gave a spasm-like squeeze of the trigger.

The stock jerked in his hand, and the flash of fire blurred his eyes. A high-pitched explosion of thunder resounded through the sleeping neighborhood.

Tony crumpled silently to the ground, most of his head blown away.

Bill turned and started through the parking lot. A limping, reeling ghost, he ran through it and up Elm Street, his rubber-soled loafers making no sound. At the corner he turned left and continued his erratic race to the station wagon, panting and still wracked by cramps.

During the long minute or two of running and staggering forward he was conscious of the absolute quiet. No cries, no alarms, no doors opening, no footsteps. Surely the noise would have brought some one out?

He scrambled into the station wagon. In his panic he immediately released the hand brake and flipped the shift lever from "Park" to "Drive". The wagon began rolling down a long, gradual hill he hadn't even noticed when he parked. He turned the ignition on, and as the car gained speed, the engine turned over and began its quiet rumble. Inadvertently he had left the scene with no noise whatsoever, not even that of a car starting.

The house seemed to be exactly as he left it. He wiped the shotgun carefully with a dust cloth, and trembling, crept upstairs and put it back in the corner of Jack's closet.

Clutching walls for support, he made his way back to the station wagon and drove, shaking and groaning, to the Emergency Room of the Green Valley Hospital. He got just inside the door before he collapsed, unconscious, his jeans soaked with blood.

XVII

John Tate stood by his bed, white-faced and un-steady. He put his hand on Bill's shoulder gently. "The doctor says you'll be okay in a few days."

Numb and slightly euphoric from drugs, Bill nodded sleepily. He had been trying to figure out whether he shot Tony on purpose, or whether it had been an accident caused by the pain. Both, he decided. Anyway, he was glad he had killed the son-of-a-bitch.

"The police say you haven't been able to give them any help on these guys who jumped you."

"No." He had told the police that the group invaded his car when he paused at a stop light on Main Street.

"We've got to find them. We can't have apes like that running around loose," said John. "Can't you remember *anything* about their appearance?"

"It was dark."

"But surely—"

"It was dark and I was scared." It was partly true. While he could remember Tony's face, he had no idea of what the other two looked like. In the bar he had avoided looking at them closely, because to stare would have only invited more trouble.

"Where were you headed for, Dominick's?"

A small chill of panic penetrated the euphoria. "Dad, will you please drop it."

John removed his hand. "No, I won't drop it. I want to kill the bastards. If it's the last thing I ever do, I'm going to find them and see that they're punished." He rubbed his aching forehead for a few seconds. "Green Valley isn't all that big. We'll find them."

If he talked to Dominick, he'd find them fast enough.

"Dad, if you don't drop it, you're going to get me in a lot of trouble."

John stared at his young son's bandaged head. "Why?"

In a husky whisper Bill said, "Because I killed one of them."

"You *what*?"

Continuing to whisper, Bill said, "After they left me I went home and got Louise's shotgun. Then I went to Tony Urrachek's rooming house and waited in the bushes until he came home. Then I blew the lousy bastard's head off."

The whispered words floated past John frighteningly, and they might be sailing down the hall to one of the nurses. Whispering himself, he asked, "Louise has a *shotgun*?" He pulled a chair close to the bed and sat down, his head spinning. "You shot him? Really?"

"Yeah. I'm not sure I meant to, but I did."

The room seemed to be tilting a little. Bill was just a child. He couldn't possibly have *killed a man*. It just wasn't credible. It had to be a mistake.

The police had thought Bill was concealing something, maybe because he was ashamed about what had happened to him. They had asked John to try to get more information. Anything about the attackers he could pry from Bill. So he had pried a confession of murder. He didn't want to hear it.

He bent over and whispered, "You *really shot* this man?"

"Yes."

"My God."

"Nobody saw me."

Damnit to hell, he had had provocation enough to kill all three of them. A jury would never convict him. On the other hand, he might spend the last two months of his life in jail waiting trial. If he was charged with murder, no bail would be allowed.

He shakily put his hand back on Bill's shoulder, pity sweeping through him. "Don't worry about it. I think you're right. I think maybe we'd better keep quiet."

Bill said, "Dominick might guess. But I don't know if he'll say anything."

"Dominick knows?"

"It was there they started in on me. He can't prove anything. He doesn't know they caught me."

The poor, battered, unlucky kid. "I'm glad you shot him. Don't feel bad about it."

"I do, sort of."

"Don't. You had overwhelming provocation."

"I just wish it was clear-cut. I wish I could get it straight in my mind."

"Try not to think about it."

"I went there planning to. Then I wasn't so sure I would when I talked to him. Then this terrible pain cut through me, and my finger jerked almost like I didn't have anything to do with it. I wasn't even aiming at his *head*."

A small shudder ran through John. "You've got to get it out of your mind. Forget it."

Something like panic flickered in Bill's eyes. "Dad, it blew most of his head right off."

John bowed his head, wondering what he could say. A psychiatrist would know, probably, but he didn't. He remembered that Heather was waiting. He had asked her to let him speak to Bill alone, thinking he might learn more. A man doesn't want to talk in front of his girl about being beaten and raped. But Heather might be better medicine than a psychiatrist. Bill had had his manhood cruelly violated, he had acted even more violently in retaliation. It was the kind of revenge that might have helped reestablish his confidence in his manhood, and having Heather as a reason might help.

"Heather is waiting. I wanted to talk to you alone."

Bill nodded.

"Don't say anything about it to her. To anybody."

"No, I won't." Bill's eyes dropped. "Does she— Does she know what they did to me?"

"No. And no one's going to tell her. All she knows is that you were beaten up because you have long hair."

Bill looked relieved. "The other thing is so degrading."

John squeezed his shoulder. "Don't worry. Put the other thing out of your life. Concentrate on Heather."

Bill smiled weakly.

John left the room and told Heather to go in.

He strolled to the waiting room, wondering what he could do to protect Bill. He doubted that the Green Valley police would be able to give much time to Bill's attack. Crime was running the small force ragged in the Township, which embraced the four villages of Green Valley, Edgeford, Pugh and Falling Hill. Edgeford in particular was boiling over. According to the local paper, the police had during the last two weeks accumulated eleven unsolved cases of arson, fifteen murders, twelve rapes, thirty-five burglaries, seven muggings, and twenty-one armed robberies. A record that would be about average for a whole year in ordinary times. The paper had editorialized that perhaps the Township should consider asking for a company of National Guard. John hoped it wouldn't come to that. With the military mind at work, the first thing they would impose would be a curfew. The kids wouldn't obey it. In fact, neither would he. Be shut up in the house every night, at a time like this?

He paced up and down, chain smoking and waiting for Heather. Through the big wall of glass at one end of the room he could see the dawn breaking, an ugly muddy red through the smog. He was hungry. He couldn't remember whether he had eaten any dinner the night before. Of course he had. Fried chicken. Fran had cooked it, joking about it being Soul Food. He smiled, thinking about how she and Terry had taken over management of the house. It was like having a live-in couple. Except that, of course, no one asked them to do anything. They just did it. And because they were guests, and black, everyone tried to pitch in and help, and usually just got in the way.

Terry and Fran, he decided, were simply energetic, supercharged types who couldn't sit still. Also they had a passion for neatness. Everything had to be tidy. The first morning Terry had taken one look at the living room and said, "Man, this place is one big mess," and had gone to look for the vacuum cleaner.

At first John had found the situation upsetting. It looked as though he had offered hospitality to his black friends, who were in trouble, and had then made servants of them. The traditionally abhorred occupation of blacks. Actually it wasn't really that way. They occupied the master bedroom, they sat at the table with him and they drank his whiskey. And they were pretty bossy about keeping the place clean.

Heather finally appeared. "They threw me out. They have to make some kind of tests."

He drove to an all-night diner on the Boston Post Road where they ordered enormous breakfasts of pancakes, bacon and eggs.

Halfway through her pancakes Heather stopped eating and said, "Sometimes I wonder if Bill and I were wrong in trying to have this, this kind of relationship. Maybe we're too young.''

Suddenly the food was too much. He lit a cigarette and poured himself more coffee. Who knew what kind of trauma the attack and the killing would leave with Bill? What if Heather left him?

''Are you terribly unhappy?'' he asked.

''No.''

''If it were not for the *situation*, I would certainly agree that you're both rather immature for marriage, or whatever you have in mind.'' He sipped his coffee. ''However, under the circumstances, well, it seems to me it might be less boring for you than being alone.''

She tilted her head to one side, smiling. ''I don't know. I get pretty bored.''

''Do you think you'd be less bored at home?''

''Probably not.''

He looked at her for a moment. ''Then I hope very much you'll stay. Bill has had a very bad experience. His pride has taken an awful beating. If you leave him—'' He reached across the table and put his hand over hers. ''Besides, I'm enjoying having another daughter.''

She playfully put her other hand on top of his. ''Oh, I wasn't thinking of leaving him. I mean, I think he's more bored with me than I am with him.''

''All couples go through this sort of thing,'' he said, wondering how to remove his hand without awkwardness, and wondering whether the other diners thought he was an old goat trying to make this child.

She released his hand and picked up her coffee cup. ''I suppose so.'' She sipped her coffee, watching him over the top of the cup. ''Anyway it's sort of fun being away from home and not having Daddy on my neck all the time.'' She mimicked her father. ''Wash your face. When did you last trim your nails? For heaven's sake, can't you wear a dress once in a while instead of those dirty jeans? Did you brush your teeth? Your room is a *mess*.''

John smiled, remembering his own problems with Marcy. Why shouldn't a father want his daughter to look sweet and clean and feminine? "I suppose fathers do get out of hand."

They drove home with the sun well up.

Terry met them at the front door. He was carrying a pair of long garden clippers. "The shrubbery around this place is a jungle. You don't mind if I—?"

John frowned. "I hate to see you working so hard all the time, Terry. Why don't you relax and be a guest?"

"I like to keep busy. Besides, this is a nice house, and you're letting it run down something awful."

John shrugged. "We had a guy who used to come around once or twice a week, but—" He turned to go in the house. "Help yourself."

He wondered if it was too early in the day to call Ginny. He had to tell her about Billy being in the hospital, though he planned to minimize Billy's injuries. It wouldn't be right to use this to bring her hurrying back.

He glanced at his watch. Seven A.M. Ginny's parents were early risers. He decided to go ahead.

His mother-in-law answered. After exchanging somewhat stilted pleasantries, she said, "Ginny isn't here. She's gone to Majorca."

"Majorca? Alone?"

"No, she went with a friend."

"I didn't know she had any girl friends in Sarasota."

There was a long, awkward pause. "Or boy-friends," said John.

The silence continued. Then she said, "I don't know where she's staying. But if we hear from her, I'll tell her you called."

"Tell her Billy is in the Green Valley Hospital. He was in an accident, but his injuries are not too serious. He'll be home in a few days."

He answered a few anxious questions about Billy and hung up.

So Ginny had found herself another man.

XVIII

Another day of wondering what to do with himself stretched ahead. John roamed around the house restlessly. Without being able to write, or work at his job, he had nothing to lean on but companionship, and there was damned little of it of interest in the Tate house. Heather was in Billy's room listening to records. Jack and Louise were either alseep or incommunicado behind their closed door. Archibald was in New York. His committee duties kept him busy almost around the clock, and he had managed to rent a room at the Waldorf to use when the sessions ran late.

Fran was in the big kitchen painting. She had set up a make-shift easel, and using the photograph of Ginny from his dresser as a model, was doing a portrait on canvas. A gift for Ginny when she returned.

Just looking at Ginny's picture made him feel suicidal. He had to get out of the house. There was no where to go but New York.

He found Wendell Harlow frantically trying to spend money. Getting rid of the big budget allocated to the Gold Bullet was not easy. Newspapers were short of newsprint and help, and were accepting less advertising. Radio and television stations were short of help, and were thus curtailing broadcast hours. Weekly magazines were also suffering from the paper shortage. Salesmen who three weeks ago had been begging for orders were now being begged.

Wendell gave John a dozen Gold Bullets, then pressed him into service. He found himself telephoning newspapers all over the country, begging that the Gold Bullet orders be honored.

What the hell, it was something to do. Not that he really cared whether they ran the damned advertising or not.

In between begging calls he got up enough courage to call Rattigan Derwent.

"Mr. Derwent, this is John Tate," he began, his voice a little shaky. "We've never met, but I thought you might remember my books. You've reviewed most of them favorably."

Derwent laughed. "Of course I remember your books. Four of them, right? I have a phenomenal memory."

"Mr. Derwent, I—"

"Call me *Rat*. Most novelists do." Derwent chuckled loudly.

"The reason I'm calling—"

"I know why you're calling, and the answer is 'probably not,' though I sincerely wish it could be otherwise. John, you don't mind if I call you *John,* do you? Of course not. John, we're only being allowed a hundred and twenty-five cubic feet for literature, and they are cramming everything in under literature that isn't *science*. That means we have to take care of philosophy, history, and every other damned subject you can think of. Even cook books, for Christ's sake." He paused briefly for breath. "Now you probably think a hundred and twenty-five cubic feet is a lot of room for microfilm. Well, you can get a hell of a lot of microfilm in that space, it's true, but remember, it's still only a box five feet by five feet by five feet—"

"You mean five feet square."

"Exactly. Maybe you belong in the *science* section."

John laughed politely.

"I really wish I could offer you some hope. I liked your books, all but the second one. In fact, just the other day I was saying to Campi, 'I wish we had room for some good minor writers such as John Tate.' "

"Campi?"

"Campanile Fraser, the critic. You know him, of course."

"Oh yes." Campanile Fraser had been one of John's English professors.

"Well, poor old Campi is sweating out the logistics of this impossible job, and my heart goes out to him. You know, he's getting along in years, and it really is a ball-breaker, trying to fit everything in that should be in." Derwent sighed deeply. "However, that's the situation."

John thanked him and replaced the phone. He should have known.

Dr. Campanile Fraser. John hadn't seen him for more than twenty years. He would be a very old man now. In college he had seemed old. White hair and a big, loose face that he kept continuously sun-lamp tanned, and showing wrinkles even then. In his fifties, at least. Campanile must be almost eighty by now.

Was it possible that he might make an exception for a former student? Especially if John credited him with the success John had had as an author? John had not been just an ordinary student. He had been part of an inner circle invited almost every week to Dr. Fraser's Sunday night suppers.

Would it be held against him that he was the only one who consistently refused to take off his pants?

Campanile Fraser never invited girl students to his suppers. His thrill of the evening came when, with the meal finished, several cups of coffee, cigarettes and considerable conversation disposed of, he could say,

"All right boys, time to clean up. Take off your pants so you won't splash greasy water on them."

The first time he had been invited, John could see no real need to remove his pants. The three fellows at the sink washing and rinsing dishes were the only ones in danger of being splashed. John was drying, a good four feet from the water works.

"Take off your pants," Campanile had urged him. "They'll get spotted."

"Not this far away," John had said, naively unaware that it made any difference.

Even today he could remember the disappointed but resigned look on Campanile's face.

No one seemed to find it incongruous that of the ten or twelve students there, all would take off their pants, even though only two or three were close enough to be splashed. They sensed that it pleased Campanile, of course, and some were looking for "A's" the easy way.

Looking back, he marveled at his own naivete. He was certainly aware of homosexuality at the time, and not shocked by it. But very few men dared be openly gay in those days, and the penalties were so severe that, if you were a decent sort, you didn't label a man lightly. In fact, you even made excuses for those suspected. "Oh, so-and-so is sort of effeminate, all right. But he's okay. Probably raised by a couple of old-maid aunts, or something."

He had thus been aware, somewhere in the back of his mind, that Campanile Fraser was gay. But he never consciously accepted it, or put this tag on others in the group who shucked their pants with alacrity. He went because he was fascinated with what Campanile had to say, and his remarks were even more interesting outside the classroom than in.

As far as John knew, every guest put on his pants and

left unsullied, though he never lingered to be among the last two or three.

As a measure of how deliberately unknowing people were in those days, even John's girl friend, who despised Campanile as a stupid misogynist, had nothing derogatory to say about his sex life, or had ever suggested that this had anything to do with his refusing to invite girls to his Sunday night suppers.

Anyway, what could he lose? He would see Campanile and try to persuade him to slip at least one of the books aboard. He absentmindedly fingered the tiny round metal container in his pocket. About a quarter of an inch thick and no bigger than a nickel, it contained the thirty-four inches of film needed for the entire twelve hundred pages of his literary output. He hadn't believed it when the clerk had handed him the container, and had insisted upon having the film run through a viewer. There were nine pages on each quarter-inch frame, and every page from each book had been photographed, even the title and copyright pages. Surely Campanile could find room for something so small.

On the other hand, why should he? Literally thousands of students had passed through his classes over the years with hundreds special enough to be members of Campanile's inner circle.

Shrugging it off, he spent the rest of the day helping Wendell carry on his fight to buy advertising space for the Gold Bullet. They were more successful than either expected, probably due to the apathy of stronger contenders for space. Then, too, the publication people exhibited a sort of macabre fascination with the product. One jokingly acknowledged a duty to make the space available as a public service.

As he was about to leave, Wendell came into his

office. "Want to go to an orgy?" he asked, dropping a card on John's desk.

"Orgy?" John glanced at the card. It had the initials "SPUV" centered in large letters, with smaller type underneath reading "Society for the Preservation of Unlimited Vice."

"I don't know. I've never been to one."

"Neither have I. Jim Ferguson gave it to me."

John read the card aloud. "Admit One Guest, Royal Festival of Vice. Cocktails 6:00 PM, Dinner 8:00 PM (No tie). Grand Ballroom, Pilgrim Hotel."

"I don't know what it is, but I certainly can't go. I have a dinner meeting with some people from CBS." Wendell turned to leave. "If you can't use it, throw it away or give it to someone."

John nodded, smiling, and slipped the card into his jacket pocket. Trust Wendell not to let vice get in the way of business. He was entertaining the CBS people to try to wheedle them into selling him more spots for the Gold Bullet.

Aside from two lone drinkers unknown to him, the Press Club bar was empty. Even the bartender was unknown to him.

"Where's Jesus?" he asked.

"Not here."

Not rudeness. The substitute, another member of the Spanish-speaking minority, had too little English for explanations.

He brooded silently over a drink. Why not go to the orgy? Organized vice had never appealed to him, and it would probably be boring and perhaps even uncomfortable. However, he had nothing else to do, and he could always leave.

The Pilgrim, uptown on the West side of Central Park, had once been a luxury hotel catering to the elite of New York's organized crime. In recent years, pressure from the I.R.S. and various investigative bodies had driven these executives into low-profile establishments in the suburbs. The Pilgrim had deteriorated. Shabby and poorly maintained, it had become the habitat of lower level racketeers, senior citizen pensioners, and even some welfare cases. It's once elegant greystone front was now decorated with the spray-painted signatures of grafitti artists. Old newspapers, candy bar wrappers and other windblown debris littered the sidewalk and cuddled the base of the building.

At the entrance to the Grand Ballroom he surrendered his ticket to a red-cloaked devil wearing a mask. How square could you get?

A devil's helper whose tail was dragging, half unglued, led him to a locker room and handed him a key on a neck chain and a red plastic mask.

"What's this for?" asked John, holding up the chain.

"This is a 'no tie' party. Put all your clothes in the locker and wear the key," said the attendant.

"All my clothes?"

"Sure. I guess you ain't been here before."

John nodded. "What about cigarettes and stuff like that?"

"You'll find everything you want inside."

John shrugged. He had expected something like this. After all, how much vice could you have with your clothes on?

The lockers were small, and looked as though they might have been stolen from Grand Central Station. He found his number and undressed, his eyes wandering to two women across the large room who were doing the same, giggling loudly. On his side of the room several men were self-consciously undressing nearby. The locker room was coed, but different areas were allotted the sexes, probably for purely practical reasons. The women required dressing tables and more mirrors.

Stripped, John tucked his shoes and clothes into the locker and closed the door firmly, hoping his microfilm would be safe. He slipped the key chain over his head, then put on the small red mask. It covered only part of his forehead, his eyes, and the bridge of his nose. He tugged it to position the eye holes better, and then headed for the ballroom.

As he neared the door, the two women approached. They were both in their late thirties or early forties and sagging a little, though not offensively. One was a red-head, and the other a blonde, both dyed. They had both solved the problem by shaving off their pubic hair.

They glanced at John's mid-section and laughed. He looked down, momentarily wondering if his zipper was open, and was immediately confronted by his own nakedness.

Were they laughing at his member? It was average size and had no unusual attributes as far as he could tell. But you never knew. Maybe there was something peculiar about it. Probably just nervous laughter, he decided.

He held the door open and let them go through, giggling.

Dimly lighted with candles the ballroom seemed to be an endless, vast chamber. The floor was covered wall-to-wall with old gymnasium mats, and mingled with the smell of candle wax a faint odor of stale perspiration still clung to them. In the half-light John could see a horde of naked bodies sprawled around low coffee tables. Glasses glittered in the candlelight, and a blanket of cigarette and cigar smoke hovered about five feet above the floor.

As his eyes became accustomed to the light he could see the general outlines of the whole large hall. About a hundred and fifty feet long and seventy-five to a hundred feet wide, it contained a small, low platform in the center of the room, a makeshift but empty stage with multi-colored revolving lights playing on it, a number of bars dispensing liquor and food scattered along the walls, and, unless his ears deceived him, a big swimming pool at the far end. While he couldn't see the water, the noise of splashing bodies, and the special echo of laughter in or around water, drifted toward him through the haze.

He made his way along the periphery of the room towards one of the bars feeling slightly ashamed of himself. Vice in the mass, and dispensed commercially, was beneath him. Yet it was a new experience, and as a writer, he had spent much of his life doing things that bored him, were tedious, painful, dangerous, nauseating, depressing and sometimes shamefully enjoyable, always in the name of "necessary" experience. Tonight he could only be motivated by sheer curiosity, since he'd never have a chance to write about it. And what did it matter anyway, this opinion of himself? If Ginny, after twenty-two years, found it necessary to go off to Majorca with another man, who really cared whether John Tate demeaned himself. Somehow the time had to be filled in. At least this evening would be different.

The bartender, another devil's helper, asked, "What Hell Juice is your pleasure?"

Oh man, was this ever going to be a drag. "I'll have some molten lava on the rocks. From a Scotch volcano," said John.

The devil's helper tittered. "Say, that's pretty good." He bent to pour the Scotch.

"I take it there's no charge?"

The bartender pushed the drink over to him. "No. Everything is included in your ticket. Booze, food, cigarettes.'' He shoved a box of cigarettes across the bar.

A loudspeaker nearby coughed and sputtered. ''Fellow denizens of Hell, greetings,'' said a voice clearly amplified. ''Some of you have expressed concern about fire. Let me reassure you. The floor mats have been double fireproofed, and you'll note that the tables are metal. Almost nothing in this room can burn but your candles and cigarettes. Enjoy yourselves. We promise to save you for the big one.''

A cackle of laughter erupted, then died quickly.

John pulled one of the candles over and lit a cigarette. ''I've never been to one of these things before. What goes on?'' he asked the bartender, then, noticing the startled look, added quickly, ''I mean besides the varieties of fornication I see around me.''

The bartender poured more Scotch in his glass. ''That's about it. Later there's a show. What more do you want for two hundred bucks?''

''The tickets cost two hundred dollars?''

''Yep.''

''A guy *gave* me mine.''

''Yeah. Well, you know how it is. Money don't mean so much today.''

John nodded. ''What's the procedure? Wander around until you find an unattached woman?''

The bartender said, ''Either that or wait until one finds you. But watch it. Man, some of these chicks are animals. They'll tear your balls right off if you're not careful.''

Smiling, he finished his drink and strolled off in the direction of the swimming pool. The mats were firm, but walking on them was strange, and brought back uncomfortable memories of his school days. Gym, being compulsory, was one aspect of school he had detested. It was not that he had been a ninety-nine-pound weakling. He had played football with creditable mediocrity, and had achieved some recognition on the tennis team, but gymnasiums made his nostrils curl. The group exercises, the leather horses and the shiny wooden parallel bars, the pointless arching of the body this way and that, the preoccupation with muscle-building, all combined to produce boredom that was almost painful and led him close to open rebellion.

He sighed. That had all been a long time ago.

At the swimming pool he paused and watched the guests playing in and out of the water, feeling more like a voyeur here because the area was better lighted. In action, the bobbing breasts and flopping penises, not to mention the occasional erections, were somehow much more obvious and arresting. He decided that he should leave or go into the water, not just stand there and watch, and the idea of a brisk swim seemed a bit ridiculous. He belonged back in the dim candlelight.

He walked away slowly, looking for someplace to light, for companionship. He passed three women who were alone, but the presence of two glasses on each table indicated the temporary absence of a man, or woman—for the gays were almost as numerous as the straights—who had staked a prior claim.

Eventually he found a woman who seemed to be by herself. He circled her cautiously, pretending to look elsewhere, and made a detailed inventory. Reasonably slim with big breasts and well-shaped legs, long black hair, about thirty-five or forty, he estimated, though it was difficult to tell with the mask and the dim light. What he could see of her face appealed to him. Her mouth was rather large, and somehow he had the impression that she was intelligent and would have a sense of humor. Still, wouldn't she be a little kinky, coming here alone? On the other hand, he was here, and was he kinky? Male chauvinism at work.

"May I join you?" he asked.

She looked up, pretending to be startled. "Well, a true gentleman at last. With it all hanging out."

He sat down next to her. "Did I say something wrong?"

She smiled. "You're supposed to creep up, pounce, and grunt, "Hey baby, you wanna ball?"

He toughed his voice. "Okay baby, you wanna ball?"

She shook her head. "I never ball with anyone in the first ten minutes of a date."

He laughed. "What brings you to this kinky place?"

"I'm probably getting kinky. Why are you here?"

He sighed. "I'm lonely, and I couldn't think of anything better to do."

She adjusted her mask to get a better look at him. "You look married to me. Isn't your wife kinky enough?"

He glanced at her drink, wishing he had thought to bring one. "My wife, after twenty-two years, has flown the coop. I think she's in Majorca with another guy. It was a very uncivilized thing for her to do, with so little time left."

"Oh." She picked up her glass and drained it. "Well, you know what George Meredith said."

"Offhand I don't."

"He said, 'I expect that woman will be the last thing civilized by man.' "

So she was intelligent. Or at least, educated. "They didn't worry much about male chauvinism in those days, did they?"

"No."

"My I refill your drink? I'd like to get one."

She handed him her glass. "Scotch on the rocks. And bring back some cigarettes."

He got to his feet. "If anyone pounces, cool it."

"I'll try."

He made a fast trip to the bar and returned quickly with the drinks and a handful of loose cigarettes, relieved to find her still alone. He didn't want to lose her. How many women would you find in a place like this who could quote George Meredith?

He put the cigarettes on the table, taking care to find a dry spot, then handed her one of the drinks and settled himself down on the mat beside her.

"Thanks." She reached for a cigarette and pulled the candle close to light it.

"Are you married?" he asked.

"Was."

"I hope you didn't leave him after twenty-two years to spend your last months with someone else?"

"No."

"That's good."

"It could have worked that way. Actually he left me."

Subdued groans and little high-pitched female cries were coming from the semi-darkness nearby.

"I'm sorry. Was it recently?"

"No."

"I mean, since the *situation*."

"It was several years ago."

"In other words, it was a normal break-up."

She lifted her drink. "You consider yours abnormal, obviously."

"Of course. Ginny wouldn't have left me under normal circumstances."

Faint slurping, slapping sounds drifted to them, the noises of love carried on wetly and at great length.

"Maybe she would have."

"Never."

She lit another cigarette. "You consider what was happening before the *situation* normal?"

"What do you mean?"

"The world was going to end anyway."

What had he picked up, a nut? An educated nut, to be sure. "Did you have a day set?"

She blew smoke in his face. "You know what I mean. They were going to blow the fucking world apart anyway. Russia and the United States. Stupid idiots."

"Oh that. I always had hope it wouldn't happen."

"Then you were very naive."

A steady sound of grunting reached them. It went on and on as though coming from a stuck record, neither increasing nor decreasing in volume.

"Oh I don't know about that. If we could survive the years of Dulles' brinkmanship, I think we had a pretty good chance."

"Oh shit. You *are* naive."

"Well—" He reached for a cigarette. "The question is sort of academic, anyway, isn't it?"

"We survived Dulles because Russia wasn't ready and we weren't ready. The probability was there, and would always be there. When the world is run by idiots, sooner or later—"

He searched his mind for a way to abandon the subject. She could be right, of course, but what difference did it make now? She was over-simplifying. Governments were chameleons, in constant movement and change. In his own short life many countries had evolved into totally different entities. The Russia of Stalin was not the Russia of today. Britain of the forties was not Britain of today. China, India, the United States, all fluid, all moving, changing.

"It was inevitable. As—as inevitable as death," she said.

He stared at her naked body, her rather full breasts, her stomach with the faint lines of an appendectomy scar, her dark bush and plump thighs, and thought how peculiar it was that they were lounging there in this condition discussing world affairs. He supposed it happened all the time in nudist colonies. But not with the sounds and sights of Sodom and Gomorrah all around.

He thought of an old Russian joke and reached for her. "Enough of this lovemaking. Off with the clothes."

She pushed him away. "Sometimes I don't ball even in the first hour of a date."

He reached for a cigarette, lit it, and then took a long drink of Scotch. Should he move on? Strangely enough he didn't particularly care whether he made love to her or not. Talk would do just as well, if he could get her away from now irrelevant international politics. Face it, he was lonely for female companionship. But what was still relevant? Human beings, their hopes and their despair.

"What did you do besides being a wife?"

"How do you know I did anything?"

He put his glass down. "I think you had a profession or something that made you feel self-sufficient."

"Why?"

"It's just a feeling I have. You could have been, let's see, an English teacher?"

She smiled. "My God, it shows? Even naked?"

"You were?"

"A teacher. Not English. Mathematics." She reached for her glass. "I was a mathematics teacher. Still am, but hardly anyone comes to class."

Mathematics. Why couldn't it have been anything but mathematics? History, psychology, philosophy, social studies, even home economics. Anything. What could you say about mathematics except that it was a necessary evil? How dare she quote George Meredith? Mathematicians were inhuman. Their minds floated in stratospheres of pure science. The numbers game, abstract and cold.

If she noticed his disappointment it wasn't apparent. She downed her drink, then handed him the glass. "Get me another, please."

He finished his own drink and got to his feet. "Where did you teach mathematics?"

She cocked her head to look up at him. "I'm an associate professor, and I think I'll stay anonymous. Not that it really matters anymore. However, habit dies hard, as we say at the faculty club."

He walked towards the nearest bar. A professor. That was even worse. However, she was still probably the most intelligent woman he would find here, and intelligent women were not all that numerous.

On the way back a girl blocked his path and when he stopped, helpless with a drink in each hand, grabbed his penis rather roughly.

"Dearest," he said, "we can't keep on meeting like this."

She was too drunk to respond to the old gag and simply held on, trying to lead him away like a dog on a very short leash.

"Drop that thing," he said, his voice stern. "My wife is watching."

She dropped it. He stepped past her and hurried back to his table.

"So who are you?" she asked, accepting her drink.

"As a famous writer, I suppose I should remain anonymous." He put his drink on the table and slumped to the mat.

"I know, you're Eugene O'Neill."

"Thanks. Unfortunately, he's dead."

"Aren't we all?"

"Not by a long shot. I have plans for transmitting

myself to another planet by fifth dimensional guru methods.''

"Good. As long as I don't have to go with you.'' She leaned over and sipped her drink, her breasts falling into enticing roundness. "What do you write?''

"I doubt if a mathematician would have read any of my novels.'' He instantly regretted the remark and hurried to say, "I didn't mean that in a snotty way. What I meant was I expect my books would not have much appeal to the scientific mind.''

She straightened up. "I've probably read more novels than you have.''

Unlikely, but why argue?

"What's your name?'' she asked.

"I prefer to remain anonymous.''

She laughed. "All right. My name is Cynthia Blaufeld.''

"Are you related to Judge Marcus Blaufeld?''

"My uncle. Why?''

"My father is serving on his committee. The Greater New York Committee to Coordinate the Situation.''

She brushed his comment aside. "All right, now I told you. What's your name, damnit?''

"John Tate.''

"Tate? Never heard of you.''

So much for fame. He wasn't even discussed around the faculty club.

"Famous author? Where do you get that bit?'' she asked.

Obviously she was still annoyed at his remark. Now he was becoming irritated. "Look, my novels are not only published in this country but in England, Italy, Denmark, The Netherlands and Japan. That's five languages. Three of my four books have been reviewed very favorably by Rattigan Derwent, the absolute dean of American literary critics. Not only that, Rat told me today that there is an excellent chance microfilms of my book will be included in the culture space ship.'' He paused for breath. The last statement was untrue, but she deserved it. ''So the fact that you have never head of me is only indicative of your ignorance.''

The monotonous grunting which had been continuing on their left ceased suddenly, terminated by a long, whistling sigh.

She stared at him, unbelieving. ''You may be a good writer, but you are not *famous*.''

He was suddenly struck with the ridiculousness of his school boy bragging. He smiled. ''You're right. I'm not famous. I used the word facetiously.''

''Are you really translated into all those languages?''

''Yes.''

''Maybe you're famous in Denmark.''

''Who knows?'' As a matter of fact, his foreign sales had produced little in royalties beyond the initial advance.

''Maybe you're a hit in Japan.''

He ducked his head, weary of the subject. ''I'm afraid I'm not really a *hit* anywhere.''

She touched his arm. ''I'm sorry if I was bitchy. I'm a Jewish princess, and we're entitled.''

He pulled her close and kissed her, then began a careful exploration with his hand.

She stopped him.

''I know, you've got a headache,'' he said, smiling.

She patted his cheek. ''Later. And not here.'' She finished off her drink. ''I came here fully prepared to abandon myself completely in the wildest kind of orgy.'' She put the glass down with a thump. ''But somehow it's not working. The crude types who've asked me if I 'wanna ball' have turned me off. Maybe because they were all middle-aged and pot-bellied. And you, you're just more of the non-orgy world, like being picked up at the faculty club.''

He reached for her again. ''You don't know how orgiastic I can be.''

She grabbed his hand. ''Later. In my apartment.''

He took their again-empty glasses to the bar for a refill. The bartenders were generous in their portions, and he was beginning to feel the alcohol. He walked back, a little tipsy on the resilience of the mats.

''You're a scientist. Maybe you can answer a question that has bothered me for a long time,'' he said, placing the drinks carefully on the table and sitting, tailor fashion, beside her. ''I've asked a number of famous scientists, and instead of answering me they just laugh.''

''Oh God.''

''I'm serious.''

''Why do you have to label me a scientist?''

He picked up his drink. ''Look, you have a doctorate in mathematics, right? You must have, or you wouldn't be a professor.''

''Oh, all right. What's the question?''

''Here it is. For electricity to shock you it has to go through your body to the ground. Right? If you're a little squirrel running along a high tension wire nothing happens. Touch another wire at the same time and get grounded and you're a fried squirrel, right?''

She nodded.

''Now. How does the electricity know whether or not you're grounded before it starts through you? Now. Consider this. Here's your hand touching a wire. Your feet, at the other end of your body, may or may not be grounded. You may be standing on heavy rubber soles, or you may be barefoot in a puddle of water. How does the electricity find this out without going through to your feet? Now. Don't tell me it just stands back and says, 'Ahha, I see the silly bastard is standing in a puddle of water. ZING!' "

She stared at him, her mouth slightly open. "This has been bothering you for a long time?"

He nodded.

She lit a cigarette, tipping hot candle wax on the table. "It's going to bother you a while longer."

"You can't answer it?"

"I can but I won't. It's asinine."

"Yeah." His tone expressed a sizable share of disbelief.

"You probably wouldn't understand it, even if I did explain."

"Yeah."

"I'd prefer you got your explanation from an electrical engineer, since you've been worrying about it so long. I wouldn't want to confuse you."

The spotlights playing on the stage brightened and a red-cloaked Mephistopheles appeared clutching a microphone. After clearing its throat briefly the loudspeaker near them rasped, "You heard the one about the girl who wears mink all day because she fox all night?"

There were not many laughs. He told a few more tepid jokes, then introduced a couple who would demonstrate twenty-seven different positions for making love. The participants undressed with quick unconcern, like kids in a hurry to get on the beach. She was a thin girl with long brown hair and a noticeable triangle of light showing through when she stood with her legs together; he was muscular, well-endowed and blond. Many of the positions were incredible, and the muscular strain took its toll, leaving him unconvincingly limp.

This act was followed by two homosexuals who

demonstrated thirty-seven different positions. Though many of the positions were ridiculously acrobatic, the actors drew sustained applause from the homosexual contingent.

Next two naked girls pretending to be lesbians demonstrated simultaneous cunnilingus, hating every minute of it, then entered each other with vibrator dildoes, which they seemed to enjoy more. Or maybe the vibrators just tickled unbearably.

Cynthia leaned back, stifling a yawn. "So *this* is an orgy."

John lit a cigarette. "Really only a stag show. Like they had in the days before porno films were shown in public."

He made a trip to the bar for more drinks. A feeling of numbness was creeping over him.

As he returned, the stage was suddenly blacked out, and the announcer said, "Don't go way, dirty denizens, more to follow." Rock music took over.

When the lights came up the stage was bare except for a large wooden cross. Shaped like a giant "X" instead of the cruciform, it was about six feet high and had wrist and leg irons fastened at top and bottom.

"This looks like it's going to be pretty sick. Shall we go?" asked John.

"No."

"You want to watch people being tortured?"

"Pretending to be tortured." She grabbed her drink and took a long swallow. "I came here to sink into the pit of depravity. So far I don't feel at all depraved. Only a bit soiled, as though some one had rubbed some dirty toilet paper on me."

"It's almost impossible for a sophisticated person to feel depraved. Especially when only engaged in a spectator sport," said John. The idea of torture, even simulated, sickened him, and he would have preferred to go.

But he was afraid to leave Cynthia there alone. The party had been gradually increasing in decibels, wildness and drunkenness, not to mention pot, coke and other drugs circulating freely. Groups of men were staggering around looking for new and exotic delights. So far they were amiable, but the evening could certainly become much rougher. She might find out about depravity the hard way, such as being gang-raped.

Two heavyset men dressed as devils dragged a girl onto the stage. She had long black hair and was wearing nothing but a thin, short nightgown. She struggled convincingly as they ripped it down the front, tearing it from her body. With her feet resting on the stage, they spread-eagled her on the cross and fastened the cuffs to her wrists and ankles. She continued to writhe and emit small cries of terror, twisting her hips and shaking her head so much that her long hair almost covered her face.

"*Now* you'll talk. Where is the money hidden?" asked one of her torturers with hammy ferocity.

"I don't know!"

He pushed her hair aside and slapped her face roughly.

"I don't know! Oh, please!"

He grabbed one of her breasts and pretended to squeeze. She shrieked.

"Where is it?"

"I don't *know*! God, I don't *know*!"

He reached for her pudendum roughly, covering it with his big hand. "How would you like me to shove a bottle up and split you wide open? Where's the money?"

She shrieked again, this time a little louder.

"Or maybe I'll stick a lighted cigarette up your ass?"

He lit a cigarette slowly, staring at her face, which

was doing a good job of registering terror.

Cigarette in his mouth, he pulled her hair away from her breasts and tucked it behind her shoulders. Then, removing the cigarette he pretended to burn one of her breasts, bringing the cigarette close enough to leave a smudge from the long ash.

She yelled, trying to twist her breasts away from his hand.

"Where is it?"

She continued to scream.

He leaned close to her and said, "Shut up, or I'll cut your breasts off and make you eat them."

She stopped screaming, her mouth open, and stared at him, a look of deep disgust forming.

"Talk, or I'll put a rat up your snatch." He turned to the other devil. "This is a tough one. I think we're going to need Oswald."

The other torturer brought a white shoe box to the center of the stage. He took the lid off and lifted out a small, ugly, old gray rat whose sharp incisors overlapped his chin. Holding the twisting, clawing rodent tightly he thrust it close to her face. "How would you like to have Oswald gnawing his way up your hole?"

Now the look on her face was one of genuine terror. "You never told me—get that thing away from me!"

"Where's the money?"

Her voice rose higher with fright. "Don't touch me with that!"

He lowered his hand to her crotch and thrust the struggling rat between her legs, pushing it up against her.

The shriek she let out this time was real, and it knifed through the large room with the terror of an ambulance siren. Then it stopped suddenly, and her head fell forward.

"Hell, I think she's fainted," said the first devil in a low voice.

The lights blacked out.

Nausea creeping up from his stomach, John asked. "Had enough?"

Cynthia nodded.

Large double doors at one end of the room sprang open and a ball of fire raced out. It headed straight across the room, uttering unearthly wails. It was followed by another, and then another. In seconds there were a dozen or so streaking wildly and erratically around the room, each a brightly flaming oblong of fur emitting high, piping shrieks.

John jumped up. "What the hell!"

One ran right at John, screaming. He leaped to one side, feeling the hot flames brush his leg.

"For Christ's sake! They're burning cats alive!"

He reached down and jerked Cynthia to her feet. "Let's get the hell out of here!"

A burning cat rolled to a squirming halt at their feet, screeching piteously, its charred fur reeking of gasoline, its eyes wild with pain. John grabbed the metal table and smashed its head, striking it again and again until it was a bloody pulp.

They ran toward the locker room through an uproar of human screams and yells. Ear-splitting rock music suddenly exploded from the speakers, obliterating the human cries of terror.

With shaking hands he managed to unlock Cynthia's locker and get her started dressing. She had a glazed look in her eyes, and seemed half in shock. She didn't know quite what to do next. He handed her her clothes, item by item, urging her from pants to brassiere to sweater to slacks and last, to shoes. Then he led her hurriedly to his own locker, where she stood in a trance while he dressed quickly.

Others were crowding into the room, some of the women crying, most of them white-faced and sick looking.

"Christ, I despise cats, but I couldn't do *that*," said one man, his belly as big as a clothes basket and swinging wildly as he struggled to pull on his pants.

"The whole fucking joint is gonna go up in flames!" yelled another, fighting to get his locker open.

"They must be out of their motherfucking minds!"

A woman a few feet away was vomiting, too stunned to even bend over, a cascade of half-digested food spilling over her chin and streaming down on her breasts and protruding stomach.

John felt in his pocket for his microfilm container. It was still there. He grabbed Cynthia's arm and pulled her, half-running, to the hall and down it to the front entrance.

On the sidewalk some of his panic eased. Cynthia was still in a zombie state.

"Are you going to be hysterical? Should I slap you?" he asked. Stupid question, but he wanted some response from her.

"I'll be all right," she mumbled.

"What?"

"I'll be all right."

He turned to head downtown, holding her arm firmly. The possibility of a cab was slight, but at least they could make their way towards more lights and less chance of being mugged.

The area south of the Pilgrim Hotel was under construction, and the sidewalk was blocked. They entered a long passageway of unpainted boards and planked walk skirting the new building.

Behind them someone yelled, "Hey you! I wanna talk to you!"

John glanced back and quickened his pace. In the semi-darkness lighted by an occasional bulb he could see a single large figure in a white jacket about fifty feet back.

"Hey you, wait!"

The figure pounded after them, running, his feet resounding loudly on the boards.

John tried to run, but he couldn't get Cynthia moving fast enough. She stumbled and almost fell. He caught her, and by the time he was sure she had her balance, the man behind was almost on them.

John spun around, keeping Cynthia behind him.

The man following them was huge. About six feet five, and wide enough in the shoulders to weigh close to three hundred pounds, he was wearing a white jacket with the words "Pilgrim Hotel" sewn on it in red. His big face had a vacant, retarded look, half-mongoloid and half-squashed, as though he might have been a prize fighter too long.

He stopped about five feet from them, his long arms extended, as though he expected them to try to run past him.

"You son-of-a-bitch, you set fire to my cat!"

John opened his mouth, momentarily speechless. "You're crazy."

"I seen you. I seen you beat her over the head with a table."

"For Christ's sake! I was putting her out of her misery. Wouldn't you want someone to kill you if you were burning alive?"

"You set fire to her, too. I seen you."

Cynthia pushed forward. "He did *not*! No one but an insane person would do that."

"I *seen him*. I said to myself, 'I'm going to kill that son-of-a-bitch!'" He stared at them with the hurt incomprehension of a slapped child, tears forming. "I been looking all over.''

Panic in her voice, Cynthia said loudly, ''It wasn't this man! It may have been somebody that looked like him, but *it wasn't this man*!''

A crafty look slid over his battered face. ''Oh you're tricky, but you ain't going to get away with it. I been tricked before. I wasn't born yesterday.''

''I did *not* set fire to any cat,'' said John. ''For Christ's sake, whoever was doing it must have been crazy.''

''I *seen you*.'' He lowered his arms and lunged forward, grabbing John's jacket and yanking him close. ''Fucking cat-burner, that's what you are.'' His right fist lashed out and smashed into John's jaw. The shock and pain registered briefly, then the fuse blew. He was on the ground, trying to struggle to his knees, when his short trip to oblivion ended with a return to fuzzy awareness.

A few feet from him his attacker was also on his knees. For a moment John had a blurry impression that this mentally deficient giant was playing a game with him. He would bring out a sack of marbles shortly. Then John saw Cynthia holding a short length of two-by-four, and understood dimly.

He continued his struggle and managed to get to his feet, but not as quickly as his attacker, whose dark shadow loomed quickly over him. But instead of going after John he turned on Cynthia, who was holding the two-by-four high, ready to hit him again. One long, log-thick arm shot up and he grabbed the club, wrenching it from her hands with little effort. Almost in the same motion he brought it down on her head with the ease of a man swatting a fly. The soft, slapping crack of impact brought a small scream that died almost before it left her throat.

John straightened up in dazed horror as Cynthia

crumpled to the damp floorboards, her head a bloody dark mass and strangely lopsided, as though shaped in soft clay by a mad abstract sculptor.

The monster labeled 'Pilgrim Hotel' glanced downward at his victim with no change of expression. He dropped the two-by-four casually and turned to face John, his big hands held forward as though explaining that they were going to be used to kill the man who burned his cat.

The clatter of the club hitting the wooden floor penetrated. Bending slightly, John scrambled forward to pick it up. A pile driver fist shot out and smashed into his face. The pain was excruciating. He had a hazy, split-second impression that every tooth in his mouth had been broken off. One tooth fragment felt huge to the tongue. He had a mouthful of gravel. Staggering backward he painfully tried to expel the fragments and only succeeded in pushing them out to his bloody, smashed lips. He was bleeding, but there was no saliva. He wiped some of them away from his hand.

Another massive blow slammed into his ribs. For what seemed like a hangman's five minutes, no air would enter or leave his lungs. He bent over, his mouth open, trying to snatch it from a vacuum. There was no air out there, only a wall that started at the top of his throat.

While he was fighting for breath, another blow caught him on the side of the head, sending him reeling. He crashed into one of the wooden support columns and slid to the floor.

He could hear voices approaching, the shocked, hysterical sounds of other guests from the Pilgrim Hotel. A vicious kick, aimed at his stomach, caught him in the hip, sending more knife thrusts of pain. The maniac was literally going to beat him to death.

The two-by-four was lying within reach. He grabbed

it and struggled to his feet, pain stabbing him from so many different directions that he almost collapsed again.

His attacker, who let John get to his feet, probably so that he could have the pleasure of smashing him to the ground again, glanced back in the direction of the approaching guests.

Holding the two-by-four with both hands, John raised it high in the air and brought it swiftly down on the mad man's head with all the terrified strength he could tear from his body. As the club connected, he was shocked at the force exploding from his arms and shoulders. The impact tore at his hands gripping the rough lumber, and the sound of wet wood breaking penetrated his semi-stupor.

The blow struck high on the waiter's forehead. His legs shot out like those of a man slipping on ice. He fell backwards, crashing to the walkway with a thud that rattled the loose boards. He lay there motionless.

John sank to his knees, conscious of excited voices surrounding him.

XIX

Judge Blaufeld's chambers had the look of an around-the-clock strike negotiation committee room. Coffee containers, sandwich wrappings, overflowing ashtrays smelling of stale cigar butts, paper clips, ball point pens, yellow legal size pads, a box of Bufferin, a bottle of Cutty Sark, and other debris of continuous conferences littered the large table the judge had appropriated from one of the jurors' waiting rooms.

The men sitting at the table had not only largely abandoned civility, they had slipped into personal slovenliness and an odor of sweat competed successfully with the smell of pipe, cigar and cigarette smoke.

They had ample reason to be exhausted, smelly and irritable. The *situation*, which they were supposed to coordinate, had become so chaotic that the solution to one problem lasted only long enough to see ten worse arise and clamor for attenion.

The destruction had moved out of the ghettos to luxury cooperatives on Park, Fifth Avenue and Sutton Place. Fierce fires set in the vicinity of air conditioning ducts sent hundreds to early oblivion from smoke inhalation. Through a compromise worked out by the mayor and the governor, a form of limited martial law had been established. Troops patrolled the five boroughs, but they were under the direct control of the police department. National Guard officers were apoplectic, and spent most of their time threatening to pull out, strike, or simply ignore police orders. Behind the scenes they lobbied for a complete military takeover. Mayor Schapiro held firm, and he carried sufficient

211

political clout to prevail. Especially after he appeared on television and promised the public that "there weren't going to be any damned Kent State massacres on the streets of New York while he was mayor."

Judge Blaufeld glanced down the table to focus on Harrison Ricketts. "When in the hell is Ahmid Dak going to show up?"

Ricketts held his palms up. "Who knows? He said he'd come today."

Police Commissioner Reagan said, "Judge, the city Sanitation Department is down to only thirty-one percent strength. We need to draft some more volunteers."

"This is strictly a city problem. Take it up with the mayor," snapped Blaufeld.

Reagan flushed. "The mayor said bring it up at this meeting."

Blaufeld turned to Schapiro. "Why?"

"We need help."

"You expect people from Westchester to come down and heave *city* garbage around?"

Schapiro lit another of his expensive cigars. "It's equipment we need mainly. And some skilled operators. If we could just borrow some of their surplus equipment, or even use it at night when it's not in use in the suburbs—"

"Why don't you speak to the county executives?"

Schapiro puffed his cigar. "I want an official request from this committee."

Blaufeld leaned back in his chair. "Do I hear a motion to make this an official request? Seconded. All in favor say 'aye.' Motion carried." No one had opened his mouth.

Blaufeld said to Schapiro, "Draw up your official request and send it to me for signature."

The corridor door opened and Ahmid Dak came in,

stepping jauntily. He skirted the table and took a seat next to Harrison Ricketts.

Blaufeld gave him a hard look. "Well Mr. Dak, we haven't been seeing much of you."

Dak smiled. "That's true, Judge. I don't have much time for this kind of shit."

"We can understand that. You're too busy killing innocent people."

"Innocent people? No white is innocent. Every honky has the black man's blood on his hands."

Blaufeld folded his hands on the table. "You're in effect declaring open war."

"What else, man?"

The judge's mouth turned down. "Before sentencing, I always ask the defendant if he has any statement he would care to make."

"What is this, a kangaroo court?"

"I'm giving you a final opportunity to make any suggestion you may have for alleviating this crisis. If you want to force us to imprison and kill a great many blacks, most of them innocent, we'll have to do so. If it's an open war, you'll lose."

"Shit, man."

"Do you wish to make a suggestion?"

"Yeah. We willing to play ball, but we got one final demand. We want all you white people to move out of your fine homes and apartments and turn them over to black families."

Blaufeld rubbed his chin. "I see. And where are the white people to live?"

"Oh, you move in with the rats and cockroaches and bedbugs, where we come from."

Blaufeld fumbled under the table briefly and pressed a buzzer. The corridor door opened and two policemen, both carrying shotguns, entered and took a position in front of the door. Blaufeld nodded to them.

Dak half-rose in his seat, then settled back with an angry grunt. "You touch me, you gonna have the biggest fourth of July you ever seen, baby. We not only going to burn, we gonna *blow*. We got a hundred bombs hidden around this town right this minute." He wiped his mouth, then giggled. "In fact, I think you sitting right on one, Judge."

Blaufeld calmly extracted a manila folder from a pile before him, opened it and took out some papers clipped together. "I have here the names of four hundred and twenty-one innocent people who were wantonly murdered last week. Some burned to death, others suffocated." He paused, his voice becoming huskier, "Actually 'murder' is too kind a term to use in describing these despicable acts. A murderer usually has some strong personal motivation driving him to act against his victim. You kill for *publicity*." He spat the word out like an obscenity. "You're too vicious to belong in the human race."

Dak straightened up. "You right. We don't belong to the human race. You saw to that a long time ago."

Blaufeld nodded his head curtly. "It may also interest you to know, Mr. Dak, that I have here a list of the names and addresses of two hundred and thirteen members of the Black Revolutionary Guerrilla Movement. This morning, between three A.M. and five A.M., we arrested one hundred and ninety-five of these people. We expect to pick up the remaining eighteen before the end of the day. That is, I should say 'seventeen'. We already have you, don't we?"

Dak stood up, his lips curled back and his teeth clenched. For a few seconds he could only hiss, then he said, "That fucking list. That ain't even one-tenth of our people." He turned and looked down at Ricketts. "That all the names you could think of, Harrison?"

Ricketts said, "I didn't give *nobody* no names."

"Shut up! You dead, man. *Dead*."

Blaufeld said, "Shut up yourself! You're under arrest."

Dak turned to him. "I may be under arrest, but my people gonna blow you right over the fucking East River, Judge."

Carey O'Farrell, sitting close to the door, said to one of the patrolmen, "Well, Mike, you've got a nice piece of garbage to take to the tombs."

"I'll say."

"It'd be real ideal if he tried to escape."

"You bet."

"Mike, if he tries to escape, shoot him in the guts, will you? Let him find out how some of his victims feel when they're burning to death."

Blaufeld banged the table. "Enough of that! We're not going to descend to the level of these vermin." He turned to the police officers. "If this man is shot *trying to escape*, I guarantee you both will spend your last two months in jail."

They handcuffed Dak and marched him from the room.

O'Farrell called after them, "Be almost worth it, wouldn't it, Mike?"

The door from the courtroom opened and one of Blaufeld's assistants hurried in. He bent over the judge and whispered for a moment. Blaufeld's face twisted in shock.

"Cynthia?"

The assistant nodded helplessly.

Blaufeld put his head down for a few seconds, cupping it in his hands. Then he raised his head and said, "Gentlemen, my niece has been in some sort of accident. They tell me she's been killed." He stood up. "Arch, apparently your son John was with her. He's in Bellevue seriously injured."

Archibald stood up, numbly fingering the stubble on his jaw. John injured? With Cynthia Blaufeld? Did they know each other? Perhaps it was all a mistake.

They hurried down to the street where Blaufeld's chauffeur was waiting to drive them to Bellevue.

At the hospital, Blaufeld was shown to the morgue to identify Cynthia, and Archibald took the elevator to find John's room. After he located it, the nurse told him he couldn't go in because the doctor was there.

He paced the corridor smoking, an agony of unresolved questions bombarding his tired mind. How seriously was John injured? If it was very bad it was almost a death sentence. Who would wish to spend his last two months with both legs amputated? Or blind? And Cynthia. She had been like a daughter to Marcus. Her own father had died when she was fifteen. Marcus had been her surrogate father for a long time. Her death might destroy him.

There was a uniformed policeman sitting on a folding chair by the door to John's room. Why? It was probably a two-bed semi-private room. The other patient was in trouble with the law.

The doctor finally came out. He was a round-faced Indian, smiling and short.

"Yes?" he asked, when Archibald stepped up to him.

"I'm John Tate's father. How seriously is he injured?"

The doctor thought for a few seconds. "He has two fractured ribs, a possible fracture of the collarbone, possible concussion. Many, many severe bruises and abrasions. He has also lost six of his front teeth." He smiled and shrugged. "A very bad beating."

"Can he be moved?" John would be better off in the Green Valley Hospital. Bellevue was always overcrowded and understaffed.

The doctor shrugged again and glanced at the officer. "I'm afraid you'll have to ask that gentleman."

The cop was guarding John?

Marcus Blaufeld approached, his face drawn and white. He had to telephone the District Attorney's office before the guard would let them enter John's room.

"Unbelievable," said Marcus. "It seems they think he killed Cynthia. And a man named Tiny Bales."

Heavily sedated and feeling no severe pain, John still had difficulty talking. His lips were swollen and purple and the gap left by his broken-off front teeth left his speech impeded. His mind, however, was clear, and with the help of a pad and a ball point pen he was able to give them the whole story.

Marcus asked, "Why did you take Cynthia to such a despicable place?"

John scribbled hastily that he had met her there. They had not known each other before.

Both Archibald and Marcus were shocked and could hardly conceal their contempt, particularly about the cats. Burning animals alive! How viciously sick could you get?

John wrote another long note explaining that neither he nor Cynthia had anticipated that the party would degenerate into this kind of horror, and that they certainly would not have attended had they known. Then he closed his eyes and refused to have any further communication with them. A deep depression had settled in. He no longer cared what they thought, or what anyone thought. Or whether he lived or died.

Blaufeld made several more phone calls. As a result, John was remanded to Blaufeld's personal custody. That afternoon he was moved by ambulance to the Green Valley Hospital.

XX

The warm, still summer air of Central Park was fragrant with the scent of fresh cut grass, hot dogs and sauerkraut, drifting wispy clouds of pot and hashish, and the many human smells of several thousand young people crowded together for a rock concert.

Jack passed the bottle of *Mad Dog 20-20* to Louise. She took a long swallow and handed the bottle to ·Heather. Heather passed it on to Bill without drinking. Bill up-ended it, and would have finished off the bottle if Jack hadn't caught his arm. "Hey, don't kill it all."

Grinning, Bill opened his jacket and displayed two pints of *Wild Irish Rose* tucked in his belt. He handed the *Mogen David 20-20* back to Jack.

The *Hesitant Dead* were performing. Harold Harold had personally asked Jack to attend, and to stop by to see him afterward. There might be a job in it. Harold Harold was now in charge of a government music project, the purpose of which was to set up many new groups to keep the young continuously entertained, and they hoped, non-violent.

Louise had persuaded Jack to bring Bill and Heather. Ordinarily Jack would no more have thought of inviting Bill than of asking his father. In addition to sibling rivalry and the age difference, unceasing conflict over the sharing of household tasks kept them in a state of hostility they concealed with difficulty.

But Bill, since returning from the hospital, had been depressed and silent, unresponsive to all efforts to bring him out of it. With Ginny away, and his father in the hospital, Jack felt a stronger responsibility for Bill, and gave in with only mild argument. Though hostile, Bill was much impressed with his brother's status, and Louise had been right. This unexpected attention from his older brother had brightened his life. He had laughed and joked during the drive down, and was now becoming amiably drunk.

A vendor selling wooden pipes carved in the shape of a penis and testicles elbowed his way up to them. Louise wanted to buy one as a present for John.

"Don't. Believe me, he won't appreciate it," said Jack.

Louise persisted. "Hasn't he a sense of humor?"

"Sure. But he wouldn't like it."

"Why not?"

"Well—" He thought for a few seconds. "I just know he wouldn't. He'd think it was in bad taste." For that matter, Jack himself thought the pipes were in bad taste. He questioned Louise's sense of humor. Suppose they had been carved in the shape of a woman's vagina, would she think they were so damned funny?

A youth with a heavy overlay of acne, scraggly chin whiskers and a squint, offered to sell them mescaline.

Louise wanted to buy some.

Jack shook his head and told the vendor to fuck off. "That's angel dust he's selling. They call it mescaline or any other damned name because dust has a bad rep."

Louise said, "Now I remember why I always thought of you as 'Tut-tut'."

He handed her the *MD 20-20*. "You got enough bad trips in that dim brain of yours without dust. Stick to something you can handle."

The loudspeakers sputtered. "You kids flipping out from bad dope come to the O.D. Tent. Nobody will bother you, honest. Come in and talk. We'll listen."

Louise uncapped the wine bottle and drank.

The loudspeaker spoke again. "You people swimming in the lake, get the fuck out, will you? That water's got everything in it but the bubonic plague. We already got eleven cut feet in the First Aid Station."

The crowd began to clap rhythmically, and eventually the group began to play.

They finished off the *MD 20-20* and one of the pints of *Wild Irish Rose*. Louise revealed that she had a half-ounce of fine Colombian pot. They rolled joints and passed them around. Heather, who didn't like wine, dragged at the pot eagerly.

The music flowed, thundered, crashed, sang, vibrated, engulfing them in hypnotic but violent enchantment. Jack, the almost professional, lost his technical objectivity, letting his body take over, jerking and swaying and snapping his fingers.

"Man, this is really heavy!"

"Heavy, man, heavy," they heard all around them.

Toward the end of the concert they pushed through the crowd to the roped-off area near the stage. The guards, recruited from Harold Harold's school, recognized Jack and let them through. Inside the enclosure, however, people were spread thicker than peanut butter. Jack craned to see the stage, wondering if he could even get to Harold.

The music came to a disorganized halt.

A young man had appeared on the stage. No one saw him arrive. He was suddenly just there, in front of the group, holding up his arms for silence. He was dressed in shades of red. A bright red leather jacket with leather pants to match, a lighter red shirt, a dark red tie, and shiny red boots. His hair, long and billowing down his shoulders, was dark copper. Even his face was a light reddish brown. He had a big, kindly mouth, very white teeth, a long, straight nose and large, dark eyes.

He grasped the vocalist's microphone.

"I am Aidan Grain. *Aidan* means holy fire. I was born of fire. I bring you fire to save you from fire." His deep voice boomed out over the crowd, speaking slowly, caressing it, electrifying it, soothing it. The musicians left their instruments and fell to their knees.

Jack wondered briefly whether it was some new stage business. The fellows would pick up their instruments, and the newcomer would begin to sing. Then he noticed that most of the people around him were kneeling. He felt a tingling at his nerve ends, then the bright, sharp joy of pure coke in his nostrils. A deep feeling of peace invaded his whole body. He lowered himself slowly to his knees.

"My Father sent me here to bring you love and peace, for he loves you, even those of you who have followed the paths of evil."

"Are you Jesus?" a kneeling figure asked.

There was a long pause. "No. Jesus was born of woman. *Aidan* was born of fire. My Father has many sons and daughters. Their numbers are legion."

The kneeling figure shouted, "The Holy Trinity admits of only one son. The Father, the Son and the Holy Ghost."

Aidan Grain smiled. "Do not let it concern you, my brother. The ancient scribes and apostles were confused. They *knew* of only one son; they assumed the rest. Man's knowledge of the secrets of the universe cannot even fill the hull of a sunflower seed."

The questioner bowed his head.

"My Father has loaned me certain powers. The power to heal and the power to destroy. I have come to heal your spirit and to destroy your fears and your apathy. I shall set you free."

He reached down and gently touched the center of the thick metal pole supporting the microphone. It bent away from his hand like paper bulging in the wind. He touched it on the other side, and it became straight again.

A groan went up from the crowd, but it was a joyful groan, full of awe and wonder.

"This is my first visit with you, my brothers and sisters. We shall mark this occasion, for it is truly an important one." He pulled his jacket sleeve back and glanced at his wristwatch. "The correct time is exactly four forty-five. Those of you wearing or carrying watches will please set them."

He waited. "Are all your watches synchronized?"

An affirmative roar filled the air.

"At four forty-eight your watches will stop. They will never run again. They will remain forever frozen, hands pointing to this moment of our joyful meeting."

He glanced at his watch again, waiting for its slow movement to register four forty-eight. Then he raised his hand, as though blessing them, and said, "Now. Your poor mechanical time has ceased. You will learn later of other measurements of time."

Jack looked at his watch. The second hand had stopped exactly on twelve, the minute hand indicating twelve minutes to five.

"Jesus, my watch has stopped," said Bill.

Heather was not wearing a watch. She scrambled to look at Bill's.

Another roar went up from the crowd.

"Treasure your watches as blessed mementos. My Father's power has stilled them."

The crowd moaned joyfully.

Aidan Grain turned to the kneeling musicians, and motioning upward with the palms of his hands, had them rise. "Play my brothers, while I walk among my beloved."

They rose quickly, went to their instruments and began to play, but with muted softness.

Aidan left the stage and started through the crowd. It parted slowly, leaving him a path a few feet wide.

One girl took off her shirt and spread it on the groud for him to walk on. Quickly others followed, tearing off jackets and shirts to make a many-colored carpet for his feet.

When Aidan paused, most of those nearby kneeled.

The path wound its way to the Tates. Aidan stopped and put his hand on Bill's head. "Your head has been hurting for a long time, my brother. You were cruelly beaten, in spirit and body. Your pain is gone. Your spirit is free."

Louise, who had taken off her shirt and spread it on the ground, knelt like a slave girl, her big breasts exposed.

Aidan put his hand on her head. "My sister, your poor mind is a cesspool of torment. You are healed. Your thoughts will no longer torture you."

He lifted his hand and moved slowly on.

Louise continued to kneel, her face dazzling bright in the later afternoon sun. "I'm free," she whispered.

Bill stood up. He grasped Jack's arm. "My head doesn't hurt anymore! Did you know, it's never stopped hurting until today?"

XXI

The best Green Valley Hospital had been able to provide for John was a two-bed semi-private room, but it was large and comfortable. Located in the new wing, it had the most modern facilities, including piped-in oxygen and individual television sets suspended from the ceiling.

His roommate was a middle-aged auto mechanic who had been shot in the right buttock climbing a fence. A hot-tempered husband had come home unexpectedly.

"One lousy second more and I would've been over the goddamned fence. One lousy second," said Fred, puffing on a soggy cigar. "I was right ready to drop to the other side."

John stared at the ceiling. The subject of Fred's bad luck had been covered thoroughly, a number of times. "Yeah. That was tough," he muttered.

"You know, it's goddamned uncomfortable, having to lie on your side all the time."

"I'm sure it must be." John reached for the proper button and flicked on the television set. Not that he wanted television, but it offered relief from Fred, who not only repeated himself, but prefaced any new comment with a complete replay of everything that had been said before.

John adjusted the padded earphones, turning the volume down so low that he couldn't hear it. He lay watching the silent figures move, talk, gesture, smile, frown in a world that totally deaf people would know.

Some he recognized. The woman who had been unable to have a good bowel movement was still there, and her friends were worried about her. The happy ending when she found the right laxative was joyous.

'Am I even indirectly responsible for this kind of shit?' he asked himself, mentally noting that no pun was intended. It really made no difference. His life was a total failure, and there was now no time or reason to make it otherwise. Why worry about his wasted years writing advertising copy? Suppose he had put aside the desire for family, affluence, a house in Green Valley, and had lived a monastic existence working at his writing, improving it, and in the end achieving a genuine literary contribution? The *family* he had wanted had certainly not been a success. The children were strangers, and the strong bonds that had tied him to his own mother and father seemed to be missing. And Ginny. Apparently their life together had been a fraud.

He continued to watch the figures going about their silent business of entertaining or selling, his mind becoming blank. As soon as the pills were issued, he would take his. Why prolong this tortured boredom?

His tongue probed the gaps in his front teeth. The six broken ones had been extracted. The dentist had offered to grind them down and cap them, but it would take weeks to fit this much work into his busy schedule. A quick solution would be removable bridges, which he could have a day or so after he left the hospital. He would not go to his death toothless. It was strange that he cared.

Archibald appeared suddenly on the tube, apparently in conversation with a newscaster. John turned the sound up. As a spokesman for GNYCCS, Archibald described the plight of the thousands of blacks made homeless by fires. They were camping in schools, libraries, and abandoned buildings. He urged all those who had extra room to "adopt" a black family. John turned the sound down. They already had their black family.

He wondered if Ginny was enjoying Majorca with her lover? And what sort of man was he? Did he have a wife at home whose world had suddenly been pulled out from under her? Or perhaps she didn't care, and was glad to be rid of him?

Now they were examining charts. Probably something to do with the SOW rockets. He turned the sound up. The Russians had revealed that they had their own *Save Our World* project. The Russian concept was different, and John did not understand it, other than it also would attempt to put the world in a safer orbit. The commentator mentioned that Russian and American teams of scientists were coordinating their efforts closely. He turned the sound off again. He wouldn't be around to find out whether it worked or not.

Ginny came in the room.

John slowly removed the earphones.

"I'm sorry you were hurt," she said.

He shrugged imperceptibly. "How was Majorca?"

"Lousy."

"I'm sorry."

"Sorry I'm back?"

He shook his head. "Of course not. I'm sorry you didn't find the happiness you were looking for." He spoke with his lips together to conceal the gaps in his front teeth.

She pulled a chair close to his bed and sat down.

"I'm not going to ask you to forgive me, if that's what you're waiting for."

He glanced over at Fred, embarrassed, and was relieved to see that he was asleep, snoring gently. He pushed a button, raising the bed slightly to sit up straighter. "Why should you ask me to forgive you? Apparently I should be asking you to forgive me. For twenty-two empty years." He fumbled for his package of Marlboros and got one out.

"That's a woman's trick."

"What?"

"To throw up a statement someone's made when they were emotionally upset. As though it were a literal truth."

He lit the cigarette, puffing it slowly. Exaggerations were one thing. Sometimes you accepted them as that, and at other times they hit home, and you had to believe them. "Ginny, I'm sincere when I say there's nothing to forgive. I don't blame you for going away to try to find some happiness elsewhere. I was hurt by it, but I don't feel *wronged*."

"Then why are you so cold?"

"I don't mean to be cold. I'm just—deeply depressed."

She grasped his hand. He let it lie in hers, unresponsive.

"When will you be able to leave the hospital?"

"Tomorrow. Or maybe the next day, they say."

She lowered her head. "I put Fran and Terry in Marcy's room. I thought you'd prefer that to having them in your study."

He was silent for a moment. It really didn't matter anymore. "Yes, I suppose that's better."

She opened her handbag. "Archibald gave me your valuables. Your wallet and watch. Do you want your watch?"

"I suppose so."

She handed it to him. "Do you need any money?"

"Leave me a couple of dollars for cigarettes."

She got out two one-dollar bills. Then she fished

around and held up the tiny microfilm container. "What's this?"

He stared at it. "Oh, that. You can throw it away."

"What is it?"

He grimaced. "It's my entire literary output on microfilm. All four books."

"Really? *All* of them?"

"Umm. I had some wild idea of getting them aboard the culture space ship."

She glanced at it, unbelieving. "Well, I certainly wouldn't throw it away."

What else would he do with it? Have a private showing? "Rattigan Derwent told me they wouldn't have room for it, though he would like it aboard as an example of an excellent minor twentieth-century writer."

"He *did*?" She was impressed.

He nodded. "Then I had the crazy thought that I might drive down to Cape Canaveral and try to persuade Campi to sneak it in. He's in charge of the actual loading."

"You know him?"

"Campi? He was one of my English professors. Yes, I knew him quite well."

She sat holding the small container, still marveling at its size. "John, I think your books *belong* in the space ship."

The loyal wife.

"I really do."

He said, "I don't know whether they belong there. But for a while I desperately wanted to get them aboard" He stared past her to the window with its green leaves brushing against it outside. "Now I don't seem to really care."

She carefully tucked the container back into her pocketbook. "You owe it to yourself to try."

"Why?"

"Because you worked hard writing them. Creating them. You owe it to yourself to try to save them."

He shook his head. "Vanity. And pretty stupid vanity at that, I'm afraid."

She stood up. "We'll go to Cape Canaveral. And you'll see your friend. What's his name, Campi?"

"Dr. Campanile Fraser."

The name brought a smile of recognition. "Oh, I remember your telling me about *him*. He's the one who made all the boys take off their pants."

He wasn't sure he wanted to bother to go to Cape Canaveral but the question did not have to be settled right at that moment. He said, "Yes, that's the one."

She bent over and kissed him quickly, then left.

Fred woke, and before John could get the earphones back on said, "You know, the funny thing about my gettin' shot in the ass. There wasn't nothing' going on between me and Oscar's old lady. I'm not kidding. We was just sittin' there in the kitchen having a cup of coffee."

XXII

The major cities were gradually becoming disaster areas. The slow breakdown in communications and other vital services brought increasing anarchy. One major irritant was the government's refusal to put liquor on the free list, or even to issue scrip for it. Liquor stores were looted of every last bottle, and when the mobs could find no more liquor stores with stock, they descended on the warehouses.

Full martial law was declared in New York's five boroughs, and this precipitated the resignation of Mayor Schapiro. The Greater New York Committee for the Coordination of the Situation was also disbanded. With the military in charge, who could coordinate anything?

Accustomed to working a schedule of fourteen to twenty hours a day, Archibald suddenly found himself idle and exhausted. He flew to Mexico to take a series of *Fountain of Youth* injections of a serum made from crushed lamb's testicles.

Aidan Grain and his followers bought the old McGraw-Hill skyscraper, which had been standing empty for several years. The first thing they did to the gigantic green building on West Forty-Second Street was to paint it red. This might seem an impossible project, considering the size of the building, but Aidan had in a matter of days accumulated many thousands of followers. The sides of the building were laced with hundreds of window-washer platforms, all loaded with cans of red paint and volunteers.

On one of these platforms thirty stories above the ground, Jack and Louise stood swaying in a breeze which bumped the platform against the building frighteningly from time to time. Louise looked down.

"Isn't this far out? What a view!"

Jack, who suffered from slight acrophobia, clutched the railing and looked up instead of down. He cautiously dipped his roller in the paint container and continued applying red pigment to the side of the building. "Come on, paint. We're not up here to look at the view," he said.

"If I jumped, I'll bet I could fly right to Paris," said Louise, flapping her arms.

He grabbed the rail. "*Quit* jostling the platform. This is not the subway you're in, you know."

"It's a long way down, isn't it?"

"Yes it is."

"I'd splatter good."

"You would. And I'd miss you."

She turned to him. "Would you? Really?"

"Sure."

She picked up her roller. "But you don't love me. I'm just a slob."

"I wouldn't say that." He slapped his roller against the building and worked it up and down. "Sometimes I feel like I really do."

"You do? Why?"

He glanced at her out of the corner of his eye. "Who knows? You don't ask *why* when you love someone."

"I do."

"Then *you* analyze it. Do you love me?"

"Yes."

"Why?"

"If I told you, you'd get mad at me."

She moved closer and threw her arms around him.

The platform tilted. He pulled himself away and grabbed the ropes frantically, adjusting the pulleys. "Watch it, damnit!"

Louise leaned against the rail, smiling. "Why don't you fuck me up here? I think I could even stand your being on top."

"No."

It was a temptation, he reflected briefly. He had never quite adjusted to their lovemaking, though it was better than it had been in the apartment over the Strobe Bar. Some atavistic instinct in man, he supposed, demanded the feel of physical mastery. The woman underneath, pinned to the mattress. More and more he had to control a strong urge to rape her, for taking her in that position would certainly be rape, and would probably cause her horrible anguish.

"If we rolled off, we'd go flying through the air fucking, and what a *bang* for a climax," said Louise.

He smiled. "I thought Aidan had freed you from your bad thoughts."

"That was a *good* thought."

"It was good until you get to the part where we hit the pavement. That's definitely bad."

They went back to painting.

Thirty floors below, in what had been the bookstore, Bill and Heather sat stuffing envelopes.

"Do you think Aidan is really God's son?" Heather asked.

"Yes."

"Will he save us?"

"Yes."

They stuffed envelopes silently for a while.

"Aren't you sure?" asked Bill.

She bit her lip. "Sometimes I am and sometimes I'm not."

"Why?"

"I don't know."

Aidan Grain had been appearing in unexpected places all over the country. No one knew how he did it, because no one ever saw him board an aircraft. But somehow he managed to be in Cleveland at eight o'clock, Pittsburgh at nine, Topeka at ten, Phoenix at eleven, and on across the country to San Francisco, Los Angeles, San Diego, Portland, Seattle, and then back to New York with the speed of an angel.

Had he been willing to say he was Jesus Christ returning, the Catholic church would at least have been willing to investigate his credentials, the situation being unusual enough to suggest that it might indeed be time for His return. But when Aidan insisted that his Father had many sons and daughters, they could only label him a fraud. The Rabbinical Council was certain Aidan was a fraud. He didn't even *look* Jewish. He had the complexion of an Indian, and the facial features of a *goy*. The fundamentalist Protestant churches also refused to accept him. His complexion was too dark, for one thing. He might well be part black. Mainly, however, they objected to his flaunting the Holy Trinity as an error of historians. Many of the liberal Protestant churches, however, urged a "wait and see" policy; anything was possible, and certainly if ever the world needed God's help, it was now.

The Army didn't care whether Aidan was a fraud or a real son of God. He was a good influence. A man of peace and good will, a man who had the power to keep millions non-violent, law-abiding, and happy. The Army extended every courtesy to Aidan Grain and his followers. His followers wore bright red armbands, and could move freely about the city during curfew hours. When they needed transportation to meetings, the Army provided buses and trucks. It was even rumored that the Army had been secretly flying Aidan around the country, and that this was the explanation of his miraculous appearances out of nowhere.

"My Daddy says he's a fraud," said Heather.

Bill's mouth twisted down. "You saw all the watches stop."

"They say some of them didn't."

"All three of ours did. That's good enough for me. Not only that, he stopped my head from aching."

"Daddy says—"

"Heather! If you don't believe, you shouldn't be here."

"I *do*! Honestly, I do."

XXIII

John and Ginny left for Florida on Christmas Day, August 3rd. A weepy columnist, widely syndicated, had suggested that since the world would probably never see another Christmas, a special one should be proclaimed. President Fargo had accepted the idea with enthusiasm. It offered endless possibilities for keeping people occupied. There could be a special Valentine's Day, new Washington and Lincoln's birthdays, another Veterans' Day, a Mother's Day, a Father's Day. Labor Day would actually fall in its right slot, but he could proclaim another Memorial Day.

As they drove through Green Valley to the Thruway they found most of the homes and stores decorated with Christmas displays. Sleighs, Santa Clauses, red and green bunting, gaily decked trees, and nativity scenes. John appreciated only one. Some cynic had tied up a life-size dummy of Santa Claus leaning with one arm around a porch pillar, in the traditional position of a drunk clutching a light pole.

"Now there's a man who knows what this nonsense is all about," he said.

Ginny, who had been looking the other way and didn't know what he was talking about, said, "I hope no one bangs into us." She was still worried about the five-gallon can of gasoline in the trunk compartment. Buying gasoline was uncertain. Some stations had it, and others were dry. There had been repeated warnings on television against carrying extra gas in the trunk compartment, with gruesome footage showing wrecked, burning cars with blackened, mangled occupants. drivers who had ignored these warnings and had been blasted by a rear-end collision.

Driving to Cape Canaveral was probably a bad idea, John thought, but then air, rail and bus services were equally unreliable. There had been a number of horrible plane crashes. These catastrophes no longer came in threes, but in nines. After the ninth crash in a week, pilots and other aircraft personnel breathed easier for a few days. Rail travel, once so safe, was precarious. Several head-on collisions had killed thousands. And buses were smashing into turnpike abutments with frightening frequency. Experts attributed these accidents to the lowered morale of transportation employees, aggravated by the widespread and no longer controllable use of alcohol and drugs.

The trip to Cape Canaveral in the Mercedes had another purpose. At least so John told himself. He wasn't ready to admit the primary importance of putting his microfilm aboard the culture space ship. He told himself that his relationship with Ginny needed straightening out, and that it should be resolved before *Gold Bullet Day*. Since his return from the hospital they had been living in a cool impasse of courteous friendliness. He had avoided her bed, and she had avoided his.

The trip, he thought, with its forced intimacy, might help him untangle his own conflicting feelings. He had asked her nothing about the trip to Majorca, and she had volunteered nothing. One strong urge was to leave it that way; the other demanded to know everything. The side that argued ignorance reminded him that under the present circumstances it was ridiculous to dig into and reopen the wound. She had been briefly unfaithful to him. So what? On the other hand, to leave it at that was not to know how bad the rupture had been, and why, and what her feelings were now. Did she come back to him only because of the family situation, or because she loved him and their twenty-two years together had meant something to her? Or did he merely seem the lesser of two evils? Assuming the trip had been a disaster, her lover a disappointment, would knowing make any difference in the depression that engulfed him? Was it only because he was a tidy person, and wanted to leave this life with relationships tidy and understood? With one hand on the steering wheel, and the Mercedes floating down the Jersey Turnpike at seventy, he fingered the Gold Bullet dangling against his chest. It made a small lump under one button of his shirt. He moved it to the left of the button. In it was the pill that offered eternal relief from any pain.

In the vicinity of Newark Airport they ran into a bumper-to-bumper jam up. Up ahead, all lanes were blockaded by the National Guard. In the distance John could see people milling around under clouds of tear gas. He got out and walked past the line of waiting cars until he reached the barricades. Two National Guardsmen holding Thompson submachine guns were supervising that section.

"What's up, Sergeant?" he asked one, who had rosy cheeks and a big moustache.

The sergeant looked him over carefully and then said, "Some crazy bastards trying to take over the airport."

"What for?"

"Who knows?"

The other Guardsman, who had only one stripe, said, "I heard they wanted to commandeer all the planes to take them to the North Pole, where they're gonna be safe from the big burn."

"They do any serious damage?"

Keeping a wary eye in the other direction, the

sergeant said, "They're holding about fifty hostages. I don't think they've damaged any aircraft."

The private added, "They've got Aidan Grain coming out to talk to them. He'll get 'em squared away."

A national slogan, "Nobody goes against the Grain," was taking hold.

"Any idea how long before the turnpike is cleared?"

The sergeant shrugged. "Shouldn't be too long. Maybe an hour or so. We're hauling them away as fast as we can."

The North-bound lanes had been closed off for military use, and as John watched, truck after truck rumbled past packed with yelling, crying men and women, some shaking their fists, while others offered the military a rigid middle finger.

He walked slowly back to the Mercedes.

"Looks like we're going to be delayed here an hour or so." He explained the attempted takeover of planes to fly to the North Pole.

She looked at him blankly. "Good God."

He lit a cigarette and sat, his hands resting on the steering wheel. "Who did you go to Majorca with?"

"You don't know him."

"Well?"

She glanced at him and then looked away. "I suppose we have to have it out. His name is Dilly Thompson, and we used to go out together. His wife died of a heart attack when they announced about the sun."

"*Dilly*, for Christ's sake?"

"Dillon Thompson."

He crushed out his cigarette and immediately lit another. "And obviously it didn't work out?"

"No."

"Why not?"

She shrugged. "It was an impulse thing. It just didn't."

They were silent for a while as he struggled against the urge to cross-examine her.

"Did it, uh, clarify your feelings about our relationship?"

"Not particularly."

"What do you mean, 'not particularly'?"

She reached for one of his cigarettes. "Just that. I'm still confused."

He lit it for her. "In other words, coming back was just the path of least resistance?"

"No, it wouldn't be fair to say that."

"Why not?"

She thought for a moment. "The main reason it didn't work out was that I felt a strong need to come back to you and the children."

"But?"

She shook her head. "Oh, John, I really don't know. I just don't know."

He saw that she was weeping, and put his arm around her shoulders and pulled her close. "Don't cry," he said in almost a whisper. "It'll all work out."

She murmured something.

"What dear?" He leaned closer.

"Sometimes I'm so *frightened*."

"Of dying?"

She spoke again and he couldn't hear her.

"What?"

"Some. And some of having missed everything."

"You're frightened of having missed everything?"

"Yes."

He stared out the window. The trucks were still rolling by. "I can understand your being dejected, but why frightened?"

"I feel like I'm running through a maze, and there's no end to it."

The rear door on the passenger side jerked open and a youth with long blond hair tumbled into the car. He closed the door and slumped back on the rear seat. "I gotta knife. You tell the fuzz I don't belong here, and I let you have it. I don't care what happens. Even if I get killed." The words tumbled out in a hoarse whisper.

John turned to look at him. He was about Billy's age. "You want us to get you through the blockade?"

"Yeah."

"And that's *all* you want?"

"Yeah. I ain't a hold-up man or nothing."

Ginny, who had also turned, asked, "Are you one of the people trying to get to the North Pole?"

He brightened momentarily, then his face fell. "Yeah."

John said, "It's damned cold up there right now. Fifty to a hundred degrees below zero."

"Yeah. But when the sun comes, it will be a Garden of Eden where the earth will be reborn. Those chosen will be there to start another world."

Any hope, however foolish, was better than none, John supposed.

"The unbelievers laugh at us. When we get there, we'll be laughing while you cry."

Ginny said, "We're not laughing."

The line started to move. John eased the car into gear and crept forward. At the checkpoint a National Guardsman came up to the car to look them over. His interest perked up when his glance took in the rear seat. "Hey, I seen you before. Like maybe when you was heaving a brick at me?"

"Not me," said the youth.

"That's my son. He's been with us all the time," said John. He tried to put just the right amount of indignation in his voice. Firmness, but recognition that longhairs are frequently suspect.

"Yeah?"

"Yeah."

The soldier moved away, motioning them forward. "Fucking longhairs all look alike."

They drove along in silence until the youth finally spoke. "Lemmee off at the next exit. I gotta start hitchin' back the other way."

"Okay," said John.

As they neared the exit road, John pulled off to the side and stopped.

The boy opened the back door. "Thanks for not turning me in. I hope you get to the North Pole in time."

"Thanks," said John.

"Do you need any money?" asked Ginny.

"No, ma'am."

"You should dress more warmly than that. It's going to be bitterly cold up there for more than a month."

The boy nodded, holding the door. "I had my sheepskin coat. It got lost in the hassle." He closed the door and hurried away.

"Poor baby," she said, slumping back.

After they crossed the Delaware Memorial Bridge it started to rain. At first it was only a drizzle, but it gradually became a deluge. Barely able to see, John slowed to a crawl.

Suddenly he jammed his foot down on the brake and came to a skidding stop, hardly two feet from a big container truck. It loomed over them like a skyscraper. "Keeryst!"

"Maybe you'd better pull off until it stops," said Ginny.

Muttering, he cautiously pulled around the truck, which had slowed to move onto the shoulder. "I suppose so,'' he said, now creeping along at twenty.

A screaming shriek of brakes behind flashed a warning of impending disaster that sent them both clutching, John the steering wheel and Ginny the instrument panel. The crash followed with a loud jangling of crumpling metal. In the next lane.

John pulled over, well off the turnpike, and awkwardly struggled into his raincoat.

''Be careful, you'll get hit.''

''Yeah.''

''People can't *see* you.''

''I know.''

He walked back along the verge until he was parallel with the accident, water pounding him like a shower-bath running wild. Out on the road people were yelling at each other, and no one seemed to be hurt. He slogged back to the car and got in, removing his wet raincoat with difficulty.

''Nobody hurt.''

Ginny nodded. ''Let's stay here until it lightens up.''

He lit a cigarette, then sat tapping the steering wheel with his still damp fingernails.

''Must you?'' asked Ginny.

He looked at her, astonished. With the water thundering on the roof in a continuous roar, she surely couldn't hear those tiny clicks? He shrugged and switched on the radio.

''Torrential rains in Delaware, Maryland and Virginia during the last twenty-four hours have produced six inches of precipitation. Flood warnings have been issued in areas adjacent to the Deleware and Potomac rivers. Stretches of Route 95 in the vicinity of Washington are being closed to vehicular traffic.'' He turned the volume down.

''What the hell other kind of traffic is there on Route 95?''

"Maybe they're keeping it open for people who want to riot," said Ginny.

The radio's volume gained strength, as though a commercial was about to be aired. "Thousands of followers of Aidan Grain today descended upon Newark Airport to lend support while he negotiated for the release of fifty hostages held by a group calling itself *Witnesses for the New Garden of Eden*. After laying the hand of God on ten of the leaders, Grain convinced the would-be hijackers to release the hostages and abandon, temporarily, at least, their attempts to fly to the North Pole. Grain told reporters that if his Father wants everyone to go to the North Pole, he will supply the necessary aircraft."

"Another coup for Grain," said John.

"I hope Jack and Billy don't get hurt running around with that fanatic," said Ginny.

"He seems to be a peaceful man."

"I'm afraid of mobs."

The car was becoming very hot and stuffy. He lowered the window a bit, then closed it quickly as water slapped his face.

"Mobs are incited to violence by leaders who are violent. Try opening the window a bit on your side."

She opened the window. Water came driving in. She closed it.

"Now how in hell can it be blowing from both sides?"

He slumped back against the headrest and tried to take a nap.

After a while, Ginny nudged him. The rain had tapered off to a light shower and traffic was whirring by on the wet concrete.

By nightfall they had had two very bad meals, and had spent hours detouring around flooded sections of the highway. They had also tried for accommodation at six motels, only to find each hopeful inquiry met with a 'Sorry, full up.' Neon *No Vacancy* signs floated by with discouraging frequency.

"I hope we don't have to sleep in the car. I'm exhausted," said Ginny, then called suddenly, "There's one!"

He braked and swung in past the still lighted *Vacancy* sign and up the driveway to the office of the *Bida Wee Cabins*.

"Crummy looking joint, isn't it?"

"We're desperate. At least, I am."

"Okay." He parked and entered the motel office.

The manager, a youngish looking man with a large bald spot on the top of his head, was obviously drunk. He pulled himself out of an armchair and lurched to the registration counter, propping himself behind it with difficulty.

"You have a double room?"

The manager stared at John, trying to focus his eyes. "What?"

"Do you have a room for my wife and myself?"

The manager leaned on the counter, burying his face in his hands.

"Hey, wake up."

The manager peeked at John through his fingers. "Why?"

"I want a room, damnit. Your sign says you have a vacancy."

"Mebbe we do, mebbe we don't," came through the fingers.

"Sure you do," said John, trying to encourage him. "You wouldn't leave the sign on, and have people disturbing your sleep, if you'd rented your last room."

"Sometimes forget the sign.

John jostled his elbow. "Well, let's figure it out, huh?"

"Don't go pushing me."

"Look, we're tired and we need a room."

An idea seemed to penetrate dimly. The manager pulled himself straight and turning, reached for a key. "Just remember. The room next to mine not rented." He handed the key to John. "Gimmee fifteen."

John handed him a ten and a five.

"Try not to rent the room next to mine."

"Why not?"

"Don't like strangers close to me."

John held the key, waiting for him to produce the usual registration form. "We're quiet. No loud parties."

"Just remember, I told you."

"All right. Don't you want me to sign a registration form or something?"

"You wanna?"

"Nope," said John. He turned and left quickly.

Their room was at the end of the row. It was shabby and threadbare, and smelled vaguely as though a pet poodle might have hidden an accident somewhere under one of the beds.

John carried the suitcases in and immediately brought out the bottle of Scotch he had tucked in his own bag. The glasses were stained with toothpaste residue, and even though he washed them with soap and hot water he couldn't get them entirely clean.

"Keeryst, what a *dump*."

"I don't want a drink," said Ginny. She had slipped quickly into her nightgown and was now crawling into bed.

He pulled the covers of his bed back, thinking he would sit in it and have his drink. The chairs were greasy looking and stained.

"Good God! These sheets are filthy."

Ginny sat up and examined her sheets more carefully. "These are fresh. They're even still starchy.

He stared at his bed unbelieving. "These sheets look like they haven't been changed for three years. One or two people could never get them this soiled."

It would probably be impossible to get any clean sheets. He poured himself a drink and sat down in one of the greasy armchairs. "I can't sleep in that damned bed."

Ginny slipped back under the covers. "Well, you can sleep with me. But don't mess around. I'm too tired."

He was on the verge of explaining sarcastically that she was flattering herself, but stopped short of speaking. It had been an exhausting, depressing day. Also it had been more than kind of her to insist upon a trip which was nothing but a prop for his vanity. Everyone knew traveling was hell these days, however and wherever you went. And what was she getting out of it, this attempt to provide him immortality as a *minor* writer? Beetle-eyed denizens of the planet Orizon would learn nothing of Virginia Tate, wife of the author, even though she was in his books in hundreds of ways.

He lit a cigarette and poured himself another drink. On the other hand, why did she have to go whoring off with a man named Dilly Thompson? Who said he wanted to *mess around* with her anyway? It wasn't likely that Dilly Thompson was the kind of man he would care to share a wife with. Offhand, he couldn't think of *any* man he would care to share a wife with, even President Fargo, who would probably spend his time in bed praying. So to hell with her. Let her go back to Dilly Thompson if she wanted someone to make love to her.

For some reason the Scotch tasted sour and unpalatable. He rolled it around in his mouth and swallowed. Taste buds probably shot. The Scotch was the same. He was deteriorating. And who was he kidding? After having been celibate for several weeks, crawling into that narrow twin bed with her would be a disaster. Conditioned responses would certainly take over. He switched off the lamp, slipped further down in the greasy armchair and went to sleep.

The toilet flushed loudly, waking him up. In the light from the open bathroom door, he could plainly see Ginny in her bed asleep. He sat there paralyzed, wondering who was in there flushing the toilet?

The manager walked clamly out of the bathroom. He was wearing a long white nightgown.

John jumped up. "What the hell are you doing in here?"

The manager walked calmly out of the bathroom. He stopped up. I use this one."

"The hell you do!"

"It's a long walk to the office," he said, his voice rising to a whine. "I told you."

"You did not."

"I did."

"You stay the hell out of here."

The manager edged over to the door which connected with his own room and opened it. "I *told* you. I told you I hated coming into a stranger's bedroom to use the bathroom."

"You come back in here, I'll brain you."

The manager skipped through the door and closed it. John moved a heavy dresser in front of the door, which he found he couldn't lock. Ginny slept through the entire incident.

He settled back into the chair and finally got to sleep a second time.

In the morning, after a night of waking again and again with the need to adjust to another uncomfortable position, he found that his neck seemed to be permanently bent to one side. He undressed and stood in the gritty shower steaming his stiffness for a long time. It helped some, but his neck still pained him when he held it straight, and eased somewhat when he tucked it quizzically to one side.

Ginny woke up and got languidly out of bed. "I'm sorry you felt you had to be a martyr," she said.

"Shut the hell up."

"Why are you looking at me like that?"

"I'm looking at you like that because my goddamned neck is bent, that's why."

Ginny stared at him for a few seconds, then began to laugh.

"What's so funny?" He had never hit her, but he was unconsciously doubling his fist.

She hurried into the bathroom, trying to contain her laughter.

After driving some distance they found a diner. John felt a little less hostile when he finished his breakfast and coffee, though the elderly waitress tucked her head to one side everytime she spoke to him. Maybe she was trying to outdo him in diffidence, or perhaps she felt the need to line up their eyes, the way some people have to straighten a picture on the wall.

The day was spent largely in silence, with neither road-block nor flood to delay them. The Mercedes ticked along at a safe, effortless seventy, and as the hours passed John's neck became less rigid. By evening, when they were finally in northern Florida, the tilt was slight and hardly noticeable.

They stopped for dinner at a luxury motel, and were surprised to find it only lightly tenanted. With the preceding night's experience still vivid, they decided to go no further.

The room was large and comfortably furnished in Motel-Mediterranean. Glass doors opened onto a pink concrete patio adjoining the swimming pool. Two teen-agers, a boy and a girl, splashed around in the otherwise empty pool.

John sipped a Scotch, idly watching the girl who, in her bikini, was nubile enough to catch any man's attention. Ginny watched him watching the girl.

"Quite an improvement over last night," said John.

"Ummm."

"That crazy idiot." He told her about the manager invading their bedroom."

"I know," said Ginny.

"You were *awake*?"

She nodded.

"Why did you pretend to be asleep?"

She smiled. "I knew you'd protect me. Why get upset?"

John shifted his attention from the bikini-clad girl. "Really? You weren't frightened at all?"

She got up and strolled to the glass doors. "We should have brought our suits. We could go for a swim."

He swirled the ice around in his drink. "I think I saw a store in the lobby."

"Probably closed."

He glanced at his watch. "Nine-thirty. Probably is."

She went back to her chair. "I think I'll have a drink after all. We're drinking too much, you know."

He shrugged. "What difference does it make?" He poured her a Scotch and added some water.

"Do you want to come to bed with me?"

He handed her the drink. "Do you really want me to?"

She sipped the Scotch. "Why not? It's a physical thing. We've been doing it for twenty-two years."

"Relief for the sex-starved male?"

"I didn't mean that. Anyway, females can be sex-starved too."

He lit a cigarette. "What are you trying to say?"

"I'm not trying to say anything. I merely, for Christ's sake, asked if you wanted to come to bed with me." She gulped her drink angrily.

"What you're intimating is that there doesn't have to be any real commitment involved."

She finished her drink. "I wasn't aware that I was intimating any such thing." She got up, and snatching her nightgown from her opened suitcase, went to the bathroom.

He poured himself more Scotch. It was a peace offering he thought, no pun intended. He supposed he should take advantage of it. Perhaps it was a first step instead of a last one in resolving the real issue of trust and commitment. While it wasn't quite the same thing, she had trusted him implicitly in the matter of the strange man walking around in their bedroom. He felt rather proud of that. Most women would have been sitting up screaming their heads off. On the other hand, maybe she was cracked. Suppose the intruder had had a gun or a knife? How could she lie there with her eyes closed, confident that good old John could take care of it? The answer, of course, was that Ginny was very quick to grasp any situation. Something in the tone of his voice, when he first challenged the drunken manager, probably indicated that the incident was not frighteningly serious.

She came out of the bathroom, and without looking at him, got quickly into bed.

He tossed off the rest of his drink, undressed and went in the bathroom to brush his teeth, including the removable bridges which filled in the gaps left by a pathetic mental defective named Tiny Bales.

Everytime he detached them for cleaning the nightmare evening came back in fragments. So he had actually, for the first time in his life, killed a man. In the Korean war, as a Signal Corps officer, he had never been close enough to the enemy to shoot at anyone. If the world somehow survived, he would face a trial for man-slaughter, though Archibald had assured him it would be a formality, since the case was so clearly one of self-defense. Still, it would be humiliating. Especially if the whole story of the so-called orgy had to come out. He tried to remember Cynthia Blaufeld. Her face remained a blank. Her breasts, thighs and appendectomy scar made up the only image he could recall, like a snapshot cropped at the shoulders and knees.

Suppose they had gone to her apartment and made love? He had intended to. And it would not have been a no-meaning encounter, such as the incident in the office with Marilyn. Cynthia was not the kind of woman you made love to casually. In effect, he had been unfaithful to Ginny.

He turned out the light and crawled into her bed. Half-asleep, she stiffened and turned her back to him quickly. A tussle followed which culminated in a non-violent rape. Physical necessity won over emotional rejection, and she responded fully, though seemingly contemptuous of them both for doing so. In the struggle, however, he badly bruised his still strapped and healing ribs, giving the orgasm a peculiar adjunct of real pain, and his groan was not entirely from relief.

XXIV

About ten miles from Cape Canaveral numerous tents and tightly packed trailer camps began to appear on both sides of the road. Five miles away every available square inch of open space seemed to be occupied by campers.

John groaned. "Every damned writer, artist or musician in the world is here."

"Maybe some are just people who want to see the launching."

"Writers," said John, moving along slowly in the jammed traffic. "Ninety-nine percent will be writers."

They crept into the city at five miles per hour. The streets were congested with twenty times the traffic they were built to accommodate, and pedestrians, crowded almost solid on the sidewalks, spilled out into the tangle of cars, creating more paralysis. Most of the people on foot were carrying things—paintings, pieces of sculpture, records, books and odd shaped packages that obviously housed other treasures.

"Good *God*!" said John, unable to go forward or back up. He lit a cigarette and sat there tapping his fingernails loudly on the steering wheel, daring Ginny to complain.

A bushy-haired man wearing a beret perched on his thick crown worked his way between the cars. He was carrying an oil painting.

As he approached the window, John asked, "Any chance of getting a room in this place? Anywhere?"

The stranger stopped. "You kidding? There hasn't

been a room here since they announced the fucking culture ship."

"What would you advise a visitor to do?"

"Go home."

"Other than that?"

The artist rubbed his stubble-covered chin. "There are no rooms even in towns fifty miles from here." He smiled, shifting his painting to a more comfortable position. "I hear Framer's Hardware still has some sleeping bags."

"Eeyuch," said Ginny.

The artist shrugged. "It's not all that bad. They've put up some public showers and toilets down on the beach." He scratched his ribs absentmindedly. "The sand fleas and mosquitoes get kind of active. But there's no discomfort a good joint can't alleviate. You wouldn't happen to have any grass, would you?"

John shook his head. "My pain relievers are old-fashioned, like Scotch."

"Yeah man. That helps if you haven't got pot."

"Would you know where Dr. Campanile Fraser is staying?"

The artist laughed. "All roads lead to Dr. Campanile Fraser. But you ain't going to get to see him, man. They got that place tied up tighter than Fort Knox. Forget it. Save your sanity."

"I couldn't leave here without at least trying."

"I can dig it."

"So how about telling me where to go?"

The artist nodded. "You got a cigarette?"

John handed him the pack of Marlboros.

"Follow this street down to the third stoplight. Turn right and go about four miles. You'll see a big pink stucco house surrounded by barbed wire, sandbags, soldiers and machine gun emplacements.

"Machine guns?"

"Shit yea, man." The artist took a cigarette and returned the package to John. "Didn't you hear about the big massacre last week?"

"Massacre?"

"Shit yeah." He lit the cigarette. "We tried to storm the place. Mowed down fifty of us."

"You're kidding."

"Shit no."

"There were people *killed*?"

"You'd better-believe it, man. Thirty-three."

Traffic began to creep forward. The car behind him honked. John muttered a hasty thanks, waved and moved on.

It took the better part of an hour to crawl the five miles to Campanile Fraser's house. A large Spanish style structure, probably with an interior courtyard, the house stood in the center of an approximate acre of ground lush with palm trees and other tropical plantings. Completely surrounding the property was a barbed wire fence nine feet high with a top shelf tilting outward. Each corner had a concrete watchtower similar to those found on prison walls. Sandbagged machine gun emplacements dotted the periphery, complete with helmeted soldiers manning them.

"Unbelievable," muttered John.

There was nowhere to park, of course. He slowly circled the area and finally double-parked at the end of a wide residential street. Since it was a corner, the car he was blocking could pull out by moving straight ahead.

They walked back to the gate where some fifty people were standing in small groups, aimlessly talking or just staring at the house. John approached a sergeant, who seemed to be in charge of the guard.

"I'd like to see Dr. Fraser. He's an old friend of mine."

The sergeant laughed. More of a small, sneering yelp than a laugh. "So would fifty thousand other *old friends.*"

"He'll want to see me."

"Get lost, will you."

John's face flushed. "Who is your superior officer? Maybe General Moore would like to know how you're treating honest citizens. This isn't Nazi Germany. Yet." General Moore was Chief of Staff, but his was the only important military name John could recall.

The sergeant's jaws chomped unperturbably on a wad of gum. "I got my orders, *citizen*. Nobody goes in without a pass."

"How do you go about getting a pass?"

"That's your problem."

"Who gives out the passes?"

"Dr. Fraser."

"How can I ask him for a pass if you won't let me in to see someone on his staff?"

The sergeant studied John's face, his vacant blue eyes unwavering. "Telephone him, you twit." He reached in his pocket and pulled out a stack of mimeographed slips bearing Campanile's name and phone number. He handed one to John.

John tucked it in his pocket angrily. "Why didn't you tell me the proper procedure in the first place, instead of going through all this crap?"

The sergeant tapped John's chest with one very hard finger. "Listen, *citizen*, my orders are to discourage anyone who wants to see Fraser. Now get moving, or I'll arrest you for harassment of the military." He pronounced it 'ha*rass*ment'.

John stared into the blue eyes for a few seconds. Had this soldier been one of those who had helped slaughter thirty-three frantic authors and artists? It seemed impossible. He shuddered slightly, turned and left.

Ginny, who had been waiting about twenty feet away, asked, "Well?"

"Goddamn fascist."

An elderly lady with buck teeth asked him, "Why should I rent you a room in my house?"

John stared at her, bewildered.

Ginny said, "I asked her if she had a room we could rent."

"I wouldn't dream of *renting* a room in my house. Thank God Horace provided for me very well, and I've never had to take strangers into my home," said the old lady. "Is it true that you're a close friend of Dr. Campanile Fraser?"

John started to answer truthfully, then hesitated. Sleeping on the beach had very little appeal. He nodded. "Yes. A very old and dear friend." Campi was certainly very old.

"If I let you stay in my house as guests, will you talk to him about my *History of the Crandell Family*?"

John smiled. "I'll try."

Agnes Crandell's antebellum mansion had obviously been in Florida long before Flagler discovered the state. It still had some seedy elegance, but neglect was pushing it down the road to frayed decrepitude. The shrubbery was overgrown, and the zoysia grass lawns were rough and patchy. The house itself, a dirty graying white, had needed paint for many years.

The location was convenient, at least, John thought, since it was hardly a half-mile to Campanile Fraser's fortress.

They turned into a semicircular driveway of cracked, weed-infiltrated blacktop, and pulled up to the long porch with its tall gray columns. Paint had peeled to show large areas of weathered wood, and the steps leading to the porch were cracked and sagging.

John got out and opened the door for Mrs. Crandell.

She pried herself creakily from the rear seat while he opened the front door for Ginny.

A very old black man opened the huge front door, and peering nearsightedly around, decided that he was needed. He tottered across the porch and down the steps, one at a time.

"This is Raymond," said Mrs. Crandell. "I'm afraid you'll have to carry your own luggage. Raymond's back isn't what it used to be."

"Of course," said John, opening the trunk compartment. He would have been embarrassed had this doddering old man tried to carry anything for him.

"Raymond, show Mr. and Mrs. Tate to the guest room."

Raymond nodded, grinning over toothless gums.

She turned back to John. "Most of the house is closed off. Just too much work for Raymond and me to keep up. Lordy, it's such a big house."

"I can see that."

"My stars yes, it's just too big."

The guest room was on the second floor at the front, and had French doors opening onto a long balcony directly over the ground floor porch. It was furnished with heavy Victorian pieces and the carpet was badly worn, but it seemed to be clean.

"Safest room up here," said Raymond, opening the doors to the balcony. "This old firetrap go up, you just skedaddle out here and shinny down one of them pillars."

John cleared his throat. "That's reassuring." Then, trying to fill in an awkward pause, said, "I suppose you've been with Mrs. Crandell a long time?"

"Been with that crazy fuck-up all my life," said Raymond. Then, remembering that Ginny was there, put his hand over his mouth. "Scuse me, ma'am." He tottered back into the room. "Miz Crandell, she all right. Don't know which end's up, but she all right.''

"Hmmm.''

"Keep your nose keen for smoke. Crazy old fool smokes in bed. Drinks her pint of wine and goes right to sleep, cigarette burning or not.''

John followed Raymond to the hall door, glancing apprehensively around.

"I put her out three times already,'' said Raymond.

With Mrs. Crandell's eager approval, John settled down by the telephone in the library and began dialing Campanile Fraser's number. As he expected, it was busy. He tried several times at five-minute intervals. It continued to be busy. Obviously nothing would do but to keep dialing continuously. Sooner or later his call would squeeze in. He worked at this until his arm was tired, breaking the connection as soon as he heard the busy signal and redialing immediately.

"Damnit, it's impossible to get through,'' he said to the empty room, unaware that Agnes Crandell had left. He lit a cigarette and then angrily twirled the dial again. He couldn't believe it. He had almost broken the connection when he realized that the phone was actually ringing.

A voice at the other end said, "This is a recorded announcement. When you hear the tone, state your name and your reason for requesting a meeting with Dr. Fraser. You will have twenty seconds for your message.''

John searched his mind frantically for the right words. Should he say, "This is John Tate, a former student of yours who would never take down his pants and is now willing?'' The tone sounded. He said, "This is John Tate, one of your former students. I'd like to talk to you about my books. I can be reached at 343-7382. That's 343-7832. Mrs. Agnes Crandell's home.'' He hadn't written a thousand commercials for nothing.

He replaced the handset, suddenly aware that he had said the wrong thing. He shouldn't have mentioned his books. His approach had been all wrong. He sat seething with frustration, wondering what he could have said to get attention and action. Campanile was no fool, and whatever he said, Campanile would guess that the books were the basic reason. Assuming, of course, that Campi knew about them. Hadn't Derwent said they had discussed his work?

He paced up and down in the moldering old library trying to think of a way to get a proper message to Fraser. Probably some secretary listened to the recordings and then cleaned the tape for the next day's batch. Mentioning his books would immediately consign him to oblivion. More books they could do without. In fact, it could be that no one even listened to the messages, that this particular phone was merely a pacifier installed to fend off artists without infuriating them with blunt turndowns. Perhaps the tape was even spinning away in some military office, the messages being screened for indications of approaching violence.

Suddenly he realized why so many people had been standing outside Fraser's house. Unable to get through the recorded message barrier, they hoped to see him, speak to him, when he came out. He surely had to leave the house from time to time, if only to visit the space ship.

He supposed he would have to join the supplicants at the gate. What a fool he had been not to anticipate that every idiot who wrote or painted or composed would be here making it impossible for anyone to even talk to Fraser. His own scenario had been naive indeed. He had pictured a brief meeting with Fraser. They might even have had a drink together. Then Fraser would say, "Sorry, old boy, I wish I could include your work, but I'm sure you know how it is. We've had to leave out a tremendous number of really fine writers because the space is so terribly limited." And John would say, "Certainly, I understand. I wanted to see you again anyway." Then they would shake hands. John would leave, pick up Ginny and drive back to Green Valley, comforted slightly by the knowledge that at least he had spoken to Campanile, that he had done the best he could. Now he was going to be deprived of even this small consolation.

What was the next step, if any? Ginny was upstairs napping. Should he discuss it with her? He wandered aimlessly around the old house. Some of the rooms were locked. Others were empty of furniture with wallpaper hanging in shreds, the ceilings partly collapsed. Termites had been busy for a long time.

The large high-ceilinged kitchen still had a huge coal-burning range. Next to it was a smaller gas stove with a tea kettle hissing on it. Agnes Crandell sat on a high stool by the big wooden drainboard joining the sink. On the sink were jars of baby food. She was peering at the labels through a large magnifying glass.

"Just fixing Raymond's dinner," she said. "Crazy old fool won't go to the dentist and have false teeth made. If I've told him once, I've told him a thousand times, 'go to Dr. Bowman and have false teeth made and I'll pay for them.' " She put one jar aside with a thump. "Lamb. Now why in heavens name did I buy lamb? Nigras can't stand the taste of mutton. That fool at the store knows Raymond won't eat lamb."

John said, "I can't seem to get through to Dr. Fraser."

She turned. "Would you care for a cup of coffee?"

"I suppose so. Thanks."

She spooned instant coffee into two cups and filled them from the boiling kettle. "No one gets to speak to that *man*. But surely he won't be discourteous enough to ignore an old friend. You did speak a message into that contraption, didn't you?"

John nodded, accepting the cup she handed him. "I hope his secretary doesn't just throw me out with the hundreds of others trying to get through."

She put milk and sugar in her coffee. "I want you to explain to that *man* why the 'History of the Crandell Family' belongs on that space ship."

John sipped his black coffee, trying to appear interested.

"My grandfather, Elias Crandell, was one of the first settlers here. The 'History' starts with some very interesting selections from a diary he kept." She opened a cabinet and brought out a slim volume with a plain white dust jacket.

"Then Crandell wasn't your husband's name?"

She handed him the book. "Of course it was. We were first cousins."

He riffled the pages. It had been privately printed and was poorly designed. A photograph of the author, Reverend Beaumont Crandell, appeared opposite the title page. His luxuriant face whiskers framed a benign, thoughtful face. "Very interesting," said John.

She took the book from him quickly and turned to a section in back. "Here's where it tells about me."

He read, "Agnes Crandell, daughter of Richard Lewis Crandell and Theodosia Crandell (nee Boyle) was born February 11, 1890. Educated at Miss Dalton's School for Young Gentlewomen, Agnes grew into a beautiful young woman, proficient in music, an accomplished pianist and water colorist. In June of 1915 she married Horace Lewis Crandell, son of Barton Ricks Crandell, brother of Richard Lewis, and a

first cousin. This happy marriage began in an era
fraught with anxiety over the catastrophic state of the
world, for indeed the guns of the first world war were
already resounding, and Major Horace, as he was affec-
tionately known to his friends and loved ones, was to
see action in this bloody conflict—''

John put the book down. "I must read this more
carefully," he said. "Later."

"You give it to that silly old man and see that he puts
it on that ship."

He smiled. "I'll give it to him if I get to see him. But
I certainly can't guarantee he'll put it aboard."

"I want you to *see* that he does."

John shrugged. "I think I'll stroll over there. Maybe
I can catch his attention when he comes out of the
house. *If* he comes out of the house." He stood up,
slipping the book into his jacket pocket. "It seems a bit
futile, but I don't know what else I can do."

Outside Fraser's house the crowd was now larger,
and John recognized several writers. There were many
there, he was sure, that he didn't recognize. In one
group Francis Ellis, a TV playwright, stood chatting
with Eric Levy and Patrick Connell. Surely they hadn't
left out Levy's work? If they were passing up an author
as brilliant as Levy, what chance had he?

The hot Florida sun penetrated his lightweight jacket
like a wave from a far-off blast furnace, bringing an
unpleasant reminder of next month's date with another
part of the sun. He took off his jacket and folded it over
his arm, then began strolling aimlessly around. Fraser
might not come out for hours, if at all. Some of the
supplicants had brought canvas folding chairs; others
were sitting on the ground. How many hours should he
devote to this nonsense before giving up?

He was dabbing his perspiring neck with an already

damp handkerchief when Gregory Marsh strolled up, his face grim.

Secretly elated, John said, "Surely they haven't left your work out?" His voice, he hoped, expressed serious concern.

Gritting his teeth, Marsh whipped a letter from his pocket and read a portion aloud to John. "While your work has achieved a certain amount of widespread contemporary notoriety, it is our feeling that you have very little to say about life in this period that is fresh, true, honest and real, and will be of value to future historians appraising our human cultural achievements." He spat out the words bitterly in disjointed groupings with no particular emphasis, in a way one might read a foreign language he hated.

"Do you know who wrote this asinine letter? That goddamned miserable shithead of an old fag, Campanile Fraser."

Campanile had expressed John's own opinion of Marsh's writing perfectly, but he tried to look sympathetic.

Marsh read another sentence. "As for literary merit, we have concluded that your work ranges from pedestrian to unfortunate."

John shook his head sadly, trying to repress a smile. "*Rat* Derwent told me they have only one hundred and twenty-five cubic feet of space. Many good writers have to be left out."

Marsh's eyesbrows lifted. "Do you know Rattigan Derwent?"

"I've spoken to him—"

"If you would only—"

Marsh broke off as a big white Continental came rolling up. Soldiers hurried to clear a path about fifteen feet wide from the car to the gate. They pushed bystanders back with considerate firmness.

John recognized Campanile immediately. He had changed little over the years. His hair was still luxuriant and immaculately white, his suntanned face still firm, though the flesh was loose around the jowls and he had a sizable turkey wattle hanging between chin and throat. His eyes were bright and alert, and they shifted quickly around, peering at the faces lining the path to the gate. A soldier carrying a submachine gun walked ahead of Campanile, and another followed, both scrutinizing the crowd carefully.

From the moment the car door had been opened for Campanile, entreaties rang out. "Please, Dr. Fraser, give me just five minutes. Dr. Fraser, I'm Jason Jergens. I've got to talk to you. Dr. Fraser, will you read—. Dr. Fraser, I'm Michael Reepes; I know you'll want—"

As Fraser and his guards approached John, he joined the clamor, calling loudly, "Professor Fraser, remember me, John Tate? I'd like to talk to you."

Campanile glanced at him blankly, without recognition.

Out of the corner of his eyes, John saw Gregory Marsh pull something from his pocket and raise his arm. He turned and saw with horror that Marsh had a revolver in his hand.

Campanile saw the pistol, too, and hunched his shoulders instinctively, his face tight with fear.

John frantically threw his arm out and upward, hitting Marsh's wrist hard. The gun exploded, pointing skyward.

At that instant, both soldiers opened up with their submachine guns. The racket was deafening, a whole fleet of trucks backfiring with maniacal speed. John felt a searing burn on his left leg. He dropped to the ground, flattening himself, wishing he could claw a hole and crawl in.

The firing stopped. Campanile rushed over to John shouting, ''This man saved my life and you've shot him, you bloody idiots!''

John sat up, holding his leg.

''Idiots!'' screamed Camapnile. ''Look what you've done!''

In addition to a riddled Marsh with a hundred bloody and fatal wounds, three spectators on Marsh's right lay on the ground chewed almost beyond recognition by the spray of hot lead.

At Campanile's insistence, two of the soldiers carried John into the house and then went to fetch a medic. The other casualties were beyond help.

Campanile bent over him. ''I'm trying to remember you, dear boy. You were a student of mine, were you not?''

''Yes. I'm John Tate.''

''John Tate, the writer?''

''I was also a student of yours. But I can see how you wouldn't remember,'' said John, his leg burning. ''You've seen so many students come and go.''

The medic arrived. Loosening John's belt, he unzipped John's trousers and pulled them down. The bullet had made a bloody crease about two inches long on the outside of his thigh. Quickly cleaning the shallow wound, the medic coated it with disinfectant and taped on a small bandage.

''That it?'' asked John, reaching for the waistband of his trousers.

The medic straightened up. ''Hold it. Better give you a tetanus shot.''

John then had to pull his shorts down while the medic attacked one buttock with a syringe.

Campanile, who had been watching, said, "*Now* I remember you."

John pulled up his pants sheepishly.

XXV

Campanile insisted that he stay for dinner. He telephoned Ginny, who was cheered by the news that he had succeeded in penetrating the fortress. He didn't tell her how, and she would not know about the four people slaughtered in the process unless she happened to meet an eyewitness, because strict censorship of the press kept a tight lid on nasty news of this type. She could find out about his slight wound later.

Always a gregarious gourmet, Campanile now apparently preferred to dine in lonely elegance, for there were no other guests. Probably he was weary of the importunities of writers.

The large table with its snowy, embroidered cloth was set with Tiffany silver and there were four wine glasses at each place. The room was softly lit with candles. Campanile sat at the head, and John had been placed about a yard away on his right.

"Thank God this awful task is just about completed. Had I anticipated the heartbreak and bloodshed to come, I would never have accepted it," said Campanile.

"Is it true that thirty-three people were killed last week?" asked John.

Campanile shook his head sadly. "Alas, only too true. It's madness, absolute madness."

A white-jacketed waiter wheeled in a cart of hors d'oeuvres and served them rillettes, caviar, smoked salmon with capers, shrimp in mustard sauce, and sliced galantine of chicken.

Campanile brightened. "My only consolation in this miserable assignment has been an excellent chef."

"I'm sure it has been terribly difficult," said John, cutting a piece of smoked salmon. "I'm just amazed that anyone could become so violent. I mean, it's a highly uncertain immortality they're seeking."

Campanile spread caviar on a wedge of toast. "I think it's frustration, primarily. Literally thousands have poured in and out of this town. Hundreds arrive every day." He shrugged and ate the caviar. "It would be impossible for me to see them, or even talk to them on the phone." He began on the shrimp, eating it with great enjoyment. "In any event, a writer's work is the only thing we judge. What can a man say to me about his writing that will change the panel's evaluation? What's to be gained by my seeing these poor people?"

Truite a la Marguery arrived, with a vintage Chablis to accompany it. John stared at the fish, sinking into a mild depression. Campanile was right. Why was he there?

"That was a devastating letter you wrote to Gregory Marsh. I'm not surprised he tried to shoot you."

Campanile cocked one of his bushy white eyebrows. "Were we not doomed, I should indeed have Mr. Marsh on my conscience. The truth is I have always despised the man and his cheap, sensational books. The letter was petty and spiteful, and I should never have written it."

John smiled. "You're entitled to be human as well as the rest of us."

Campanile sipped his Chablis, the glass twinkling in the candlelight. "Yes, dear boy, we're all too human." He sighed. "If only I had been a young man in the seventies. You can't imagine how utterly frustrating it has been, being a closet queen all the best years of my life."

John, somewhat startled by this sudden admission, just nodded sympathetically and ate the trout, which tasted as though it had been caught only minutes before dinner. At least he was getting a superb meal.

Tournedos Beauharnais arrived, along with an excellent Burgundy. Campanile cut a small wedge of the beef, ate it, and nodded appreciatively. "So you were the boy who would never take off his pants."

John said, "You won't believe this, but at the time I was so naive I had no idea it was even important to you."

Campanile nodded. "I can believe it."

"Of all the hundreds you must have entertained over the years, was I the only one?"

Campanile smiled. "The ploy had to be abandoned. Others wiser and more cynical than you began to talk. Alas, the pants-off-while-you-wash-the-dishes was possible for only two terms."

John helped himself to some cauliflower with anchovy butter. It was delicious. So were the new potatoes. "Perhaps if you had been able to be openly gay all these years, it might not have been nearly as exciting."

Campanile put down his fork. "My dear boy! Excitement? You can't begin to conceive of the agonizing fear, the soul-destroying worry that accompanied every brief affair. One slip and my career would have been ruined."

The gargantuan meal ended with Crêpes Suzette blazing merrily. John ate them, though his stomach had already begun to feel like an over-inflated basketball. They adjourned to Campanile's study.

Over coffee, strong and freshly ground, accompanied by cognac and many cigarettes, Campanile launched a continuous flow of anecdotes about authors the panel had eliminated. Milburn McTwill had sent him a poisonous coral snake. An anonymous bad loser had posted a letter bomb; fortunately, the post office had intercepted it. Another, Trevis Track, had sent him a beautiful boy. Campanile had kept the boy and returned the microfilm, whereupon Trevis had sent a box literally writhing with live scorpions. Frank Freddis had hanged himself from the top of a telephone pole highly visible from Campanile's bedroom. Campanile had had to move to a room opening on the inner court, and not nearly as cool at night. A bottle of chutney containing cyanide had been received. He had also been given a dusty bottle of Napoleon brandy liberally spiked with arsenic. A Molotov cocktail had even been thrown at the limousine. The fire had been extinguished, but so much bloodshed had followed!

In one of the lulls, John said, "I can see you have been having a really rotten time."

There was a long pause. "Yes. And now you're here, and you desperately want me to put your books on board."

John shook his head. "I haven't asked, and I won't. But I must admit this was the purpose of our trip down here."

"That I guessed, of course."

"So let's say no more about it."

Campanile lifted his brandy snifter. "You are a true gentleman, John Tate."

John made his way back to the Crandell house half-staggering, three quarters drunk, and painfully stuffed, resolving never to eat and drink so much at one sitting again, and relieved that at least his project was completed, though unsuccessfully. Campanile had invited him to visit the space ship, which would be interesting, he supposed, and following this, they could head home for Green Valley.

He slept badly, his new wound burning, his old

wounds aching, the too-rich food and drink he had consumed conjuring up nightmares in which he found Cynthia's crushed head in his bed, Gregory Marsh's bloody body in his car. He struggled awake intermittently to sniff the air, certain that he smelled smoke and that old Mrs. Crandell had begun the process of incinerating them, to repay him, no doubt, for completely forgetting to mention her book to Campanile.

It was almost noon when they breakfasted in the shabby old kitchen, John substituting an Alka Seltzer for the orange juice Mrs. Crandell offered. Grits, eggs, bacon, chicory coffee and thick toast made from home-baked bread followed.

"Im sure he was pleased when you called his attention to my book," said Mrs. Crandell.

"Delighted," said John, putting butter on another steaming helping of grits. No more worries about cholesterol. "Unfortunately selections must be made by the entire panel, and this work is done. The space ship is full."

"He couldn't take your books either?" asked Ginny. "No."

"The man is a fool. He could have slipped the 'History' in somewhere," said Mrs. Crandell.

John reached in his pocket and brought out his tiny container of microfilm. "Mrs. Crandell, this is microfilm of eleven hundred pages of my four novels. He can't even find room for *this*. How would you expect him to squeeze in your volume, which would take up a hundred times the space?"

Mrs. Crandell stared at the container, biting her lip. "He could slip it in somewhere. There must be a lot of nooks and crannies in a space ship."

John shrugged, sipping the muddy but strangely pleasing coffee. Nooks and crannies. It was a thought. He was still hungover, and had a headache throbbing over his right temple. He had not told Ginny about his new wound or the bloody scene that preceded his highly civilized dinner with Campanile. There would certainly be time for that later. If she knew, she might be apprehensive about his visiting the ship. In the meantime he might as well go back upstairs to bed. Campanile was not scheduled to pick him up until three-thirty.

Though John had seen many photographs of space ships, he had never seen, much less toured, the real thing. The elevator ascending the side of the launching platform was open, stirring some faint pangs of acrophobia and reminding him of the rickety old crate that traveled up the legs of the Eiffel Tower. He and Ginny had once eaten dinner on the terrace of the restaurant on the first level. In the dusk, they'd watched the lights of Paris come on below, and been gayly excited over their first trip to the most beautiful city in the world. A fullness settled in his throat. His eyes became hot and threatened tears, for there would be no more intimate discoveries for Ginny and himself. Lately he had found himself becoming increasingly sentimental. He had had to fight back tears on several occasions. Perhaps he needed to lock himself in the bathroom and have a good cry.

The cabin was small and smelt of metal and electrical wiring. A narrow aisle ran between six large bins of heavy aluminum.

Campanile, who had gone ahead of him into the cabin, said, "Would you believe five bins for science, and *one* for the arts?"

"I would," said John, glancing around curiously. There were no nooks and crannies. Nothing but smooth, uncrannied metal. "What happens to all the space in the aisle and above the bins?"

Campanile leaned against one of the bins. "Dear boy, every square inch has been allocated. That space will be filled with artifacts. A small computer, President Fargo's grandmother's harmonium, one or two priceless paintings and pieces of sculpture, many small items of everyday use. Toothbrush, comb, lipstick, candles, silverware, cooking utensils, costume jewelry, a vibrator, and so on." He leaned closer to John and asked, "Will you treat it as confidential if I tell you about three other items that are to be included?"

"Certainly."

Campanile whispered, "The embalmed corpses of a woman, a man, and a child. Orizonites will be able to see exactly how we were constructed."

"My God. Will they keep for a thousand years?"

"Of course. All air and moisture will be expelled, leaving a complete vacuum. After the ship leaves the earth's atmosphere, there will be nothing to cause decay."

"I see. Why does this have to be so secret?"

Campanile raised the lid of one of the bins. "Some religious leaders would no doubt object. Others would pester the life out of us to be included." He chuckled. "Can't you just see it, a nationwide contest to pick 'Miss Space Corpse of Eternity'?"

John smiled dutifully, staring into the open bin. "Is this the arts bunker?"

"Yes. Tidy and tight, isn't it?"

The round plastic containers of film were wedged snugly, and even the space left by the curvature of the containers was filled by small square boxes with curved sides specially molded to fit perfectly. Wasn't there even a half-inch for John Tate? If there was, he couldn't see it, surely he could squeeze that tiny container in there somewhere? But where?

"Dr. Fraser," called one of the soldiers on guard at

the entrance way, "the president's harmonium is here."

Campanile muttered under his breath, then said, "Damn the president's harmonium! Can you imagine the millions of beautiful words I could have crammed into that space?" He walked the ten or so feet to the door and said, "What the devil has that go to do with me?"

"I think it's busted, sir."

John snatched up one of the small square boxes and opened it quickly. Inside there were three rolls of film, each about as large as the one in his pocket. He removed one roll quickly, stuffed it in his pocket, then substituted the film from his own container, hoping that he wasn't depriving posterity of Shakespeare's sonnets.

"I really can't see what I can do about that, dear boy," said Campanile. "It's been ages since I repaired a harmonium." He turned and came back to the bin just as John was replacing the square box.

John held it up. "Neat. They've been specially molded to fit, I see." He pressed the box back into position.

"Naughty, naughty. Mustn't touch," said Campanile.

"Sorry."

"No one is allowed to touch but Campi." He closed the huge lid carefully. "Tomorrow we seal the bins. Then the artifacts will be loaded. When that's done, my job will be over, thank God."

"That'll be a relief, I'm sure." He was still flustered over his near miss. A split-second sooner and Campanile would have seen him closing the container. He bent over and pointed to some metallic protrusions on the front side of the bin, trying to hide his nervousness. "What are these?"

"Those are valves. One to be used in sucking all the air out. The others, well, I understand they will be used to introduce preservative gases, powders, that sort of thing." He turned and headed for the door. "Let's go. There really isn't much to see here, is there?"

In the limousine, Campanile insisted that John return to the fortress for dinner. His mission complete, John wanted to be with Ginny. He also wanted to find a microfilm viewer. If he *had* removed Shakespeare's sonnets, or something of equal importance, he would have to confess and rectify his misdeed. Would they mow him down, he wondered?

Campanile said, "You can't imagine how lonely I've been, dear boy, You're the only decent person I've entertained. Every other guest I've had has literally sweated me for *hours* in special pleading. I've had my fill of tears, of authors on their knees, of suicide threats, of personal threats. The tension has been *unbearable*."

John said he would stay. It was too late to leave for Green Valley anyway, and while he had hoped to take Ginny out to dinner, she would understand. Then too, if he refused, Campanile might begin mulling over the matter of the box he had seen John handling, and perhaps even recheck the contents. Furthermore, his hangover was gone, his queasy stomach was now steady as a rock, and he would never be able to buy a dinner in town to equal Campanile's hospitality.

The meal was even more elaborate than yesterday's. It began with Oeufs en Cocotte à la Jeanette, baked stuffed mushrooms, snails Bourguignonne, Quichede Saumon Fumé Parisienne, and canapés Rochelaise, any one of which would have been sufficient as an appetizer. Following the hors d'oeuvres, filets of Dover Sole Sauté Amadine appeared, accompanied by a fine Pouilly Fuisse. The sole, Campanile claimed, had actually been flown from Dover that morning.

"You *do* live well," said John.

Campanile surveyed the table despondently. "There's little pleasure in it when you have no one to share it with. I'm a prisoner here."

"Well, in a day or so you'll be able to go home."

"Home? Dear boy this impregnable blockhouse is my prison from now to the end of my life."

John held his glass for more Pouilly Fuisse. "Why?"

"Why? At least a thousand enraged authors want to kill me, that's why." He filled his own glass again. "Should I return to New York and sit chewing my nails on the terrace of my apartment, waiting for a sniper's bullet? A bomb? Poisoned caviar?"

"What happened to the boy Trevis Track sent you?"

Campanile ate his sole mournfully. "He became bored and left. Really, at my age, you must understand that the fires of sexual desire burn very low indeed. Hardly enough to make the tea kettle whistle."

"Surely there must be some old friend who doesn't write?"

Campanile smiled. "Those who don't write always seem to have a loved one who does. In any event, most of my real friends are dead. When you reach your eighties, this is a condition you must expect."

They moved on to the main course, Breast of Capon Drouant, with a superb white Beaujolais. Endives Braisées en casserole, stuffed baked potatoes and a simple salad completed this portion of the meal.

Campanile clutched his chest briefly. "Ooof! My doctor says if I keep gorging and drinking so much I will surely die. Isn't that ridiculous?"

John cut a portion of the tender, succulent endive. "Why ridiculous? Sounds like sound medical advice."

"My dear boy, why in hell should I care?"

It was an impossible question to answer. John concentrated upon his eating and drinking for a while, sorry for Campanile, but even sorrier for himself, for Ginny, for Marcy, Jack, Billy and Archibald.

The meal ended with fruit and cheese. John's stomach warned him that he was not accustomed to Roman orgies of eating and drinking, and suggested that he go out and walk a fast three miles.

When they left the table and moved again to Campanile's study, he brought out a bottle of Johnny Walker Black. "No brandy sipping tonight. I intend to get royally spiffed."

"Why not?" thought John. Ahead there was only the long and uncomfortable trip back to Green Valley, his uncertain relationship with Ginny, and *Gold Bullet Day*.

Campanile poured large drinks, adding only a little water. "You know, if you had taken off your trousers, nothing would have happened. You understand that, don't you?"

John nodded.

"It was silly voyeurism. I never dared touch any of my students. But it did give me so much pleasure."

Forbidden pleasures. Watching the boys in their undershorts. An intimacy that outweighed prowling the beaches in summer, he supposed. Mellowed by predinner martinis, more wine than he had ever consumed with a single meal, and now beginning to feel vaguely drunk, he thought Campanile's frustrations were somehow very sad, and felt guilty that he had denied Campanile that small pleasure. He was almost ready to reexamine the banal question of why the human animal is so preoccupied with, and screwed up by, sexual relationships. Why couldn't humans settle for the simple, sensual joy of the act and let it go at that? Reproduction, he decided fuzzily, threw a bleak coat of importance over the issue, deadening the joy and complicating the problem beyond solution by the pill or any other mechanism. There would never be any answer.

"There'll never be any answer," he said.

"To what?" asked Campanile, pouring himself another Scotch.

"The frustrations of sexual relationships."

Campanile emptied about half his glass in long draughts. "Surely you're not comparing the silly little problems heterosexuals have with the torment we gay people endure?"

John poured himself another Scotch. "Since you've never been heterosexual, how would you know our problems are trivial?"

"It's quite obvious," said Campanile, irritated. "You surely can't be serious?" He took another long drink. "Incidentally, I have a bone to pick with you, dear boy. I saw your little sleight of hand trick in the space ship. It was very naughty of you."

John almost spilled his drink. Flushing, he sipped, feeling as though he had been caught shoplifting.

"Don't feel badly," said Campanile, watching John's obvious discomfort. "I've appreciated your attitude more than you'll ever know. You haven't argued with me, you haven't implored, you haven't begged, you haven't tried to bribe me, you haven't threatened. You saw an opportunity and simply couldn't resist temptation. It was all neat and painless."

Not painless. Now his books would not be included. It was too much. He couldn't go back to being nothing. Having achieved immortality, he would not give it up. He lifted his glass again, drinking and staring at Campanile over the rim. How he hated the miserable old bastard. Should he kill him? Could he kill him without being caught?

"Oh dear, you are taking it hard," said Campanile.

John forced a small smile. Maybe Campanile would let the substitution stand. Not likely, but—

Campanile was distressed. "Promise me you won't cry. I can't stand seeing an attractive man cry."

John said, "I promise not to cry."

Campanile brightened. "So be a good boy and give me back the film. I know exactly where it belongs. First row, second from the right."

John shook his head slowly.

"Dear boy, don't be silly. You'll just delay me several days while I have a new microfilm made."

John poured himself another drink.

"Of course, I could have the guards search you. But it's such an unfriendly thing to do. And I do so need to think of you as my friend."

John reached in his pocket and brought out the film, hesitantly, like a schoolboy surrendering a packet of contraceptives. He laid it on the table, then looked away. It was too painful.

"Good, good," chirped Campanile. "Now we'll say no more about it. We'll just drink and enjoy the evening. Agreed?" He looked at John, smiling hopefully, but aware that the evening was spoiled.

John lifted his glass in a silent toast, hoping his hate was not showing through.

Campanile stood up. "I must go and pee. These situations are so distressing." He left the room, walking unsteadily.

John eyed Campanile's half-empty glass. Suppose he dropped his Oblivion 123 pill in it? He had read that the drug was virtually undetectable in an ordinary autopsy. Campanile's doctor expected him to depart this world at any time. And even if they recognized the Oblivion pill, he could say that Campanile had been terribly depressed all evening. His job was done and he had nothing to look forward to but this lonely prison.

Many people were using their pills early, so why shouldn't Campanile?

He reached inside his shirt and pulled his gold bullet and chain out between the buttons. What difference did it make whether Campanile died now or a month from now?

Murder. Could he accept himself as a murderer? Why this pusilanimous hesitation? The important thing was to give his work a chance to survive. The label *murderer* meant nothing. Neither his nor Campanile's life meant anything.

Was he afraid of some just, anthropomorphic god dealing with him later? No. He did not believe in an anthropomorphic god. These gods and their rules had been created by men for obvious, self-serving reasons. Including the demand for praise. All man-made gods demanded an inordinate amount of praise. It was strange that these lords of the universe felt so pitifully insecure.

He fumbled with the bullet, separating the two pieces of metal and shaking the pill into his palm.

Actually, he would be doing Campanile a favor. An unhappy, miserable old man with nothing to live for but his gluttony, gluttony that would surely bring a very painful illness and death. This route would be quick, without pain. And Campanile, he suspected, would not have the courage to do it himself.

No. He dropped the pill back in the bullet and snapped the two pieces together. He couldn't do it. To hell with the survival of his novels. He tucked the bullet back under his shirt.

Why, he asked himself, was he throwing away this chance because of some petty need for self-esteem? In this special situation, of what earthly use was integrity?

Campanile came tottering into the room, holding his palm against the wall for support.

"I don't feel at all well, dear boy." He gasped painfully, leaning against the large desk. "Will you call Dr. Fried? The number's there, by the telephone."

John got up hurriedly, and after helping Campanile settle in a chair, dialed the doctor. The telephone rang a long time, but was finally answered. Dr. Fried sleepily agreed to come immediately.

With the help of a Cuban houseman who spoke no English but was the only servant left on duty, John carried Campanile to a guest bedroom only a few feet down the hall. They propped him up in bed with several pillows. He was breathing easier now.

"Is there anything else we can do?" John asked.

"No," Campanile whispered. "Fried will pull me through. He always does." He turned his head to look at John. "Tell Security. It would be unseemly of them to shoot Dr. Fried."

Smiling, John went to the front door and told the guard to relay this information to the soldiers at the gate.

Back in the bedroom he found Campanile resting quietly. The Cuban houseman had perched himself on the edge of a straight chair, and with his hands clasped together, was praying in Spanish.

"If I die this time, you'll have your immortality," said Campanile, his voice soft.

"I don't want it."

Campanile waved one hand weakly. "Take it. I have a confession to make." He was speaking in such a low voice that John could hardly hear him. He leaned closer.

"I spliced a whole volume of my poetry to the end of *Madame Bovary*." Campanile chuckled, then clutched his chest, his face twisting. "Fuck them all."

Dr. Fried, who was fat and almost as old as Campanile, came briskly in with a nurse he had somehow collected quickly. He hustled John and the Cuban from the room.

John strolled back to the study and poured himself a fresh drink. The small roll of microfilm still lay on the table, a black, disgusting disc of shame. He picked it up with thumb and forefinger, like someone else's dirty handkerchief, and carried it to Campanile's microfilm viewer. Flicking on the light, he moved the first frame into view. "*The Joy of Cooking* by Irma S. Rombauer" appeared on the screen.

He removed the film carefully and dropped it in his jacket pocket. "To hell with you, Irma S. Rombauer," he muttered. "I hate to do this, but that's the way the soufflé sags."

XXVI

The panel show was considering the question, "Is God a Woman?" John sat watching, muttering to himself. The silly idiots were at it again, or still, and they damned well would be finding out soon that whatever God was, if he-she existed, he-she was probably not a man *or* a woman.

"It's quite obvious that St. Augustine hated women because of his mother," said one of the panelists.

John groaned.

"The very concept of divinity being male is sheer sexism," said another.

He groaned louder, and turned back to the family Bible. It was a big, thick volume, and more than half of it was devoted to collation, summary, concordance, and other indexing. He had been studying and copying from a page headed, "The Miracles of Our Lord." There were forty-two listed, and they were cataloged under various headings. Miracles of raising the dead; miracles of exorcising devils; miracles of healing; miracles of supply; miracles of judgment; miracles of deliverance; and miracles wrought not directly by Him but to attest to His divinity.

The miracles of healing were the largest group, with seventeen incidents annotated. He had raised three from the dead, exorcised devils from five, provided wine and fishes on six occasions, demonstrated two miracles of judgment, and three of deliverance. Seven had occurred to attest His divinity. This added up to forty-three miracles, the discrepancy explained by the exorcising of devils from two people in a single incident.

Aidan Grain had sent his followers home to spend
their last days with their loved ones, and the house was
again full. The quiet faith of his sons and their *wives*
—*mistresses* seemed an overly pretentious and sophisticated item for these children—had interested John
enough to start him thumbing through the Bible. Not
the modern English and American translations of which
there were several among his books, but the old St.
James version, which he preferred.

He was now trying to compare the miracles per-
formed by Christ with those attributed to Aidan Grain.
Grain had healed the sick, largely psychosomatically
sick, John suspected. He had bent any number of metal
things by touching them lightly, and he had stopped
thousands of watches and clocks. He had confused a
great many computers. In fact, it was rumored that he
had almost put Visa out of business. Corporate executives were reluctant to let Aidan Grain approach within
a quarter of a mile of a computer. He had exorcised no
demons, at least none that were reported, though
Louise claimed his touch had made her more tranquil.
Jack said she was as potty as she had ever been. Miracles of supply had not been necessary, since millions
had sought to give Aidan Grain everything he asked
for. The miracles of judgment puzzled John and he was
not able to compare. Both incidents so described
seemed to be demonstrations of power rather than
judgment, but who was he to question the scholarship
of theologians?

Then last, the miracles of deliverance. That remained to be seen. Aidan Grain's followers believed he
would deliver them from the holocaust.

"Why are you sighing and grunting like an old
goat?" asked Archibald, who had been reading a
shockingly abbreviated edition of the *Times*, completely deaf to the television program. He had returned

from Mexico tanned and full of his old vitality, and whether the crushed lamb's testicles had helped him physically or psychologically, he had managed an affair with a thirty-five-year-old expatriate widow living in Acapulco. They had parted regretfully, she unwilling to leave her five children, and Archibald not quite ready to take on the chores of fatherhood again.

John looked up and smiled. "And who do I hear talking about old goats?"

"A real old goat."

"I was sighing because religion baffles me."

"If it didn't baffle you, it wouldn't be religion. When you try to explain a mystical experience, it no longer is a mystical experience."

John shrugged. "But scholars still write thousands of volumes."

"Not to explain, but to propagate the faith."

"Would you classify Aidan Grain as a genuine mystic?"

Archibald lit a dark Havana cigar. "I would classify Aidan Grain as a massive electrical disturbance."

John glanced down at the Bible, amused. "Do you think he carries a secret power cell or something?"

Archibald shook his head. "Who knows? Where he would hide it, I can't conceive. Perhaps his viscera is wired, and he plugs himself in for recharging every night."

John looked at his watch. "In five minutes he will be making an important announcement."

"Oh, that's why you have it on."

John lit a cigarette. "Well it certainly wasn't to listen to those silly biddies worrying about whether God is yin or yang."

"That's what they were worrying about?"

"Ummm."

"God is yang all the way."

There was considerable noise on the steps, since Fran had taken up the carpeting to have it cleaned, and the rest of the household crowded into the living room to see and listen to Aidan Grain. Heather and Billy sat on the floor; Ginny perched nervously on the edge of a chair, chain-smoking; Jack and Louise slumped on a sofa. Terry moved some chairs to the very center of the group. He and Fran sat down primly, as if they were not quite certain that the family they had adopted was going to measure up to their expectations.

Aidan Grain, still dressed in shades of red, appeared suddenly on the picture tube, his long copper hair gleaming, his face radiant with serene joy. In the background a guitarist softly strummed a rock hymn.

"Verily, verily I say unto you, the hour cometh, and now is, when the dead shall hear the voice of the Son of God; and they that hear shall live."

A small chill flitted up and down John's spine.

"For the lightning cometh forth from the east, and is seen even unto the west; so has been the coming of Aidan Grain."

John lit a cigarette. Jack glanced at him disapprovingly.

"I am Alpha and Omega, the beginning and the end, the first and the last." Aidan Grain smiled, turning his head slowly as though to take in the millions watching him. "I have come to you tonight to talk to you about the end. Omega. It is not to be an end, but a beginning. Alpha." He paused for a few seconds. "As a father pitieth his children, so my Father pitieth them that fear, for he knoweth our frame; he remembereth that we are dust."

Grain was now concentrating his attention straight ahead. "*Be* ye not fearful, O ye of little faith."

Ginny coughed, and crushed out her cigarette.

"My Father has spoken to me. He has taken pity on his children. We *shall not* burn." Grain's face brightened, as though a spotlight had suddenly shifted. "I say to you again, *we shall not burn.*"

The guitar gained in tempo and loudness, then softened.

"My Father has promised, earth shall not pass into the sun's deadly rays, but rather in another direction, to another sun, where life will not be so easy, but where those of the human race who have faith in my Father will survive. So will the innocent animals of the field and forest, and the fish of the sea, for my Father loves them. On this trip to another sun, those who have faith to live will sleep for a thousand years. It will pass like a second of dozing, but when those faithful wake they will be fully aware of a new world, a new sun, and a life to be reshaped to meet God's will."

He paused and his face became stern.

"Ye of little faith will destroy your bodies and souls with the *pill* you have been issued. Take it if you wish the oblivion it promises.

"If you wish eternal life, then forgo your deadly medicine, for it promises nothing but the destruction of your body. My Father has instructed me that you will need your body when earth blossoms again under a new sun."

Aidan Grain stared unblinking at his audience for a long minute, then holding up his hand in a gesture of blessing said, "Thy faith hath saved thee; go in peace."

The sound disappeared and the picture tube was suddenly blank.

"Now he's knocked out the whole damned network," said Archibald.

"This is no time to be flippant," said Jack. He lit a

Marlboro angrily. "If we can't change your skepticism, well okay, but you don't have to make fun of our faith."

Archibald cocked one eyebrow. "Sorry."

"I'm beginning to wonder if this man is a monster," said John.

The eyes of the faithful turned on him, shocked and incredulous.

"I mean, he is asking millions of people to *burn to death* to demonstrate their faith."

Billy yelled, "That's *not* what he said!"

"I know what he *said!* I'm talking about what is really going to happen."

Jack stood up. Speaking in a low voice, he said, "You don't know what's really going to happen. If you had faith, you'd trust in Aidan Grain. We do."

John looked around at the group to see if there was any support for his position. Archibald, of course. Fran averted her eyes, and Terry returned his look self-consciously. Were they becoming Aidan Grainites too? Ginny jumped up and left the room.

He went to the small portable bar and poured himself another Scotch. The eighth or ninth or tenth that day. He had lost count. Spaced well apart, the drinks did not make him drunk, only mildly anesthetized. But this was a pain that would need an anesthetic stronger than alcohol, the thought of Jack, Bill, Louise and Heather remaining conscious in the coming inferno. It was unbelievable cruelty, or madness, on the part of Aidan Grain.

How could a father allow his children to suffer in this incredibly horrible way? If he had the courage, he would destroy them one by one, painlessly. He wondered if he had the courage.

XXVII

John found Ginny on her knees scrubbing the tiles of the upstairs bathroom.

Feeling guilty, he asked, "Why do you have to do that?"

She looked up. "If I don't, Fran will. They make me feel like we're exploiting them."

"To hell with it. They're happy. Anyway, you should make the girls do some of the housework."

She continued her scrubbing.

"Look, I think I've figured out Fran and Terry. They're lonely people. They were brought up by middle-class parents who were white oriented. They tried the Afro bit and it didn't fit. They were too immersed in the white life style." He leaned against the door frame and lit a cigarette. "They're pretending this is *their* house. This is the way they've always wanted to live. Neater, of course, and on a more splendid scale, but this will do as a temporary expedient." He sighed deeply. "As long as they don't try to throw us out, I say let them have their fun. Terry can even sit at the head of the table and be paterfamilias for all I care, if it will make him happier."

She shrugged. "Maybe I just need something to do." She brushed a wisp of hair from her eyes with the back of her hand. "I thought I had almost adjusted to being a prisoner in a cell on death row. Now this. Aidan Grain." She began to cry. "I can't stand it! I simply can't stand it."

He knelt beside her on the wet floor and put his arm

around her shoulders. "Don't cry. A lot can happen in eighteen days." Living from day to day in this strange limbo, eighteen days seemed another lifetime. Even a minute dragged out forever.

"The *Save Our World* project may even work."

She tried to smile, tears still rolling down her cheeks. "Well you *did* get your books on the space ship. That's worth something.

He helped her to her feet. "I hope those crummy Orizonites appreciate what we went through." Though Campanile Fraser had survived the night, he was still hospitalized, and John was sure his novels would remain aboard. Having confessed his own malfeasance, and having virtually invited John to retrieve the film he had made him surrender, it was unlikely that Campanile would take any further action. Now that the world-shaking important deed was done, John was surprised to find himself almost indifferent about it.

Ginny emptied the bucket of dirty water. "Maybe Aidan Grain is—well, maybe his prediction will come true."

He stared at her. Her eyes were still shiny wet from tears, and there was a flicker of hope in them that he could not destroy. "Maybe it will. Let's hope so."

They wandered back to the bedroom. Her feeling of being a prisoner on death row was apt, he decided. Time meandered so slowly and heavily, with sixty seconds in every minute stretching out to an eternity of awareness. Could a man on death row be entertained by reading a book? John could find no book, or for that matter, anything else, that entertained him. He smoked and drank and ate lightly, and slept badly, and many times each day he was tempted to swallow his pill out of sheer, agonizing boredom. The only thing that inhibited his premature withdrawal—a phrase that now made bank advertising almost sexy—was the one-in-a-million chance that *S O W* might work.

How does the condemned man feel about sex? How does the condemned woman feel about sex?

At times he felt completely sexless. His mind could bring into focus no erotic images, and physically he seemed bereft of any sexual apparatus. There were no testicles, there was no penis down there, only an emptiness that wasn't even cool flesh, just a sort of airy void.

At other times the urge was so great he wondered if the anticipation of death was not a strong aphrodisiac, with nature demanding that he impregnate as many females as possible before it was too late. In this mood he could think of nothing else, and mentally made love not only to Ginny, but Louise, Heather, Fran, and even Marcy, feeling ashamed that he could allow this incestuous coupling a place in his mind. Were there any need for it, he would even offer his sperm for artificial insemination, free, without the customary fee.

He watched Ginny undressing. She was preoccupied and not conscious of his stare. She removed her clothes with slow awkwardness, her face somehow more youthful though worried, like a schoolgirl wondering whether she was pregnant.

She stalked past where he was perched on the edge of the bed, about to pick up her nightgown, when he reached out and stopped her, grasping her hips with both hands. He pulled her around to face him.

Slightly surprised and now awakened from her preoccupation, she stood silently, glancing down at him. Holding her firmly, he leaned back and looked at her, his glance moving slowly from her face to her toes.

"Why are you staring at me?"

He smiled. "I'm just looking over the only real treasure in my life, a body I know better than my own."

He kissed her between her breasts. "Isn't it strange that I still find it fascinating, since I've been surveying it inch by inch for twenty-two years?"

She frowned. "I don't feel particularly flattered. It's nice that my body has been such a fascinating plaything for you. But I can't really take much credit for that, can I?" She pulled away gently and sat beside him on the bed. "Suppose I had been born ugly and misshapen?"

He nodded. "You think it's somehow demeaning? That your body should be a thing of exquisite pleasure for me? It's not a *plaything*. And the body without you in it, your personality, your mind, your sensitivity, would be nothing."

She moved her feet around him and stretched out on the bed, waiting for him to undress. "I know, it's all grand and soul-shattering and above sex."

"I think so."

"How?"

He unbuttoned his shirt slowly. "I don't know. Maybe the whole impact of love between men and women is completely sexual. To me, though, it seems to be much more." He kicked off his loafers, removed the rest of his clothes, and lay down beside her.

"Obviously, entirely apart from sex, my feelings for you are very similar to those I have for the children and Dad. This is love, isn't it?"

He pulled her close, kissing her lips. He went through many other rituals of foreplay, but his midsection remained an airy void.

It was the first time in his life that he hadn't been able to make love to her on the slightest provocation.

She sat up, distressed. "This horrible situation. It's made you impotent."

"Only at times."

She put her hand on him, then her lips and tongue, and he felt nothing.

He stopped her. "Don't worry about it. Tomorrow will be different."

He pulled her to him and they lay clasped together, sexless, for a long time, until Ginny drifted off to sleep.

John finally got up, dressed and went down to his study. It was time for his hourly potion. He poured the Scotch, his hand shaking a little. Maybe he had become permanently impotent? Maybe he wouldn't find himself as horny as a sex-starved sailor tomorrow? Maybe he was through?

He poured water in the whiskey and then drank, suddenly amused at his own terror. Suppose he was deprived of eighteen days of sex? Big deal.

He lit a cigarette. The house was deathly quiet. How could the others sleep so easily? Of course the children felt secure in their faith, including his two black "children," Fran and Terry. Archibald was secure in his old age and cynicism. Ginny was no doubt exhausted from the lovemaking that didn't occur, more tiresome than the real thing, probably.

Only he had to sit nipping the bottle and smoking. Toward morning, he might become tired enough to sleep a few hours. Some nights he did. Others he only dozed, sitting in his chair, and soon after dawn went to the kitchen to make toast and instant coffee.

He pulled the big, battered old Bible close to him and switched on the Tensor lamp hovering over it like an ugly bird. Opening the book he began to read passages at random, turning a half-inch thickness of pages at a time. Fatigue, blurry vision, the lateness of the hour and the substantial amount of Scotch circulating through his veins and arteries brought a certain fuzziness of perception. Squinting, he began reading aloud, hoping this would, by adding sound to sight, bring increased comprehension. He began to enjoy, as he always had, the grandeur and poetry of it, but no dazzling flash of inner awareness lit his tired, dusty brain.

In fact, the high intensity lamp went out, leaving the page a gray blur in the dim light from the lamp across the room. The bulbs were always blacking out on him. They seemed to last only a few hours, and he kept a supply of them in his desk drawer. He found one, snapped out the old bulb and clicked in the new. Nothing happened.

"Damn," he muttered.

"I'm afraid I've ruined your lamp," said a voice.

John jerked his head to the left, and there was Aidan Grain sitting beside him, hardly two feet away. He half rose in his chair, then settled back.

"You frightened me. You came in so quietly."

"Yes. However, you were reading so loudly and beautifully, you could not be expected to hear."

John stared at him. He had never seen the great man in person. He felt his nerve-endings tingling, for Aidan Grain's magnetism was a highly physical thing. "I'm afraid your disciples are upstairs asleep. Shall I call them?"

"No. It is you I came to see."

"Why?"

"Your children are worried about you."

John reached for his cigarettes. "I'm worried about them." He put a cigarette in his mouth and reached for his lighter. A tiny flame flickered suddenly in the air at the end of his cigarette. He drew in, lighting it. Aidan Grain had not moved. The flame, which disappeared quickly, had not been connected with anything he could see. "Thank you," he said to Grain, shaken.

"You're welcome. My Father has given me many parlor tricks to impress the naive."

"Do you consider me naive?"

Grain stared at him, a small smile rippling his large, generous mouth. "There are many kinds of naivete. Yours is of the educated variety. You refuse to believe what cannot be proved by logic or science. Yet you surely know that there are secrets of the universe that scientists will never unlock."

John puffed on his cigarette. "I've always thought that eventually they would. Find an explanation for us, I mean."

"Not with test tubes and computers."

John reached for the bottle of Scotch. "Would it offend you if I had a drink?"

"No, why should it?"

"When I was a child, and a Presbyterian, it would have offended the minister greatly."

Grain nodded slightly. "Man's interpretation of God's law is frequently trivial, and sometimes even ridiculous."

John asked, "Would you like a drink?"

Grain's smile became broader. "No, thank you. I do not require it."

"What is God's law?" John poured himself a drink.

"You know it in your heart."

John shook his head. "In my mind, possibly. My emotions only confuse me."

"What is in your mind?"

John sipped his Scotch. "I suppose I would think of God's law in very broad terms. Be kind, generous, honest, truthful, try to love and help your fellow man. Actually these are just tribal laws. Self-serving. I want people to be kind to me, to love me. I don't want anyone to kill my children. I want to live in peace with my neighbor."

"I see. You have never been touched with the love of God."

"No, apparently not. I haven't seen much evidence of Him. How can I love someone I don't know?" He drank more of his Scotch.

"Ah. Evidence."

"Call it what you will."

"There is evidence of Him all around for those who have the eyes to see, the ears to hear, the heart to feel."

John finished off his drink. "Why is God destroying the world?"

Grain's smile disappeared. "My Father has said that the world will live, though he did plan to eliminate the world because man had drifted too far away to be redeemed. In His infinite compassion He has promised His children another chance."

John shook his head wearily. "I wish I could believe that."

Aidan Grain raised his hand, as if to quiet this blasphemy. "John Archibald Tate, you have lived a shallow, shoddy life. But standing with most of humanity, you are acceptable to my Father. You have tried to love your fellow man, and you have tried to teach your children to love. You have not made material things your God, and it is in this more than anything else that the world has been corrupted by man. Spreading from west to east, and east to west, the love of *things,* not just the comforts of easy living, but *things*, has cornered man and made him earth's most vicious animal. He cowers in his cave guarding his *things*. He takes pride only in what he owns. Only his *things* bring him respect and admiration. He will do anything to accumulate them. He will kill, lie, cheat, sell his body and soul, sell his loved ones, sacrifice his very sanity for *things,* for more property than he can use, for more food than he can eat, for more strange objects than he can ever see or touch. Do you wonder that my father was ready to burn them all, man and his worthless artifacts?"

John reached for the bottle. "May I?"

Aidan Grain smiled. "Why are you asking my permission?"

John paused, replacing the bottle. "I don't know. I somehow have the feeling you're in charge here."

Grain stood up, looming over him. "John Tate, your children have saved you. Your children have worked hard for my Father, and they have prayed that you be granted understanding and belief." John felt Aidan Grain's hand on his head, heavy, as though it carried the weight of the earth on top of it, and that if not restrained it would crush his skull, and pushing downward, compress his body into one tiny atom. "My Father has asked me to touch you with the Holy Spirit."

Suddenly the weight was lifted from his head, and his body felt feather-light, almost as though he were floating out of his chair. Dawn was seeping into the room, but it was a strange golden light, not gray, and Aidan Grain had disappeared as mysteriously as he had arrived. John sat, his entire being flooded with an odd, exhilarant feeling, a happiness he had never known before. God had touched him. He sat for a long time as the room lightened, ecstatic in this serene joy.

He began to feel very hungry. He went to the kitchen and began to assemble a huge breakfast. Bacon, eggs, toast, rolls, guava jelly, coffee, tomato juice spiked with Worcestershire sauce. He threw a whole pound of bacon into the frying pan. If he didn't eat it all, the others would be up soon.

The heavy, smoky aroma of frying bacon filled the room. He switched on the ventilator fan and stood trying with a fork to separate the pieces of bacon, fat popping out and burning his face and wrists. Perhaps it had all been a hallucination? He was emotionally disturbed. All that Scotch. And the atmosphere in the house was always heavy with pot smoke. He had had to relax the rule of no-pot-smoking-in-the-house, and Jack had recently traded his Corvette for five pounds of fine Colombian pot. He simply wasn't used to breathing all that marijuana; even secondhand it probably affected the brain.

On the other hand, the feeling of serenity and happiness persisted. The Tensor lamp was broken, that was a fact. Or was it? He hurried to his study and tried several more new bulbs. None would light. Still, it could be a coincidence. He went back to the kitchen and continued preparing his big breakfast.

Jack came in sniffing. "That bacon smells good. Say, Dad, last night I had the most terrific dream. I dreamed Aidan Grain was here with you."

John finished flipping the bacon onto absorbent paper towels. "He was. Either that, or I was hallucinating from all that damned pot you kids smoke."

"He was!"

John nodded.

"Why didn't you wake us?"

"I offered to. He said he only wanted to speak to me."

Jack looked hurt.

"But it was on your behalf that he came. He came because you kids were worried about me."

"Oh." Jack picked up a piece of the crisp bacon and ate it. "And did he—"

"Convert me?"

Jack reached for another piece of bacon. "Yeah. Did he?"

He stared at his son. He would never change them, and now he was certainly not sure he wanted to. Why should they be unhappy, worrying about him? "Well, I thought there was a possibility the whole thing had been a hallucination, but since you *dreamed* about him mustn't he have been here? Then, too, he put my Tensor lamp out of commission.''

Jack's mouth slowly shaped into a broad grin. ''Gee, Dad, that's great. Simply great!'' He ate the bacon he had been holding. ''I sure hope he spoke to Mom and Grandpop while he was here.''

''Perhaps he did,'' said John.

They sat down to the big breakfast, John still euphoric and exhilarated. It couldn't have been a hallucination.

XXVIII

Save Our World Day arrived a few hours earlier than scheduled, before dawn, a full week ahead of *Oblivion Day*. Armies of technicians had been working around the clock to meet this date, which they hoped would give them time to refuel for a second try, should the first blast fail. Manned space stations had been sent into orbit to observe and report.

For the first time in history, 3:15 A.M. became prime television time in America. Even if any of the country's two hundred and twenty million inhabitants were not socked in before television sets, it was certainly doubtful that they were alseep, for there were some scientists who believed that the blasts might literally blow the earth into small pieces. In fact, it was assumed by everyone that all of the world's several billion who could get to radios or television sets were now waiting for the biggest show on earth to begin. Some of the more timid huddled with *pill* in hand, ready to pop it should mortal and painful injury result from the explosions.

No one in the Tate household had even tried to sleep. John, still alternating between serene joy and attacks of skepticism, had continued his intake of one or two ounces of Scotch every hour. God apparently had nothing serious against either Scotch or pot.

With the exception of Archibald, the entire household was now committed to Aidan Grain. Ginny wanted to believe so badly that when John described his experience, she would listen to no talk of possible hallucination. The others, with no doubts to resolve, spent most of their time smoking grass and listening to soothing stereo tapes of Aidan Grain's reassuring voice, playing some of his sermons so many times that John could repeat them verbatim. Ginny seemed to be quietly happy, though somewhat light-headed, and John suspected that she too was partially turned on from drifting in the clouds of the house's perpetual grass fires.

Poor Archibald stood alone on his rock of skepticism. He kept mainly to himself, claiming that the marijuana smoke spoiled the aroma of his Havana cigars, and that, though Aidan Grain's voice was indeed soothing and soporific, he preferred Seconal. This black, predawn morning he had, of course, joined the group in the living room. He sat smiling wryly and taking an occasional meditative puff on his cigar.

The eight sitting in a semicircle before the big color television set had moved closer together to make room for Archibald, and John had pulled a chair into position. Shaking his head, Archibald had taken a seat across the room.

"I can see well enough from here," he had said, and John had felt another twinge of pity for his father in the lonely isolation he seemed determined to keep. At least it would all be over soon.

As the minute hand moved close to 3:15 the various teams of commentators gave way to the star of the show, Dr. Harvey Michailmas, Chairman of S O W. Flanked by two newscasters chosen by lot from a panel of twenty-five leading network personalities, Dr. Michailmas was wearing padded earphones and presiding over a large instrument panel. On it were numerous dials and several small television screens and speakers which provided continuous communication with the three orbiting space stations and command headquarters in the Mojave Desert, where the earth-launch rockets were to be fired. On his right sat Sigrid Latimer, whose talk show 'Women's Stuff' was popular almost everywhere. She was an immaculately groomed, outdoorsy blonde who usually looked as though she was on her way to ride to hounds. This morning she might have just fallen off her horse. Her hair was mussed and kept falling over one eye; there was a smudge on her nose; and one set of eyelashes had disappeared. Her left cheek twitched at regular intervals. On Dr. Michailmas's left, Cassidy Cuff, a tall, big-mouthed newsman, was almost as nervous as Sigrid, and kept half-rising in his chair as though he suspected he might have to go to the bathroom but was not sure.

"Well, Cass, they say—" Sigrid paused in midsentence, her mouth open.

"Yes, what do they say, Sigrid?" asked Cassidy, rising a few inches off his seat.

"They, ah, they say we'll be able to hear the explosions even here in New York."

Cassidy settled back. "Yes, they do say that. A low rumble."

"A low rumble?"

Cassidy lifted an inch or so. "That's what they say. A low rumble."

"Like distant thunder."

Cassidy came up another inch, then collapsed. "Probably like distant thunder, yes."

"They say the weather may become very stormy. If they manage to change the earth's orbit," said Sigrid.

Cassidy stood all the way up, and the camera was caught for a second with a close-up of his vest. "The speed," he said, his prominent Adam's apple bobbing as the camera found his face, "if they can maintain the same speed in the new orbit, earth's atmosphere will not be disturbed." He sat down apologetically. "If the new movement is faster, or slower, there may be atmospheric disturbances."

Sigrid blinked her single set of eyelashes. "Like typhoons, tidal waves, hurricanes?"

Cassidy gripped the table to hold himself down.

"Hundred-foot-high walls of water crashing in from New York Harbor?"

Cassidy tried to smile, still holding the table tightly. "Let's hope nothing that severe."

Dr. Michailmas motioned for silence. "The countdown is beginning."

John grabbed the bottle and poured himself a very stiff drink. Another joint was lighted and started making its round of eager lips.

"Nine. Eight. Seven. Six. Five. Four. Three. Two. One!"

There was a low rumble from the west.

"I hear it!" shrieked Heather.

The rumble grew louder, like a jumbo jet flying low overhead.

On the television the picture trembled, came apart, came back together, then began flipping over endlessly.

The jet roar grew louder, as though the plane was heading directly for the house. The walls rattled and shook. A vase tipped off the mantelpiece and shattered on the stone hearth. John grabbed the bottle of Scotch as it rocked wildly on the end table.

Sounds were coming from the television set, but they were indistinguishable in the roar overhead.

Gradually the noise decreased, as though the plane had gained altitude and was well on its way to Miami. The house stopped shaking, and the television sound again became intelligible, though a whine, almost above audible range, seemed to fill the air with unpleasant vibrations.

The nine members of the Tate household, momentarily frozen in panic of threatened imminent destruction, were able to breathe again. They relaxed, sighing and shifting in their chairs.

Michailmas's picture stopped shaking. He was busy twirling dials and holding inaudible conversations with the three space stations. Sigrid and Cassidy were coming unfrozen. "I thought the building was going to collapse," said Sigrid.

"Didn't it?" asked Cassidy.

Her single eyelash fluttered seductively. "Funny man."

Dr. Michailmas held up his finger for silence, then turned to beam at the television audience. "Ladies and gentlemen, we are *moving*! I do not say yet that we are saved, but we are *moving*! Earth is moving toward the orbit we have plotted. *Praise God*!" He waved both arms around in a sort of idiot gesture. "Incredible! Incredible. *We must all pray*!"

Sigrid and Cassidy lowered their eyes self-consciously.

The seven thoroughly committed souls in the Tate house slipped from their chairs and kneeled, praying silently. John lowered his head and tried to pray, but his mind kept skipping off in other directions. Saved? Had man's own science snatched the marshmallow from the fire? Could he go back to a life he had already given up? He had arranged for his contribution to civilization to be appreciated on Orizon, and he had been prepared to allow Aidan Grain to save his immortal soul. He had prepared himself well for oblivion or salvation, one a black nothingness without joy or pain or regret, the other a monumental achievement, to be saved by a personal God. Now must he return quietly to life as it was before? He had burned his bridges, and he wasn't sure he could face the swim back.

The high-pitched whine grew louder, and the vibrations more noticeable. They traveled from John's feet up through his body to his brain, as though he had started moving down a sidewalk on steel-wheeled roller skates. He lifted his glass quickly, hoping the Scotch would quiet these tremors.

The others had moved unobtrusively back to their chairs. He glanced at Ginny. Her face reflected both joy and bewilderment. She had found a diamond in the Wheat Germ jar.

Dr. Michailmas had settled down and was again busily conferring with the space stations.

"I can't think of anything to say that wouldn't be completely banal," said Sigrid.

Cassidy gulped. "Be my guest."

"I'm sure we're all thankful that the world has been saved. Did you ever hear such a ridiculous understatement?"

"No," said Cassidy. He stood up.

"Why don't you *go* if you have to?"

"Thanks." He eased himself off the screen, glancing shyly at the two billion people who were watching him go to the bathroom. It was probably some kind of record.

A low moan swept through the house. The sound grew in volume to a frightening howl, and a loud wood-splintering crash outside drew all eyes away from the television screen.

John got up and rushed to a window.

"It's the wind. The big maple fell over."

"Ginny jumped up. "It fell *on* something."

"John's Mercedes."

Jack hurried to the window. "Jeeze!"

"Please fasten your turbulence. This is your seatbelt speaking. I mean, this is your captain's mother," said Louise.

No one laughed.

Jack went out to look over the damage. The others drifted back to their chairs to resume monitoring the screen.

"We seem to have quite a windstorm going on," said Sigrid. "I can feel the building swaying."

Cassidy, who had returned looking much improved, said, "There are high velocities."

"What?" asked Sigrid, clutching the table.

"Somebody said something about gusts up to fifty miles per hour."

Outside the Tate house the wind was a thunderous rustle as it ripped through the leaves of the many trees and battered the house. The old frame creaked and groaned.

The picture began flipping over again, then steadied. Sigrid was tilting noticeably. "I don't like this a bit. I don't care to be on the ninety-fourth floor of a building *bending* in the wind."

"I wouldn't quite say it's bending," said Cassidy, though his face registered some doubt.

Attention was suddenly focused on Dr. Michailmas. He was jerking his head from side to side, staring wildly at the small screens on his big panel and listening intently to messages from the space stations. He ripped off his earphones and screamed, "No!" Then he pounded the panel and shouted, "No! No!" His face began to take on a purplish hue on the bright color tube. He tried to stand, but half way up he collapsed and fell to the floor, off camera. There was a quick close-up of Sigrid.

She fluttered her hands. "I'm afraid Dr. Michailmas has fainted."

The camera pulled back to take in Cassidy, who was looking to the right, where others were obviously helping Michailmas.

"I'm afraid he's had a heart attack. The poor man looks quite blue."

"They're giving him mouth-to-mouth resuscitation," reported Sigrid.

She looked up suddenly and screamed. The ceiling was bulging downward alarmingly like a white plaster balloon being inflated. It exploded in a rain of plaster, laths and twisted metal.

The picture blacked out and the set was silenced, leaving only the roar of the wind.

Bill rushed over and began flipping channels. There was no response. The set was completely dead.

"Try the radio in the kitchen," said John.

They crowded into the kitchen while Bill worked the dial of the radio there. Nothing but static and an occasional word could be heard.

John hurried to his study and switched on the more powerful radio in his stereo. The others followed, even Archibald, who remained hovering in the doorway. Here too, static dominated. John continued to turn the station selector very slowly while the others watched impatiently.

"Let me try, Dad," said Bill.

John held up his hand. Fragments of a faint voice could be heard, hardly audible in the reverberations from outside. The speaker, who had a broad southern accent, was obviously working under an almost unbearable emotional strain. "New York City is completely devastated. Gales of unbelievable force, they say five hundred miles an hour, nobody can even measure them, have leveled the entire heart of Manhattan in a radius of ten miles from the Empire State Building. Casualties are in the millions. Every skyscraper in New

York has collapsed. The center of the city is nothing but rubble, a sea of rubble fifty feet high. The screams of the injured are unanswered, because rescue efforts are virtually impossible under present conditions—''

The voice faded and static took over.

Outside, trees in the wooded area on the hill behind the house were falling, crashing into each other. The house, which was in a protected pocket, with hills on all four sides, had always survived undamaged in windstorms. Now it was shaking and vibrating.

Should they stay in the house? John had gone through seventeen hours in a typhoon on Okinawa, and with this experience rushing through his mind, decided that it was useless to make everyone go outside. The wind, which was probably stronger than the typhoon, would simply slap them flat on the ground, and flying debris could tear through them like cannonballs. If the house started to collapse, they would, of course, have to risk it.

"Stay on the first floor," he said to the group absentmindedly.

Bill had taken over the delicate selector dial and was edging the indicator along with painstaking slowness, trying to pick up another distant station. Finally a voice broke through the static.

"Stand by for a message from President Fargo." There was a long static-filled pause, and then Fargo's voice could be heard. "Fellow Americans, this is no time for levity, but some urge stronger than I can control impels me to say to you that I have some *good* news and I have some *bad* news." He began to laugh, a sound that grew into a hysterical cackle. In the background a voice said, "Mr. President, get hold of yourself." Fargo's voice, directed away from the microphone, could be heard saying, "Get your ass out of

here, you presumptuous young fart." Then it came on
stronger, directly into the microphone. "My fellow
Americans. As I said before I was so rudely interrupted, I have some *good* news and some *bad* news.
The good news is that we will not be burned to death.
The bad news is that earth is presently traveling *out* of
our solar system at the rate of fifty thousand miles an
hour. It seems that our Russian friends unleashed their
earth-launch only minutes after ours. This was contrary
to all bilateral agreements and plain ordinary common
sense. I suppose there is no point in belaboring the
issue, no point in crying over spilt milk, but those
egomaniacs were so determined to prove that Soviet
science is superior to ours that they simply could not
face the fact that *our* earth-launch was *working*. Yes, it
was working, working perfectly. We'd be in our safe
orbit around the sun right now. The good old United
States of America *saved the world*, and *this* these—
these consummate morons, could not accept. They
pushed the button.*Varoom*! Children playing games!
Varoom! Here we go into outer space. *Varoom*! Varoom! Varoom!" Fargo's voice broke off, and after a
long pause, another came on the air. "President Fargo
seems to have had some sort of seizure, and will be
unable to continue his statement." A recording of the
Star Spangled Banner welled up to compete with increasing static.

John buried his face in his hands as excited waves of
chatter from the others broke over him.

John raised his head. Bill was waving his hands
frantically. "Aidan Grain! It's all coming true!"

Jack said, "Of course it is. We're going to travel a
thousand years to another sun."

"Frozen stiff," said Louise. "I hope they defrost me
with gentle care."

The house was becoming noticeably chilly. The roar of the wind had decreased, but the breezes creeping through the cracks were icy.

John got up and went to Ginny. He took her in his arms. Well, they said freezing wasn't such a bad death. After a period of teeth-chattering discomfort you got very sleepy, and while you were asleep, everything gradually stopped working. If this was God's plan, so be it.

They stood clasped together for a moment and then went to look for Archibald, who had disappeared from the doorway.

He was back in the same chair in the living room, and had his gold bullet open, with the pill in his hand.

John hurried over to him. "Dad. Why not take a chance? Go with us."

Archibald shook his head. "I'm too old and tired and bruised for cryogenic preservation." He smiled. "I'm bone weary, really."

Ginny knelt by his chair, holding his arm. "Please, Papa."

He patted her hand. "Bless you." He put the pill back in the container and fitted the two pieces together. "Now you've made me self-conscious. I'll have to take care of this later, in the privacy of my room."

"Don't you believe Aidan Grain now?" asked Ginny.

He turned his head away. "Dear, I don't know what I believe. If there is a God I'm sure He'll understand how tired I am." He bent over and hugged her briefly, then stood up. He embraced John quickly, then turned and went slowly from the room.

His eyes tight with tears, John walked over and turned on the heat. Damnit, they would survive as long as they could. No point in waking up a thousand years from now with pneumonia. Fast freezing did less damage to the tissues. Obviously it would be better to go when the earth had traveled far enough from the sun to bring the temperature down to deep freeze levels. How soon would that be? Was the heat even working? Possibly. The natural gas pipeline didn't go through New York City.

He went to the study where the others were still crowded into the small room, sitting on the floor and couch, the cold air heavy with pot. Bill was still fiddling with the radio, but getting nothing but static.

"I want you all to keep as warm as possible until we get far enough from the sun. Do you understand?"

Louise looked up. "Sure, Pop. You want us cutlets to be quick-frozen properly."

He smiled, his eyes wet enough to haze his vision. He waved his hand. "See you in a thousand years."

He went to one of the linen closets and got a blanket. Draping it around his shoulders he returned to the living room, found a fresh bottle of Scotch and a package of Marlboros. Then he joined Ginny on the sofa, pulling the blanket around them.

Ginny put her head against his chest and closed her eyes.

It was ironic that they hadn't resolved the matter of commitment. It would have to wait for a thousand years and another sun.

He wondered, how strong was his faith? If Aidan Grain's proposition had come to facing the inferno alive, would he have accepted it? Could he have let Ginny and the children suffer so cruelly?

No. God had to offer some logic and kindness in his challenge, some hope. Now the situation offered hope, no matter how slim. This was what mankind lived on. But then, perhaps Archibald was right. Wasn't the hope illusory? No, it wasn't. There was more than hope. There was curiosity. Man lived by curiosity, too. John realized suddenly that this motive was probably stronger in him than hope. If there was another sun to be seen, he wanted to be there to see it.

Epilogue

Earth, still rotating, hurtled through space, a ball sheathed in a rock-hard coat of ice and frozen granite. It sailed silently through the blackness of space no longer lighted or warmed by the sun.

Briefly, though, there was a great noise.

Traveling only a few miles away, the culture space ships of the Soviet Union and the United States were approaching close together on course to the planet Orizon. The Russian ship's delicate equipment "smelled" the United States ship. A rocket automatically appeared in its belly and went whistling off to greet the intruder. The American ship "smelled" the approach of the Soviet rocket, and automatically released a homing rocket of its own. The explosions were very close in time, the United States ship disintegrating first, and the Soviet ship only seconds later.

In weightless outer space, the contents of the two ships drifted and mingled together. Containers of microfilm floated in melding groups like aimless frisbees. President Fargo's grandmother's harmonium nudged a samovar. The American computer circled the Russian computer like a wary fighter, its terminals waving threateningly. The little girl corpse from Dayton, Ohio, drifted into the arms of a burly, sightless Russian from Leningrad. Space debris. Frozen angels.